LIGHT AT DUSK

LIGHT
AT DUSK

PETER GADOL

PICADOR USA

NEW YORK

Picador® is a U.S. registered trademark and is used by St. Martin's Press under license from Pan Books Limited.

Book design by Michelle McMillian

ISBN 0-312-20336-5

First Edition: May 2000

10 9 8 7 6 5 4 3 2 1

FOR SLOAN HARRIS

$$\frac{1}{}$$

FINALLY THE DAY CAME to go out into the city.

I remember that someone tuning a cello in the courtyard woke me at six that morning, a long bow-stroke repeatedly riding one troubling string, sliding from sharp to flat, sharp to flat. After a while, I realized that it was not a cello but a cat, and I lay in bed waiting for one of my neighbors to either feed or free her. But the plaint continued, and eventually I found my robe and headed downstairs barefoot, taking the oval stairwell a little too quickly after a long night of wine and play. I had to sit down at the threshold of the courtyard to catch my breath, and by then, the cat cries had ceased.

I had been renting a top-floor apartment in an elderly building on the edge of the south Sixteenth for almost three months, and I'd heard this cat many times before but only seen her twice. I knew she was brown and sleek-haunched, possibly green-eyed, and even though the day began brightly enough, finding a brown cat in a gray stone courtyard proved difficult. I looked behind some bikes, behind trash cans, and under the car parked in a corner. A tenant in the building had driven the sedan across the cobblestone one afternoon some weeks before my arrival and apparently left it for dead without explanation. I didn't know much about cars, but I could tell that it was vintage and valuable, with its sloping hood and arrogant chrome. It was burgundy and upholstered in caramel, and here was what was strange: The keys were in the glove compartment. I had discovered this one morning along with the concierge, who made it her habit to keep the car washed, its windshield free of grime, its fenders agleam, as if it were her responsibility in the way that the iron railing and floral newel of the stairwell were also hers to maintain in good shine.

No cat cowered under the car or on the ledge of a low window or anywhere where she might answer me. I called out to her the way I would call out to my own cat back home, whom I missed a great deal—travel was incompatible with cat-ship—except I spoke in French.

It was October 15 and cold. I gave up.

Before I went upstairs, I heard what I thought was an unusual shuffle of feet out on the street, and when I was back in my apartment, I looked down at the sidewalk. There were many more Parisians out and about at this hour of a weekday morning than I was used to seeing. They were all headed in the same direction, a steady stream, away from the Bois and toward the main boulevard.

My apartment consisted of two large rooms partitioned by

sliding doors, the room that I used for my bedroom and a larger parlor with tall windows. The narrow molding around the ceiling edge made it look as if the place had been trimmed with eggshells. There were traces of gilt. I stood in a window and became anxious when I glanced back at a settee layered with books about French architects and histories of the Revolution, at the table littered with snapshots of pale eighteenth-century buildings and my several notebooks. Maps, index cards, a laptop open like a steamed clam and collecting dust. Research had kept me busy me all summer and into the fall; important deadlines now were imminent, although I had done no work at all for the last three days.

Through the doorway to the small kitchen, I could see a budding grove of empty cabernet bottles on one counter along with a considerable berg of dark chocolate and a bowl of flawless pears—gifts. The man sleeping in my bed had brought them. I looked at him and some of my panic abated.

His name was William Law, and he didn't stir while I stood at the foot of the bed. Count among his enviable virtues a propensity for undisturbed sleep, which was true of him as long as I'd known him; you never wanted him in the passenger seat if you required conversation to keep you awake on a long drive. It was Friday; he had arrived early Tuesday morning, and except for dinners in a corner café down the street, we had not left the apartment. We had sequestered ourselves and successfully ignored the beat of the city, but today all that would come to an end.

Will slept, the blankets pulled back longitudinally to reveal half of him, a ruddy range of arm, back, butt, and leg. I decided to poke around his luggage, an abused leather bag containing his

worldly effects, so he claimed. I had forced him to admit that he
did maintain a storage vault elsewhere, in Washington as it
turned out, but he seemed to consider everything he kept there
dispensable, book boxes, an heirloom quilt, his childhood globe.
I looked in his bag expecting to find I don't know what. I had
seen his entire wardrobe, Will who dressed in the reds and
browns of fallen leaves. He owned a single suede jacket, which
was inappropriate for the increasingly wet weather in Paris. Most
of his clothes were draped over an armchair or carousing with
my own hasty discards on the floor, our khakis in delicto.

Will shifted and pulled a pillow over his head.

He also had brought a backpack with him, and again, I already
knew its contents. He had been reading a book related to my
dissertation topic that I'd recommended, although his bookmark
was lodged in an early chapter. I saw the wad of letters I had sent
him. There was a camera, no film. And there were some token
artifacts, proof of his recent travel—for all the time that we were
renegotiating our romance after long silence, he had moved
every month—some torn currency and thin coins, various city
plans. I had examined everything he had brought, and still I
could not answer so many questions, chief of which was this: We
had not seen each other in seven years—what made him suddenly seek me out?

Will pulled the pillow off his head, exposing his semi-
blondness and a measure of stubble. I froze. I was holding his
passport. He didn't open his eyes.

It was a regular American passport like my own, not a diplo-
matic one. I flipped through it and glanced back at his body,
more of which was available now for review—his entire back,

the span of his shoulders. I learned nothing new from the passport—or maybe I mean that I didn't discover any lies—and only verified the borders he had crossed. He carried around a date book, too, which was blank for the majority of the expired year; in fact, the first entry logged was the estimated-time-of-arrival of the plane that had carried him from Rabat to Paris, and the only other notation was for an obligatory lunch date today with an old friend of his late father's, which I knew about.

I did think it possible that William Law was a spy. It would not have surprised me.

His body, on the other hand, continued to supply me with new clues. The Will now stretching and reaching his left hand for something to grasp—the headboard sufficed—did not match the Will who I met when he was nineteen and had not yet grown into his frame. We were in college and all of us were too skinny for own good, sporting blazers and trousers that somehow looked tight, short at the cuffs. The Will with whom I had lived in the years after college, the Will who I could safely call the love of my life—he was wheatier and had more hair; he was fair, he sunburned easily. Now he wore his hair cut short, and he looked tan with leisure, his bikini line evidence of days given over to the sun and sand. Or to a rooftop deck with a view of the souk—that was what I imagined. This new Will looked as if he didn't go to bed without doing several hundred sit-ups and push-ups. When he moved an arm, you learned something about anatomy.

And then hold that image of a tall and tan, traveled man against the image of the man I thought I would buzz into my building earlier that week, a man I genuinely and maybe naively believed I would hug hello, that's it—a man in a poplin suit and

silk tie and polished cordovan oxfords. The career consul, visiting from the tropics. His father's son. Needless to say, the Will
who showed up did not match the Will I expected, and I don't
mean to imply that I was disappointed so much as cast into a
fog. Will Law had followed some turn in his life which I did not
yet understand. He had resigned from the Foreign Service,
which was a busy life; then he became a man with an empty
date book and a well-stamped passport. How did that happen?
Why had he left?

Years had gone by, I had lived my life. We were a decade out
of college; I had to check my math to convince myself that this
was fact. We'd lived together, we'd lived apart longer. We had
lost each other. Then six months ago, Will began writing me letters: Each one ran a brief page, a few jerry-rigged sentences, yet
each read true and passionately. They came to me weekly, often
before I could respond. He talked about how he wanted to start
his life over, and—here was how I figured in the ramble—about
how his best times had been spent with me: Our autumn jaunts
to the Law family house in Maine, which we would have to ourselves. A languid trip here to Paris the summer after college—
our days were so easy back then, how did we drift? He wanted
to see me, he wrote; would I meet up with him? We arranged a
rendezvous in Paris while I was conducting my research, and he
took his time making his way here but finally showed up.

There was the hug in the foyer, pro forma, but then a kiss as
well. Right away a kiss that went well beyond communicating
the relief of reunion. A kiss, a letting-go—and suddenly his letters added up. Whatever grief he had caused me vanished like a
flap of doves. Before long we were stumbling across the room,

through the sliding doors, unwrapping each other. We picked up right where we'd left off, or so it seemed. Hours later Will said, I brought you what you used to like. Red wine with dark chocolate. And pears.

"What time is it?" Will asked. He flipped onto his back and propped himself up on his elbows.

I heard someone shouting down on the street.

"What day is it?" I asked back.

I tossed off my robe.

The cat cried out again in the courtyard, a louder, more desperate wail, the cat I had seen twice and remembered as having green eyes. Naturally I would think she had green eyes because so did Will; green by day, gray at night. He blinked at me. He pulled me closer. I crawled over to him, hovered awhile, and descended.

Finally the day came. We would have to venture beyond the corner café. We would need to engage in serious talk. But what if we had stayed in one more afternoon and one more evening? I cannot help but wonder. What if we had stayed inside.

By the time we made it to the street, it was ten in the morning, and the crowd that I had noticed before had swelled considerably, which was curious in this part of town, blocks from a commercial street and some distance from the embassies that punctuated the quarter. There was a tide of citizens rolling beyond the sidewalk and into the avenue, men and women and some children, too, all headed in the same direction like families late for a parade. I noticed that the children weren't wearing book bags, nor was anyone carrying briefcases or the morning papers or any of the obvious accoutrements of the workday. No one was out walking his dog.

A man brushed past us and stared at me, wild-eyed. He was waving a skinny baguette over his head, brandishing it like a spear. When I looked at some of the other people streaming by, I noticed that they, too, seemed to be clutching partial loaves of bread. We veered off in the opposite direction from everyone else and had to pardon our way around all of the people backed up at the intersection.

Will and I were the only patrons at the café where I had made myself a regular. Three waiters watched the crowd. We sat at a wobbling table inside, pressed into a corner that was papered with tobacco-stained concert posters. It was eerily quiet; at this hour, I was accustomed to hearing the constant throat-clearing of the espresso machine.

One of the waiters approached and we ordered a light breakfast.

"The coffee, right away, Messieurs," the waiter said. "But I must tell you that I cannot bring you the croissants."

I asked why not.

"There is no bread," the waiter said. "Everyone has gone, you know, completely crazy."

A small assembly walked by, each man shaking a scrap of pumpernickel.

"But it looks like everyone has some bread," Will said.

The men were shouting an indecipherable rant.

"Yes, yes," the waiter said. "But it is the bread of yesterday."

"The bread of yesterday," I said.

"It is, you know, stale."

"So there are no croissants," I said.

"No croissants, Monsieur. But it is possible that another café will have croissants, if they are not involved. I could not tell you where—"

"Not involved?"

I looked at Will and back at the waiter.

The waiter shrugged.

"Well, just the coffee, thanks," I said.

Soon the waiter returned with two generous bowls of café au lait.

"I cannot even offer you any stale bread," he apologized. "We gave it away before you arrived. May I interest you in an omelet?"

"No thanks," I said.

"Not for me," Will said.

"It is all because of the boycott," the waiter said.

"The boycott?" I asked. "Of what, bread?"

"Oui, Monsieur. There is a boycott today of the bakeries, which is why we have no bread. It was not delivered as usual."

"I see, I see," I said. "This has something to do with that speech."

"Voilà Monsieur."

"And how long do you think that the boycott will last?" I asked.

"Only today. That is what I heard," the waiter said and joined his colleagues back on the sidewalk.

"Do you know what's going on?" Will asked.

"Sort of," I said.

I had followed French politics during my time in Paris: A few weeks earlier, the leader of the far-right French Front party, who after decades of gradual ascendance had finally positioned himself to become the next President of the Republic, had given a speech in which he called for the deportation of anyone not born on French soil and an all-out ban on granting any new visas. The party was moving well beyond its previous platform, which at best resorted to monetary incentives for the real French or French-French, as they were called, to have children in order to keep up with the growing immigrant population. Now the party had momentum, a gale of support behind it, because a new series of laws had been passed after a bomb in the métro killed eight people and wounded a dozen others, children among them. The bomb was just one more subterranean explosion in what had become a reliable subscription of terrorism, the evil work, so it was widely rumored, of radical immigrant factions who wanted to foster the kind of deep fear in France that would make it impossible, indeed dangerous, for the new anti-immigrant laws to be passed in the first place. None of it made sense to me, but then again, we were not inhabiting an age of reason.

"So what's the connection to the bread?" Will asked.

In his speech, the French Front leader called for the expung-ing of all impurities in French life, meaning all peoples from Africa, the Middle East, and Asia, whom he likened to the preservatives that some bakers were now adding to their bread; many deemed the practice of adding preservatives to French bread treason and sacrilege.

Here was how the bakers figured in: Many of them already belonged to the legion of the French Front, and they began to hang posters in their windows and behind their cash registers boasting a new slogan: Rien d'Impur. Nothing impure. Talk of a boycott of the bakeries had been blowing about among those who opposed the French Front—recent polls indicated that they formed a narrow but steadily declining majority—and now it appeared that boycott was under way.

"We should support it," Will said.

"It's hard to believe it will mean anything tomorrow," I said.

"Yes, but look," Will said.

Clusters of Parisians continued to drift past the café, fast clouds eager to amass into a storm. No one was going to work. It appeared as though the city, and for all I knew the entire country, had shut down for the morning.

"I shouldn't be so cynical," I said.

Will puffed.

"Paris has been a mess," I told him.

I had wandered the city and seen the graffiti everywhere, the slurs spray-painted along the limestone alleys of the outer arrondissements and eastern banlieue. I had watched men in trucks parked outside the mosque in the Fifth broadcast the national anthem at a deafening volume to drown out the drone of midday prayer. I had seen the gangs of white boys with the shorn heads and the unlaced black boots and the tricolor tattooed on their forearms, and I had read about the way they flung eggs at the darker-complected girls trying to walk to school. African vagrants were thrown from the bridges. Arab markets were fire-bombed. Cars were torched outside the old cafés. And there were explosions in the métro.

"But you seem fairly set up here," Will said. "You look happy."

It was true. My research had engaged me. And I will admit that I had imagined living here more permanently. Even with its maladies, Paris remained attractive to me: I was an inveterate optimist; I thought that all of this would pass, simple as that, these hard times, this season of ill will.

I reached across the table and took Will's hand.

"I am happy," I said.

He grinned and temporarily disappeared behind the broad brim of a coffee bowl.

I wanted to interrogate him, but I didn't know how to begin. I studied him awhile, and he in turn watched the crowd.

Finally I said, "You haven't really told me why you left the FS."

"We talked about it some," he said.

"You mentioned your boredom, your disenchantment. But I feel like there's something else, Will. We all expected you to be our Secretary of State."

"I let you down."

"No," I said. "To the contrary."

We were only circling back over covered ground.

"I'll be having a big lunch later," Will said, "but you. You get headaches. You should eat something."

I stared at his eyes, dry as slate.

"What should we do today?" he asked. "I have to meet this guy and then..."

I sipped my coffee.

"There was some trouble," Will said.

I waited.

"At my last posting, something happened. There was some trouble."

"Are you okay?" I asked.

He nodded. "It's behind me. It's over, I'm past it."

I didn't believe him. "What happened?"

For a moment, I thought he might answer me. But again he said, "I'm past it," and that was that.

We finished our coffee and went out into the crowd. Before

long an elderly woman was shuffling right behind us, a stiff loaf
tucked under her arm—she poked me in the back with the
bread—and two men took long steps in front of us, each clench-
ing a rock of a brioche in his fist, the glimpse of which, stale or
not, made me hungry. We followed the march, aimed due east,
and reached the boulevard, where there were cars trapped and
abandoned, buses anchored and emptied. Every street had been
given over to the impromptu march, and drivers could honk all
they wanted, which they did, but they were going nowhere. I
became dizzy, less from hunger than from the noise, the chatter,
the manic clacking, the occasional attempts at some sort of uni-
fying, rallying chant. No one seemed to know what exactly to
shout. We turned from the boulevard onto a narrower street,
then another wide channel and another street. Eventually the
Seine came into view.

All of Paris poured into the streets, a millionfold scarved and
sweatered bodies gravitating toward the river, and those who
weren't down on the street were watching from the steep apartment houses lining the boulevards, some of them saluting, some
tossing stale bread down at us. I got hit with a rather large seeded
chunk, and my head throbbed. I ducked into the vestibule of an
antique clock dealer and pulled Will along with me.

I rubbed my head. Will kissed my left temple.

All of the stores on the street were closed, each merchant
probably fearing that his particular product would be the next
surrendered to the boycott; or maybe they were afraid that in the
spirit of improvised revolution, random looting would follow.

A group of teenage boys appeared out of nowhere, moving in
a pack against the crowd. Five boys abreast, ambling like a single

beast, in a single stride. Boots to the pavement, a gang, hungry for trouble. Everyone on the sidewalk cleared a wide path, and with good reason. If you stared at them, they might attack—I had seen it happen—they might pounce for no apparent reason other than that it was time for a nosh. I thought that their buzzed haircuts, the peach fuzz inevitably growing out too fast, made them look young. Indeed they were young and lanky, unsure of what to do with their arms, jostling one another, banging against mailboxes and signposts. Lately you saw them everywhere, their legion multiplying. You learned to avoid certain corners, entire blocks. Each week, it seemed, you rezoned a mental map. They headed into a métro entrance and descended.

"Creepy," Will said.

I leaned against him. He smelled like cloves.

"I have a friend here," I said. "His family has a cottage in the country. There's no town to speak of, nothing for miles. Maybe we should head there for a few days."

Will hummed. "Sounds pleasant."

"I'll see about getting the keys," I said. And then a stab of guilt: This friend I mentioned would be angry with me; our habit was to speak every day, but I'd not called him since Will arrived.

We rejoined the march and ended up next to a man wearing a stole of child-legs. The child had chocolate smeared all over his jowls along with the remnant cream of an éclair, and I suspected that he had partaken of the forbidden leavening. Will and I tried to hang at the edge of the crowd, but we kept getting drawn toward the middle of the street, the human rapids, and we ended up staying the course all the way to the river, past an aproned man standing outside a brasserie and cradling a bundle of baguettes like illicit firearms, dispensing them freely to anyone who appeared ready to take up the cause. I took a loaf from him, and so did Will, unsure what we were supposed to do with them, and we followed the crowd down to the quay.

Parisians lined both banks of the Seine as far north and south as I could see, a wall of woolen bodies, still now against a gathering breeze. They lined the loose stitching of bridges, too. And now we understood what everyone was doing with the stale bread. New arrivals like us were able to push our way to the edge and encouraged by example to tear off a piece and launch it as far as we could into the black folds of the river.

I pitched a segment of my baguette into the water and caught myself smiling the same way a boy smiles the first time he makes a toy sailboat complete a circuit in a fountain pool. I noticed that I was not the only one grinning; everyone who stepped to the edge of the river and made a contribution to the float of crust was smiling, too.

It seemed clear to me that this protest went beyond a mere boycott of the bakeries. We were saying to the bakers, We don't need your bread at all. We were throwing it all away, whatever we had, even stale leftovers. And yet the act, what meaning we assigned it, did not seem born from anger so much as prayer. Witness how quiet the crowd at the river became, sober, full of hope, or so I wanted to believe. I imagined that the stoop-shouldered man with a white mustache standing next to me, a war medal pinned to his overcoat, was remembering a Paris that was safe at night, and a black woman a few steps down from him was thinking that even if she wanted to, she didn't have the money to go home to Africa the way all of the graffiti suggested she should. And a younger woman next to her might have been whispering, Take back the laws, take back those evil laws.

Then again, the man with the mustache could have been muttering, Why don't you people find your own ducks to feed?

And the black woman near him was thinking, The more things change—

And the younger woman: I hope they keep bombing the trains.

I tore off another piece of bread and flung it into the current and watched it bob and capsize. I lost track of which raft amid the soggy flotilla was mine. I looked at Will, and I realized that he hadn't ripped off a single piece of his baguette and instead was staring straight across the river. I couldn't tell what he had fixed on.

What I saw were the spires of the famous monuments in the near and far distance, the dome of les Invalides catching what sun there was like a gold coin in mid-toss. I could hear quiet murmurs from distant quarters, all the worry of the centuries echoing through the twisting climbs of the old city, the sorrow rising along a soprano line. Sometimes I wondered why Paris had not yet cratered and collapsed against the weight of its long and weary history.

I launched the rest of my baguette into the river like a javelin, as far toward the nearest bridge as I could hurl it. It was a good long throw. The bread skimmed the surface before settling.

I felt faint. I stepped back from the edge of the river and sat down on a bench set into the wall of the embankment. Will followed me.

"Ça va?" he asked.

"Ça va, ça va," I said, "but you were right. I should have eaten something."

He handed me his baguette, and I ripped off a piece, and to my surprise, unlike the loaf that I had just chucked, the crust of Will's bread was thin and cracked easily; the bleached white of the bread was warm, not the least bit stale. It couldn't have been baked more than an hour ago. I ate what I needed to and then a man in a soiled raincoat approached me. His eyes were hollow and dull; he looked exhausted. He pointed at the bread. When I gave it to him, he moved away, into an alcove in the wall. He plopped down. He tore at the bread and swallowed all of what I had given him quickly enough to convince me that it was the first food he had eaten in far too long.

"Pedro," Will said.

He did not look at me but back out at the river, across it again.

"I want to get out of here," he said. "I want to go somewhere else. As soon as we can, this evening."

"We can go to my friend's cottage," I said.

"No, I mean out of the country," Will said.

"Out of the country? Where?"

"I don't know yet. Somewhere neither one of us has ever been. Somewhere new," he said.

Somewhere new. These words made me breathe fast.

"I didn't know it when I came here," he said. "I thought we would just lounge around, talk—I didn't know, you have to believe me. But now I know what I want."

He faced me.

"Come with me," he said.

All of us know someone we chase our whole lives. An early heartache haunts us across the years and by some ration makes its way into any new romance. Old sorrow has a way of renewing itself in new sorrow. All of us know someone whom we lost in our youth who forever determines what we look for in new lovers. A certain habit of casual dress—unbuttoned sleeves that fall back to reveal slender wrists. The cadence with which an anecdote is rendered. We watch, we observe the most mundane tasks—the quartering of a pear, the decanting of wine—and then from there, a much more profound hunger will drive us the way it did long ago, an ineffable draft, the urgent need to know everything about that man or woman, which is to say what you can never know, the deep summer orchard of someone's child-hood. And the years fade, and you fall in love a hundred times, and after a while, you can only recognize a pattern in yourself without remembering how it began, the long wend of a long river with a distant and hidden, untraceable source.

"Will you come with me?" Will asked.

All of us know someone. Yet now it would appear that the man whom I had chased for so long was chasing me. And who was he, I wondered, who was Will Law? I thought I knew him well—but did I?

I looked up at the sky, which was a deep gray, but not because the clouds were anxious with rain, although it would rain later. A great flock of birds hung over the river; the birds were dark, and they blocked the sun. All of the gulls and the pigeons of the

Île-de-France, silently hovering, too awestruck to squawk, flapping fast, circling, and finally dropping down toward the water
to start in on what would inevitably be known among them for
some time to come as a most miraculous feast.

$\underline{2}$

WE AGREED TO MEET back at my flat and parted ways. Will couldn't find a cab, which made him late. He cut up to the Faubourg, chased a series of short streets that didn't form quite the shortcut he had in mind, and walked fast all the way to the place Vendôme, which was empty except for a small police squadron assembled outside the Justice building, half of them in riot gear. His footsteps echoed around the Napoleonic column. Inside the hotel, however, all manner of people buzzed about or waited on a twisting queue for the concierge, patrons checking out early, trying to leave the city. Will caught his breath and called upstairs; an unfamiliar voice gave him a room number and indicated that lunch had already been ordered. As he ascended the full height of the hotel in a dark-paneled elevator, he thought: What am I doing? I don't belong here.

The man on the phone met Will at the door of the suite; he

was wearing a black three-button suit and looked as if he had just finished college. Garrett Jencks appeared a moment later, the same as ever.

"William Law, that can't be you," he boomed.

Will shook his hand. "Afraid so," he said.

"The Will I know is about three feet tall and has a few teeth missing," Jencks said.

"I have all my teeth," Will said.

"The Will I know is a damn fine archer, and he hates bees."

"I'm out of practice with my bow and arrow, sir," Will said.

"Sir? Have I been knighted?" Jencks asked his assistant.

"No, sir," the assistant said.

"Well, then. Okay, you can leave us. Go pick up some heiress at the bar. Our plane is at?"

"Four," the assistant said, heading out of the suite. "The car at two-thirty." And he was gone.

"Look at you," Jencks said.

Will wondered if he had stopped blushing.

"I feel old now," Jencks said. "Very old indeed."

He collapsed into a couch. He may have left the State Department, but State hadn't left him. He was wearing the right suit for a European city in mid-autumn (gray with a reluctant chalk-stripe), the right shirt (blue with a starched white collar and cuffs, square gold links), but no tie (not yet). And black wing-tip oxfords, which he put up on the glass-topped coffee table, avalanching an alp of faxes and newspapers.

"Still don't like bees?" Jencks asked.

"No, but who does?"

"Beekeepers," Jencks said. "And me. I don't mind them really.

They perform some function in the grand scheme of things, I'm sure."

Will said, "Your assistant said that you ordered lunch."

"Do you mind? You were running late. I have a dinner in Berlin—"

"No, sir."

"Garrett. Or Uncle Garrett. Or Uncle Beekeeper."

"I'm sorry I'm late—"

"Is it madness out there?" Jencks asked.

Madness was an exaggeration, but Will nodded anyway.

Jencks reached down to his left sock and scratched a bald leg.

"We knew this would happen today," he said.

"Did you?"

"Everyone in the hotel is probably down in the lobby checking out early."

Will nodded.

"Getting out before the revolution hits. People can be such fools," Jencks said. "Excuse me, but when you leave the FS, as I'm sure you've already discovered, you become completely uncharitable. You overcompensate for all the time when you couldn't say what you truly thought."

He glanced at the paper-thin layer of gold on his wrist, his watch.

"It will be over by three," he predicted. "There will be some carousing tonight, those gangs, et cetera. Tomorrow morning, the Assemblée will pass something or other. The President on television. Yes, we knew, and frankly, this day will come and go. How long are you in town?"

Will regretted arranging the meeting. The tedious requisite

reminiscing about his father and maybe even some reference to
his sainted mother—he knew it would come soon, and he didn't
want to listen to any of it. Garrett Jencks and Will's father had
served together somewhere early on in their careers, Will wasn't
even sure where. Germany or Italy after the War. They ran a
small city. Will had been a late child, his sisters were much older,
and Jencks—now that Will got a good look, judging from the
brown atolls dotting his hands—Jencks had to be over seventy.
Singles was difficult, yet he was still good for doubles.

There was a knock at the door. It was a white-jacketed, dark-
skinned man with a silver cart and silver-domed platters. He
spread a cloth on a table across the room from the couch and, as
if from his sleeve, produced a slender silver bud vase with two
fiery roses. Jencks took a call in his bedroom while the man set
the table.

"Where is he now?" Jencks barked. "Can you get him to
Berlin tonight? He needs to go to Berlin. And tell him we've got
it under control. No, hardly, but tell him that anyway."

Then, returning to the room, Jencks tipped the waiter, who
half-bowed as he left.

"Alone at last," Jencks said, removing his jacket, unfurling a
napkin across his lap. "It's good to see you, Will. Good to see you."

Alone in a suite in a grand hotel and feeling all of a sudden
very low. Now and then Will missed his father, but mostly he
thought about his mother, who had died a long time ago. He
didn't think that she would have been able to offer him counsel,
not the kind he needed, but he could imagine calling her and
talking about nothing in particular, a crossword, a book he'd
read, and that would have soothed him. Will glanced at Garrett

Jencks's gray mane, his manicure. His permanent tan. This was a mistake.

First there was soup, some kind of melon bisque, which was creamy and rich but ultimately too sweet. Will picked out a warm roll from the basket and focused on that instead, ripping it into small pieces.

"Your father and I had a great lunch once during the Missile Crisis," Jencks said. "I was just back from—where? I don't know. He was at State. Those were tricky times."

Jencks sliced a roll in half and smeared it with the whitest butter.

"Anyway, I came in from wherever and we had a lunch date and I went up to your father's office. His secretary, a nice girl, she let me in, but your father was nowhere to be seen. Then he called out to me—Jencks, over here. I looked around, I didn't see him. Jencks, over here, he said. Jencks, over here. Well. Your father was under his desk."

Jencks tipped his head back as if swallowing a pill and gasped a laugh.

"Under his desk—get it? Because of the Missile Crisis. We ended up eating our Reubens on the floor."

Will smiled politely.

"Your father," Jencks said.

"A famous man," Will said.

That did not seem to be what Jencks was going to say, but he agreed with a single nod. He said, "We all wanted to be your father."

Now Will expected something along the lines of the standard he-would-be-proud. Will had followed in his father's footsteps.

Garrett Jencks said, "I know all about Mexico, Will."

Of course he did. Jencks had resigned from the Foreign Service and started up his own public relations firm, but naturally he maintained his old affiliations.

"It's tough," Jencks said. "You're doing your job. You see things you don't like. You know you shouldn't freelance—the policy is the policy. However. You're arrogant enough to think you can make some quiet overtures, and that's the beginning of the end, isn't it?"

Jencks didn't add more; he had offered just enough of an abstract scenario to make Will believe that indeed he knew the truth. Although he couldn't know the entire truth, the facts, such that they were; Will himself couldn't be sure about what had happened. The only concrete facts were who was dead. And all these months, every day, no matter where he traveled, the question that trailed him, that haunted him and made him crazy because it could never be accurately answered: Was he to blame? Or better put: How much was he to blame?

Jencks bused the table; he removed the shallow soup dishes and replaced them with two broad-brimmed plates, each one petaled with duck medallions and out-of-season legumes, a spray of some fruited sauce spiraling the dish.

"I'm glad you sought me out," Jencks said.

Will reached for another roll and then caught himself: They were eating bread. He returned the roll to the basket.

"Let them eat cake and so forth," Jencks said and smeared more butter across the warm dough.

Will wanted to lunch quickly and flee. Forget his original mission. He had decided that he would run off somewhere with me and therefore didn't need Garrett Jencks's help finding employment. His only goal now was to survive this meal without further discovery of his crimes.

"The duck is excellent," he said, even though he thought the bird had been roasted dry. "Very smoky."

"Le canard," Jencks said.

"And the white asparagus."

"I don't know the word for asparagus," Jencks said. "No matter the language, I have trouble with vegetables. Why is that?"

Will knew that he needed to grab the wheel of this conversation, and so he launched into a coiling tale about how, contrary to the way he was brought up—no matter where in the world his family lived, his mother always made sure she could find a cook who could whip up a sturdy hollandaise—he would habitually hang out in favorite restaurant kitchens in order to learn the nuances of local ingredients. In Tangiers, for instance, he had practically become a sous-chef in one kitchen before he understood how to grind turmeric with cumin and ginger and add the mix to whatever lamb and vegetables were stewing in the tajine. The spices temporarily left his fingertips yellow. But the real skill he had acquired was preserving lemons—

"So you're quite the gourmet," Jencks interrupted.

"I like food, that's all."

"You've done your share of traveling of late," he added.

Will swallowed an entire haricot. The beans were nearly translucent.

"Trying to figure out your next move."

Why did he think he would be able to change the subject?

"And I know what it's like, I've been there, at that crossroads. And you don't want to try to go back to the FS," Jencks said.

"I don't," Will said. "I couldn't anyway."

"You're quite sure."

"Quite," Will said. "And actually, since coming to Paris—"

"I have to say that to some degree, I understand how you feel," Jencks said. He wiped a smudge of sauce from his chin. "What you've been through."

Will looked at the man's face, his hands, measuring again how he had aged. He could picture himself on a lawn of the summer house with Garrett Jencks, in seersucker slacks, rattling the ice of an early cocktail. You'll see a lot of cricket someday, Uncle Garrett had said, and you won't get it, don't try.

"We don't live in the same world we used to," Jencks said. "When your father and I— Okay, no more war stories. But I will tell you, this is why I got out: The rules changed."

Will gave in. He knew he couldn't hold Garrett Jencks back from winding through whatever he seemed eager to discuss. He was much more practiced in the art of lunch.

"And from all accounts, once you left the FS, you built up quite a business," Will said.

"I'm a regular trailblazer," Jencks said.

"You're based in New York," Will said.

"New York and Washington," Jencks said.

"Which do you prefer?"

"Neither, but I'm on a plane all the time anyway. My current wife thought retirement from State would give me more time for the orchids, and well. I've got a dinner in Berlin, as I told you."

"Breakfast in Milan?"

"You know the drill," Jencks said. "Actually, back in Paris."

They finished their duck.

"In your note, you mentioned relief work," Jencks said. "Wanting me to find you work at an agency or—"

"That was a few weeks ago," Will said.

"Which is why you got in the game in the first place, right? To do good works? Listen, I'm a major-league cynic, but I do applaud that. Sincerely, I do applaud you."

To do good works—there was something acid in the phrase.

Dessert was a mousse au chocolat, and because, like me, Will could eat anything made with dark chocolate at any hour, he let himself enjoy this part of the lunch. The mousse was light on the tongue; the tiniest fragments of chocolate gave it some crunch.

"Your father was my best friend, Will. I've kept track of you for him. And then you contacted me. So I've been thinking about you. Your future."

Will held the spoon in his mouth. It suddenly occurred to him that Garrett Jencks would offer him a job at his firm, and he began to consider the polite ways in which he could decline.

"And I've been thinking about myself. What I've done in the last ten years, what I've made of myself. You see, I've been very introspective lately. What will be my legacy, et cetera."

Here it came.

"You don't want to turn into me," Jencks said and blinked an avuncular wink.

Will returned his spoon to his bowl. He was surprised and must have looked it.

"Truly. You do not want to turn into me."

"Garrett—"

"You do not want, excuse me, to fuck up the way I did."

Will squinted.

"I never should have left State. And you. You, Will, should make tracks back as soon as you can."

Jencks dug into his mousse.

Will didn't know how to respond. If Jencks knew the truth, he would also know that Will's career as a diplomat was finished. The day he got on a plane without telling anyone. The day he left Mexico, it officially ended.

"I can't go back," Will said.

"I know you think that. But look at me." Jencks stretched out his arms. "I am what you will become, and you do not want to be me."

"You've built up your company from scratch," Will said.

He didn't necessarily know the true nature of that enterprise, nor did he necessarily regard his father's friend with high esteem, but he suddenly found himself in the queer position of wanting to bolster the older man's self-assessment.

Jencks leaned back in his chair. "Yes, the largest crisis management firm in the world, expanding every day."

"I see you quoted in the papers," Will said.

"Oh, yes. I can chitchat about all manner of nonsense that I know nothing about. I make beaucoup d'argent that way. But do you know how I really pay my alimonies?"

Will shrugged.

"A sultan buys a country club and is accused of being anti-Semitic. We have him donate some money to a Jewish museum. The son of a mob boss is a legit businessman who wants to make movies. We do the advance work in Bel Air. We find him the right house, get it decorated with some local art, have him throw a housewarming— There's ample cash in tarnished reputations. Sometimes we simply get scandal maidens their magazine covers—they tell their side of the story while we are quite liberal with the airbrush—and their heart-surgeon daddies pay nicely for everything. Or there's the reason I'm in Paris: I have a client, he's quite the rising étoile in the Socialist government, but he could be peripherally implicated in that utility privatization scandal. My job: keep his name out of the indices of all the various books being published. That's quite a feat. I charge accordingly."

Will folded his napkin.

"That's what you do when you return to the private sector," Jencks said. "It's silliness. And I'm not a player. I talk to my old pals, but I'm not in the game. My canoe doesn't go down the info-stream. I mean, sure, I see the wire reports, I read what I read. But it's just not the same. I don't have access to the people on the ground. I don't have the satellite shots. I mean, Will. Admit it. Don't you miss it?"

"Sir?"

"The morning briefings, the midnight rumors. Don't you miss it?"

Information was the soil of any decision tree; every diplomat knew that. You collected it from the field. You sifted through it, packaged it, sent it back to Washington. And Will knew firsthand that digging your fingers into that wet loam was a powerful sensation.

But he said, "I don't miss it, no."

"You lie."

"No, I don't think I miss—"

"You lie," Jencks insisted.

Will pushed his chair back from the table.

"Do you know how it came to be that a Foggy Bottom lifer like myself left government on the eve of an ambassadorship?" Jencks asked.

Will did not.

"Look. I'm not going to show you my wounds, and I don't really need to see yours. I'll just tell you this. As you know, I worked the Balkans. I didn't like what we were doing, but I did my job, I negotiated my piece of the treaty. I was tuning the language on the interim government. Basically we were backing evil men. Basically we said that in the name of peace, we should look the other way while— I don't have to tell you. Everybody knows the chronology now. I did my job and didn't quit despite my several threats, and then, as you know, one of my colleagues resigned rather publicly. You no doubt remember all the editorials, he became a hero. I took his place, wrapped up the accord. We all knew it was useless—it wouldn't stand. And it didn't. These days, history measures our work much sooner then we'd like. However, the Secretary was suddenly very chummy. He promised me the big desk. At long last, after all I'd worked for. But I thought, I'm better than that. I still have principles, so I resigned, too. I started up my firm with some other ex-FS. Which was such a mistake."

"Why was it a mistake?" Will asked. "You maintained your position—"

"Hardly. You're not that naive. I was just jealous of the guy who got all the editorials written about him. My colleague the hero with his two-book deal who became the special envoy when the treaty did collapse. Returned to the region. Became a hero all over again for basically redrawing my borders and rearranging my timetables."

Jencks moved to the couch, but Will didn't join him.

"I was just jealous. I am not a moral man," Jencks said. "You know that. And we know how you know it—let's be frank. You've had your lapses."

Will retreated to a window that looked down on the empty square. When it was sunny, the column at its center became like a pointer on a sundial, but it was now cloudy.

"You should return to the FS. It's where you belong."

"That would be impossible," Will said.

"I asked myself: What can I do for the only son of my old friend? What influence do I still have that I can spend on his behalf?"

Will faced him, his arms crossed. Now he understood where the conversation was running.

"I made calls."

The back of Will's neck became cool.

"It's all set."

He should have seen it coming.

"You can go back," Jencks said.

Will didn't know how to be polite about his anger. How to tell off your late father's best man. How to say fuck you to someone who probably remembered your mother's favorite flower.

"Jakarta," Jencks said. "The staff of the political counselor—that's the gig."

"I didn't ask for this," Will said softly.

"I know, I know. Jakarta was your first posting. For you it

seems like a step back, like starting over. Returning to the
Indonesia team. But a lot is happening there very fast—I don't
need to tell you. Listen, here's what I got: You'll resume as an
FS2, and I suspect you could get back on the meteor track,
expect to make FS1 in a year. After that, you can open your
window. Two, three years tops, I say you're Senior FS. That
would be some kind of record. I don't think what happened in
Mexico will affect your chances. To the contrary."

"Garrett," Will said.

He swallowed. He didn't know what he wanted, but it
wasn't this.

"After what you did, what you've been through, you think
you're finished," Jencks said. "Listen to me. You're more valued
now than you were before."

Will crossed the room and sank into the couch without even
feeling his legs move. He was numb. Minutes of silence followed.

Then Will asked, "What's the catch?"

Jencks chuckled.

"You are not going to tell me— With all due respect," Will
said, "you are not going to tell me that your influence and my
family name erased what happened in Mexico."

"You proved yourself utterly capable. Maybe you got in over
your head, and yes, after you left, it became clear that you were
the source of the leaks. But by and large, truly, the feeling was
that you performed well. Everyone was very impressed."

Performed well? Impressed? People were dead. A family was
dead—Will thought about them all the time. In over his head?
Yes, he got in over his head, and so he fled, he wandered for a

year as if he were on the run. Although technically speaking, no one was chasing him; officially he had committed no felonies.

"Some of our people have been stationed in Jakarta for a very long time, too long. They kind of like the old regime. Apparently there are a few questions about some of the political counselor's—how should we put it?—business affiliations, which State wants checked out before it becomes, well, an embarrassment," Jencks said. "So I'm told. I'm sure you'll receive much more detail."

"They want me to spy," he said.

"You've worked the region. You know, you could be an Asia-hand if you wanted—you could build on that. Of course, they want you for this because you know who does what for whom and how over there. Am I wrong?"

They wanted to run him like they ran him before.

"If what you did in Mexico offers any proof," Jencks said. "Well. I'm sure you'll gather the appropriate data."

"The appropriate data."

"Look," Garrett Jencks said. "We're all spies anyway."

Will squinted: Say what you mean.

"Diplomats and the folks in foreign aid and the certified spooks themselves. It just depends on what budget line your salary comes from—what you're allowed to say at cocktail parties. Hell, journalists, too. We're all spies. We all maintain our contacts, run the locals whom we trust, pay them well. We all collect information and route it back to the Washington desks, but here's the thing that I learned a long time ago."

A gust of cool air pushed back a pair of sheer curtains.

"You observe, you spy—call it what you want. You are reliable and thorough and fleet. You know your territory and speak with authority. But you edit what you send back," Jencks said. "You edit—therein lies your true power. That is how you make policy. I know I'm not telling you anything you don't know, Will."

"And you think my father would be comfortable with this?" Will asked. "I get back in the game by spying on my boss? Maybe my father would have approved of the Mexico assignment, but to spy on my brethren, that's very different—what would he think?"

Garrett Jencks neither smiled nor blinked.

"I could find you other work," he said. "I could get you something in a book-lined office. I've got a client, a publisher. But Will. Will, please: You belong out there. It's who you are."

"Who I am," Will echoed, his voice weak.

Here was where the years had carried him. He had grown up subscribing to a simple credo that his father claimed would serve him well: If any two people talk long enough, they will find something meaningful to agree upon, no matter how polar or violent their differences. His father believed this with all his heart, although half-seriously he used to add: If nothing else, you can start with the weather. All of us against the sun—it is the same story everywhere.

Will never questioned that diplomacy made for the most significant work, and while most of the FS brats in his circle viewed their parents as a species approaching extinction, he held fast to a singular destiny for himself. He got a master's in international relations, a job at the UN. Will would go out for drinks after work with the other interns and low-level support staff and end up talking the night away in an East Side bar. They were so young then, sincere, invested. And all conversation inevitably drifted toward the same topic, the idea of the moral line that, as diplomats, they knew they could never cross.

Everyone drew his own tropic. Some believed in the use of force, even at the risk of civilian casualty, but would never stand for torture. Some said that you had to allow a totalitarian regime to apply its own law as it saw fit, if that law ensured that a dominion was fed. Some said concessions like ignoring child-labor abuses were necessary speed bumps along the road to economic maturity. Regardless of ideology, however, they all knew that they had to maintain that tropic, stay north of it, never cross it, because once it was traversed, they could never claim that they were guided by any sort of code. Once moved, the line would be moved again, and again. And years later, Will could not remember where he had drawn his own line. He had crossed it a long time ago.

What did he believe? Where did his line fall now?

Jencks patted him on the knee.

"You know you love nothing more than arriving in a new place," he said. "Knowing you've got at least two years there. It makes you lonely at first—but in many ways, you're a bit of a loner. You crave that isolation. Being cut off from what you know, from whom you know."

Jencks reached over to an end table and fingered a green silk tie.

"The wife, the kids haven't come yet, won't for weeks or even months. Or in your case—well, I'm sure you know what I mean."

It's true, Will thought. You are on your own. The puzzle of the place is all yours. Figuring out how the city works. Who runs what. Who knows whom. Where to eat, the better cafés.

"You begin to buy things for your flat," Jencks said. "Rugs. Rugs and fabric always come first."

And what you need to make your morning coffee. The dinked-up filter pot. The hand-grinder. The beans themselves.

"You don't have much in the way of things," Jencks said and began knotting his tie. "You keep it that way."

A few good suits. A few favorite objects that you carried from place to place—a carved mahogany vase, a hammered-tin candlestick.

"There's a kind of efficiency to your possessions. Every tie goes with every shirt—you keep it simple. Three pairs of trousers to every blazer. You don't accumulate too much. Doing laundry the first time is always terrible."

Until you find the man you can pay to do your wash and look after your shoes and sweep your rooms, beat your rugs, neaten the batik you've thrown over the daybed.

"And basically all you have to be is clean-cut. Temperate. Represent America's interests abroad—I believe that's still the phrase we use. But in many ways, you can be whomever you please. No one knows you."

Which makes it easy to be charming. No one knows your flash point or your truest longing. Locals are suspect, they should be, and there's the challenge. How to befriend them. How to make them believe in your goodness and therefore the goodness of the nation you come from—bottom line, that was the game. You are expected to minister your humanity.

"Every two years," Jencks said. "You start over."

Arriving had its pleasures, but so did departing.

"Fraternizing with your colleagues in the consulate—let's be honest," Jencks said through half a smile. "You're always leaving, so why not? What do you have to risk? A few postings later, you may meet up again, maybe back in Washington—but that's not so bad actually...."

Departing: You entered contracts of brief passion. It was understood: I'm leaving, you're just getting here—whatever we do, the weeks we have will be fast, they will be hot. Let me show you around. There's this one nightclub. You should see the coast. This weekend we'll get a car. You need to see the ruins.

"You love everything about that life, Will. All the details. The letters you write back to your friends."

The images you drew with airmail syntax. Describing the sponge divers, the women selling mud cloths in the marketplace, the games children invented. A certain meal. The view from your terrace. The native sunset, forever new to you.

"To these people, you've seen the world, and we know what that confers. They think you wise."

Your beat-up writing desk with its empty inkwell. The cobalt-blue bottle someone left behind, which you make a vase.

"And let's not forget the black-tie evenings for the people who show up from back home," Jencks said.

Your maps. Your pocket dictionaries. You are something of a linguist—a bricoleur of idioms.

"A splendid buffet, decent champagne for the toast. The baroque concertos performed by a gamelan."

The market and the vendors who know you. The clean black teas. The rough green fruits that ripen red and smooth. The copper lamp you never got around to restoring.

"Let's not forget about your forays into the countryside. The merchants you're helping, they feel the need to show you yet one more temple, egad. And then soon enough you're home again. You go back to your flat in the city. And strangely, it is home."

You move around so often and remake that home so many times that in an odd way, you come to know yourself quite well. You never doubt who you are, Will thought, because you understand what you need to assemble, the few essential objects that will make you comfortable someplace where you don't belong.

Jencks pulled his tie tight. He brushed back his wiry gray sideburns with his fingertips.

"And now and then," he said, smirking, "you genuinely help someone. Will, what's the best thing you ever did for someone?"

Will shrugged.

"Come on. What is it?"

Early in his career. Back in Jakarta. Two Indonesian teenagers were in jail. They'd been wrongly accused of selling drugs to American exchange students. One faced caning and a short life at hard labor and the other was scheduled to be executed. Will heard about them. He got involved. He was able to secure affidavits from the deported Americans. He got them all out of trouble, the American kids and the Indonesian boys. The mothers of the latter were so grateful—outside the prison, one mother would not let go of him. She hugged him and would not let go.

And there were other stories he could tell. He had used the power of his office. He had worked on border disputes. On easing sanctions in order to move medical supplies to remote clinics.

"Well, I'm sure you know," Jencks said. "My point is, we are lucky to live that life, and I know what happened spooked you, but. Make tracks back. Take the post. You're very much needed. You're very much wanted. Do a little nasty work and don't get innocent on me, please."

At the door, he drew Will into an old-chum hug.

Will stepped back.

"Your mother," Jencks said, "was the smartest woman I ever met. I miss her."

"Me, too," Will said.

"We need more time. You haven't told me what a young buck does for fun in Paris these days."

Will leaned back against the doorframe.

"On second thought, maybe I don't want to know. But look: You can have your life back. And I envy you deeply."

Will cleared his throat. "You shouldn't envy me," he said.

"Arrogance, my fatal flaw," Jencks said. "I keep saying we, and I shouldn't. You, they. I don't live that life anymore. I got out, I want back in, but I'm too old. I should be happy in retirement, but I will tell you that I am hopelessly restless. And it's only taken you a decade at the game to realize what it took me half a century to figure out, namely the rules."

"Garrett," Will started to speak.

He wanted to say, Thanks but no thanks. He wanted to say, This life is not for me after all. You don't know me now. I am not like you. I am trying to be a better man than you. My generation is not your generation, times have changed—we pursue a higher code.

He wanted to say: There is a man named Pedro. Did you ever meet him? Pedro from years ago. We leave tonight for I don't know where. You will never hear from me again.

"Think about it, Will. You owe yourself that, to think about it."

Will stared at his shoes, dusty and scuffed; he said nothing at all. Here was where the years had carried him: He did not like himself very much.

"I fly to Berlin now," Jencks said, "but I'm coming back here to Paris late tonight. We can talk some more. You call me."

Will took a deep breath. He stepped into the hallway.

Garrett Jencks said, "Don't worry, young Will. Everything will work out for you. You'll know how to make your way. Everything will work out for you just fine."

HE DRIFTED BACK TOWARD the Seine. His mood grayed like the afternoon. The last few days had been the loftiest in a long while, yet now, as he found himself alone again, a familiar funk weighed him down. It was the worst sort of drag: The weather had a hold on him; he felt as if he was blending into the pale stone walls.

After he left Mexico, he had traveled to many of the countries where his father had been posted while Will was growing up. He ended up renting an apartment in Athens near where he and his family had lived when he was ten. He kept his days simple. He woke when the sun came through the windows he left unshuttered; he rolled onto the floor and did two hundred push-ups, three hundred crunches; he washed his face in a basin; he wandered out into the street. He wrote part of a letter to me in a café in his miniature all-caps. He slept away a fair portion of the afternoon, then rolled onto the floor and did another two hundred push-ups, three hundred crunches—staying in shape proved to be a useful distraction. He found an English-language bookstore that was about to close for the day; he bought a novel he'd always wanted to read, although he would read only half of it. He wandered the night, listening to languages he didn't know— but by the time he got to Paris, he could not remember how he spent all those dark hours. He had no recollection.

He moved to an island in the Aegean, and before long, he began to feel like—what? Like an island slow-baked in an uncompromising sun. Isolated, forgotten. Day after day, losing his shore to the sea. So he moved on. And for about a week, he would walk around high on a new place. Revisiting the temples he admired in his youth. Making a tour of the ruins. His father had been an important man whose trade was peace, and the Laws lived in Turkey, Israel, Egypt; Will spent time in Istanbul, Jerusalem, and Cairo. He ended up in Morocco, in Tangiers. He rented a house with the last of his cash—soon he would start spending principle; not how he was raised—a narrow house with a rooftop deck and a view of the souk in the near-distance. He drank syrupy coffee all day, and yet he slept and slept, on a daybed, out on the deck. And eventually the climate got the better of him, the architecture. Imagine. You feel dry all the time, bleached. He could never quench his thirst. There was so much dust in the air. He pictured his skin flaking off and becoming that dust. Just try to imagine. You can't hold on to yourself, your sense of yourself in contrast to where you live. It is a form of disappearing.

Now it was happening all over again.

Fade, vanish. Leave no trace of where you have been.

He followed the quay and was barely aware of the spectacle around him. The crowd at the river beginning to disperse. The police out in full force. A gang amassing, looking for trouble. He crossed over to the Left Bank. Book vendors had started opening their stalls. He glanced up at the grim mass of Notre-Dame, a shadowless fortress, awkwardly buttressed, without grace. Lunch was not sitting well with him—waves of nausea came and went—but he kept walking, heading nowhere in particular.

The pont de Sully was still closed to traffic, and he crossed it back to the Right Bank and then found himself leaning against a plane tree and vomiting into the grillwork around its base. He had to sit down on the curb and close his eyes.

He stayed like that awhile, his knees pulled to his chest, while people walked past and ignored him, which was fine. However, one passerby, a little boy who couldn't have been very old, was suddenly standing next to him and staring intently. He blinked at Will and Will blinked back.

"Nico, leave the man alone," a woman said.

Then the boy was replaced by a woman wearing a heavy brown sweater of a homemade knit, a single gray flake stitched across the front, its sleeves too long, and a large silver watch with a silver band over the fabric on her left wrist.

"Ça va, Monsieur?" she asked.

A green scarf grazed the hard line of her chin. Right away, this woman struck Will as someone who had endured some rough weather and ended up the more rugged for it, but then again, she couldn't have been much older than he was, if older at all.

"Vous êtes malade?" she asked.

"No," Will said. "I'm, I'm fine. Je suis, um, un peu fatigué."

"I suspected you were American," the woman said.

She squatted down next to him, and he noted an overstuffed camping pack strapped to her back. Also, she was holding a small plaid suitcase, a piece of child's luggage. The boy reappeared at the woman's side.

"Est-il mort?" the boy asked his mother.

"Non, non, Nico. Pas de tout," the woman said.

"Not yet," Will said and laughed and tried to smile at the kid. He had a headache and no desire to stand.

"Oh, baby, baby, baby," the boy said.

"Nico, none of that," the woman said—in English—and added: "He watches television when I'm not paying attention and sees these American movies—"

"Bock-bock," the boy said. Like a chicken. "Bock-bock-bock."

He looked nothing like his mother, who was a lapsed blonde and fair. The boy had dark-almond eyes and dark bangs; his complexion was dark, too.

"Not dead yet," Will said to the boy. "How old are you?"

The boy stepped forward and then looked back at his mother. "Quinze?" he asked her.

"Fifteen," she said. "You're not fifteen. Don't tell the man you're fifteen."

"I have fifteen," the boy said.

"He's four," the woman said.

The boy seemed small for his age. He looked like one of those cloth puppets with the large wooden heads. He wore a knit hat with ear flaps that were slightly askew.

The woman set the small plaid suitcase down and slipped her

arms through her backpack straps, letting it sink to the sidewalk. She stood and stretched.

"You just arrived?" Will asked.

"Oh, no," the woman said softly.

"Then you're heading out of town—"

"Non," the boy yelled. "Non, non, non."

"We're having a little disagreement," the woman said.

Will tried to stand as well. Slowly he unfolded himself. He was dizzier than he thought and had to lean against a lamppost.

"Are you okay?" the woman asked.

"I'll be fine," he said.

"I saw you sitting here, and you didn't look so hot."

"You were very sweet to stop," Will said.

Was it possible, he wondered, that she was flirting with him? Often he missed these signals. The vagaries of mating.

"I had a rich lunch," Will explained. "And lost it, I'm afraid."

"You should drink some water," the woman said. Motherly advice.

"Yes," Will said. "So where are you two headed?"

The woman looked out at the river and didn't respond. The boy wandered a few paces away, distracted by something beneath a bench, a squirrel perhaps.

"You really should drink some water," the woman insisted. "We were going to find a café, get some lunch before we catch a train—"

"Non," the boy said, pivoting. "Je ne veux pas. Zhoree, je ne veux pas."

The woman sighed. "We were heading for a train, you see, but Nico wanted to see what all the fuss was at the river, and so we walked over, and now he's changed his mind about taking this trip. We need some lunch," she said.

"Well, thank you for stopping," Will said.

"And you? Do you live here?" the woman asked.

"Me? Oh, no. I'm visiting," Will said. "I'm leaving tonight, actually."

"You're going to think I'm very strange," the woman said, "but it's sort of relaxing me to speak English. I don't speak a lot of English. Just to Nico when his father isn't around."

Will nodded as if he understood what she was telling him, which he didn't. What he did suspect, however, what he did pick up on was that she wasn't flirting with him at all. She was a weary and handsome woman with a boy of a certain bounce who looked nothing like her, and for some reason she was lonely.

"I've had a difficult day," the woman said. "And to talk to an American—I know it sounds strange, but it's such a relief."

She pointed to an open but mostly uninhabited bistro across the street in a greenhouselike structure extending beyond a beaux-arts hôtel.

"We're going to eat something, and maybe you want to join us," she said, and then glanced again toward the river.

Not flirting, but lonely, and why not, why not? She had risked breaking the code of urban aloofness to make sure he wasn't going to expire on the sidewalk. It was the least he could do.

"Sure," Will said. "I should get some water like you said." And he picked up the small suitcase for her; it turned out to be very light.

They fit themselves around a table in a window of the bistro.

The luggage occupied the place of a fourth person. A waiter gave them menus, and the boy instantly ordered.

"Un croque-monsieur," he said. He thought to add, "S'il vous plaît."

The waiter smiled politely and spoke to the woman.

"Il n'y a pas de pain, Madame, comme vous savez. Alors—"

"Right," Will intervened. To the boy: "No sandwiches today, I'm afraid."

The boy blinked.

"Mooza," he said.

The waiter wrinkled a brow.

"I gave you one in the park," the woman said.

"Mooza?" Will asked.

"Arabic for banana," she explained.

The waiter disappeared in a puff.

"Bock-bock," the boy said.

"Don't start," the woman said.

She scanned the menu and ordered food when the waiter returned. Will asked for a bottle of mineral water, which was the right move; soon he began releasing polite burps and felt much better.

The boy managed to invest some enthusiasm in the pea soup placed in front of him. He became quiet and steadfast in his slurping. The soup was a thick swamp, and when the woman offered Will a taste, he almost but ultimately did not accept. Now she seemed vaguely familiar to him, although he couldn't figure out why, whether she occupied some public role—was she a model?

"I'm sorry, I haven't introduced myself," Will said and did.

The woman shook his hand with a firm tug. Even though she was eating warm soup, her fingers were cold. Will noticed that she wore no rings.

"The soup is très bonne," the boy announced.

"I'm glad to hear it," Will said.

"Do you want some?" the boy asked in a small voice.

"No thanks," Will said but then reconsidered. "Well, okay."

He used the spoon from his own place setting and reached across the table, sampling the boy's bowl. And the soup tasted as green as it looked, both grassy and briny.

"What a day," the woman said. "Could you believe that scene at the river?"

Wait. He had given her his name, but she had not reciprocated.

"You know, I feel as though I've met you before," Will said.

She blushed.

And he thought: Okay, now I'm the one doing the flirting. I'm the one, for all she knows, who saw her coming down the street and fell to the ground and pretended to be ill so she'd stop, talk to me—it was possible people behaved that way.

He tried to recover his fumble: "I mean...I could be wrong...."

She shook his hand again, her hand a little warmer. Her name was Jorie Cole. Which meant nothing to him. So much for that.

"I've been here awhile, four years, so I doubt we'd have crossed paths if you're just visiting," she said.

"Je m'appelle Nico," the boy said.

"I'm sorry," the woman named Jorie said. "This is Nicolas Chamoun."

"Nicolas Chamoun," the boy echoed, as if his own appellation, like all the unsteady English phrases he auditioned, were unfamiliar as well.

"I do feel as though..." Will gave up. "I guess not," he said.

A generous salad followed the soup, replete with chicken chunks and squares of cheese, which was what the boy Nico went for first.

"Ouch," Jorie said.

She began to remove something from her trouser pockets. Chestnuts. She placed several of them on the table while Nico watched.

"He collected them in the park this morning," she said.

"Did you?" Will asked.

"I make a boat," Nico said.

"Out of nuts?"

"Oui."

"You'll need a lot more."

"I know," Nico said, suddenly serious. "It will take many, many marrons to make a boat."

"You see, there's this cat that lives in our building," Jorie said. To the boy: "I'm telling him about the cat."

"Le chat est white," the boy said.

"It's a white cat, yes," Jorie said, "with black markings. We're very fond of this cat, and Nico thought that when the fountain gets turned on in the spring, and there's water again in the reflecting pool, it might be nice if the cat had a boat that it could sail around in. You see."

"I do see," Will said. "That's a wonderful idea."

"So where in the States are you from?"

Will tried to construct an answer: "To tell you the truth, the only time I've lived there was during college and grad school."

Nico was only picking at the salad on his plate. He ran his spoon around the bowl, making patterns in the coagulated pea-murk around its edge.

"So you mean you grew up abroad," Jorie said.

"Jorie," Nico interrupted. He didn't call her Mom or Maman.

"Yes," she said.

"Je voudrais une mooza."

"Banana," Will said, the fast learner.

"Une banane," Nico said.

Jorie rested her chin in her palm. "Another?" she asked. To Will: "Don't you hate it when adults make children perform?"

Will wasn't sure how he was supposed to respond.

"I do it anyway," she said. "Hey, Nicolas."

She reached across the table and unzipped a pocket of her backpack and produced a small banana.

"Où est le Prince?" she asked.

Nico squinted.

"Have you seen him? I don't see him. Do you think...? Est-ce qu'il ne se serait pas transformé en chimpanzé?"

Nico looked at the banana, at Jorie, at the fruit again. He wiggled out of his chair and into the aisle between tables.

"I think the Prince turned himself into a monkey," Jorie said.

Which was the last cue the boy needed. He slouched over and dug his thumbs into his armpits and began flapping his folded arms like, well, not like a monkey at all but rather like a chicken. He strutted around, back and forth next to the table, and Jorie continued to hold the bait, the banana, in the air without rewarding it to him.

Nico began to issue a high-pitched bock-bock-bock, similar

to his earlier chicken noises, although in a higher key, bock-bock-bock, assuming even more of a barnyard posture.

"He used to have a monkey down pat," Jorie said. "You know, the dangling arms, the frown, the jungle noise—"

"Bock-bock," Nico said, strutting.

"Tu n'est pas un chimpanzé," Jorie said.

Nico kept flapping and bocking.

"Where is the Prince? I thought he turned himself into a monkey."

"Bock-bock-bock."

She frowned at Will, and Will could only shrug. She snapped the stem and gave Nico the banana.

He received it with a sly, confident grin, as if it were a prize he knew he would win no matter what animal he had imitated, as if he were just testing his mother. He seemed quite bright about people. He sat back down, and very carefully now, very slowly, he peeled the fruit. He took a series of small nibbles on the banana. In between bites, he looked at Jorie and, his mouth full of pap, issued another bock.

"I think we need to take a trip to the zoo to sort things out," Jorie said to him.

"Oui, oui," Nico cheered. "The zoo, the zoo."

Jorie combed the boy's hair out of his eyes.

"His father doesn't speak English," Will said.

"He speaks English just fine," Jorie said.

"Oh. I thought you were saying—"

"We speak English to each other mostly, Luc and I," Jorie said, "but French around Nico because Luc has a rule. Which I end up breaking."

Her husband's edict was that only French be spoken along with a sprinkling of Arabic; no English, which the child could learn after he was five. Five was the age, Jorie's husband believed, when a child could discern languages and know what words to use when. Jorie, however, said that she had heard the exact opposite—and they had argued about it—that if you let your kid hear and speak as many languages as possible in his first five years, he would sort it out on his own and grow up with an amazing facility at learning any new tongue he might encounter.

"Luc has his rules," Jorie said. "Get up before the sun does—that sort of thing."

Will felt a strong urge to take Jorie's hand. He meant nothing by it; she just seemed to need consoling.

Nico clearly heard his father's name and the hostility in his mother's voice, but he didn't look up from his banana peel.

Jorie adjusted her scarf.

"I taught myself Arabic," she said.

"That's impressive. I've just spent a lot of time in the Arabic-speaking world and came away with so little," Will admitted.

"Were you in Lebanon?"

"Lebanon? No," Will said.

"See, I taught myself Arabic so Luc and Nico and I could live in Lebanon. Where Luc is from. But. Well…"

Luc with the rules. Will sipped his mineral water.

"Do you know the rue de Belleville?" Jorie asked.

"In the Twentieth," Will said.

Nico became attentive, watching his mother speak.

"I love it there, what with all the smoky restaurants and import shops, and Nico and I wander the street often, but never with Luc, who refers to the area as l'Asie, Asia—you know, to be derogatory. So one day, I went and bought an Arabic language textbook. A teach-yourself. What's the phrase?"

"A how-to book?" Will asked.

"It's terrible. I lose a little English every day," Jorie said.

She went on to describe how she kept the primer hidden in her night table drawer on her side of the bed. When Luc was at work, she taught herself the alphabet. When he went away on business trips, which was often, she learned fundamental phrases. Her autodidaction remained furtive.

"But I only did this for a year or so," Jorie said, "and that was a while ago. And yet, every now and then, the odd phrase occurs to me."

"Mooza," Nico said softly.

Jorie cocked her head and looked at the boy and beamed. Her eyes brimmed with tears although she didn't cry.

"Tisbah àla khayr," she said to Nico. She translated for Will: "Good night, sleep well."

He nodded. The phrase sounded familiar.

"Àna musàfir li-wàhdee."

Will had to ask: "And that?"

"I am traveling alone," Jorie said.

She was silent awhile.

"In the end, I only made myself more lonely," she said.

A connection, a link, some fundamental cousinhood—how often did one meet a stranger and recognize that kind of bridge? What were the chances? A wash of sympathy made Will warm.

"I know how it is," he said.

"Do you?"

"I do, yes."

He leaned toward her. He composed his thought.

He said: "Learning a language without travel to where that language is spoken will only deepen your sense of isolation in the world."

"Yes," she said, "yes," her eyes wide—and it was she who reached across the table and briefly gripped his hand—"that's it exactly."

Nico turned toward the people walking past the bistro.

"I'm sorry," Jorie said. "I don't why I'm boring you with all this."

Will said, "Don't apologize. Please. I..."

He what? He wanted to thank her, although he wasn't sure why. Her candor seemed like an undeserved gift.

"It's such a relief to be able to talk to someone," Jorie said.

The sky had darkened to a point of no return, and sure enough, a bit of mist began to dust the windows.

"Visiting from where?" she asked.

"Me? From nowhere," he answered, which he knew sounded strange or rude. "I mean, I flew in from Rabat, but I haven't had a fixed address for over a year."

"I see. When you had a fixed address, where was that?"

He hesitated at first, but then he said, "Mexico. I was in the Foreign Service. And one day last year, I just left."

That silenced her again.

"And your father was an ambassador," she said.

Will leaned back in his chair.

"You're Will Law. He was William Law. Wasn't he—"

"Yes," Will cut her off. "How do you know?"

"My father was in the military," Jorie said. "We moved around a lot when I was growing up. Israel, Egypt."

"Turkey, Saudi Arabia," Will said.

"Will Law," Jorie said.

"Jorie Cole," Will said.

"I have to be honest," she said. "I don't really remember you, but I think—"

"Yes," Will said. And although he didn't know who she was for certain, he did confirm his own suspicion: At some point, they had fallen into the same orbit.

"The International School in Cairo? The American School in Tangiers?"

"Could be," Will said. "We'd have to do the math."

"And that was a lot of math ago," she said.

He looked at her and tried to imagine her at fourteen, at ten—however old he himself would have been. He attempted and frankly failed to see the girl in her, smaller-nosed, floppy-banged or feather-coifed. No, he didn't see it, but in some small way, he had recognized her.

"Will Law," Jorie said, still searching, searching, possibly failing, too, to recover the year and place. "I do think it was Cairo. Or Tangiers."

"I acted in some plays at the American School in Tangiers," Will said.

"Oh, no. I remember those plays. Who were you, the Gentleman Caller?"

"I was the older *Salesman* son. I had no clue what I was doing or what the play was about."

"I think I may have missed that one," Jorie said.

Will recounted his limited time on the boards. An outside director would always be brought in from the expatriate community, a man who wore ascots and adoringly remembered the original productions of whatever Broadway classic was insinuating itself into the international-school repertoire. Jorie knew precisely the man whom Will described.

"During my time there," she said, "he made me play a Salem witch. I was wretched. Wretched at acting, I mean, not as a witch."

"Didn't they know that all of this Americana was lost on us?" Will said.

"They never got it," Jorie said.

"American history was so—"

"Medieval, distant. Much farther away than European history. So you didn't go back to the States for any length of time when you were younger?" she asked.

"Just to visit the extended family."

"You were lucky, you realize that."

Jorie recalled one year in America while her father was assigned to the NSC. She had never felt more lonesome.

"Just now, I know that I said I wanted to talk to an American," she said, "but if you had started, I don't know, talking about sitcoms or something—"

"A natural thing for two people who don't know each other to discuss," Will said.

Jorie's laughter was loud.

Nico stared at her: Who was this crazy woman?

"You know what I mean," she said.

"I do," Will said. "It's not like we didn't get the same pop music, the same television back then. We just got them all a year or two later."

"Or we didn't pay attention to it."

"I remember on one holiday in the States, I went to a movie with some cousins. The movie was about college frat antics, and my cousins were rolling in the aisles, the whole audience was breaking up. I didn't get it. Beer pranks, tricks on professors—I sat there stone-faced. Like I'd been born on a another planet."

"One year we lived in Virginia," Jorie said, "and the next we were in Athens. I wanted to stand out at my new school, so I affected this deep involvement with country music."

Will giggled.

"No, truly. I made my friends listen to my tapes. I had this cowgirl hat. I haven't thought about this in years. . . . I'd tie a red scarf around my neck just so."

"The boots, too, I bet," Will said.

"I tried to talk with a twang, but I couldn't pull it off."

"That I'd like to hear."

Quietly Jorie warbled a line from some generic country lament, a single alto lyric of heartache. Then she and Will were silent.

"Jorie," Nico chirped. He'd had enough.

"Nico," she said.

"Let's go back to the bridge."

She checked the watch on her sweater sleeve.

"There's a train I want to take," she said.

"A train?" Will asked.

"Nico, won't you go on the train with me?"

He didn't say no this time nor did he say yes. Will could

watch the child's eyes shift back and forth, watch him ponder his next move in the eternal game of chess a four-year-old played with his mother.

"If we go to the river first," Nico declared.

"Voilà," Jorie said.

Will paid for lunch. Jorie protested. He insisted, and she didn't stop him.

He thought, We could talk for hours. We come from the same nowhere.

Outside the mist had thickened into more of drizzle. The three of them made their way back across the street and toward the pont de Sully.

"We probably know a lot of people in common," Will said.

"Possibly. Although I don't know anyone anymore," Jorie said.

Will was about to test her with my name, but then he remembered that while I had hung out with him and his friends in college, I was only a part of the expat crew because I was his friend and eventually boyfriend. Otherwise I had no connection to that circuit.

While the crowd along the Seine had diminished, there were still many people milling about, and no vehicles could make it across the bridge yet, though one taxi tried. Even motorcyclists had to foot-push their bikes through the gathering. Jorie was wearing her backpack again, and Will carried the small bag. Nico wandered ahead.

Jorie spoke his name when he strayed too far.

"Baby, baby, baby," the boy shouted back.

The pont de Sully was a gentle stone span—two bridges actually that touched down on the eastern tip of the Île Saint-Louis.

Will and Jorie followed Nico to the second bridge extending toward the Left Bank, where Nico approached a tall man leaning on the railing.

A flock of gulls, white chevrons in the dark sky, spiraled down toward the water.

The river looked like cold onion soup, a brown gruel with a soggy cap of bread. A bateau mouche appeared from under the bridge and maneuvered around a bank of the Île like an ice-breaker clearing a channel for smaller vessels.

Now Will wanted to tell Jorie something that would complete a kind of pact with her, the contract of friendship that she had already signed by telling him about how lonely she had made herself with her Arabic textbook, by suggesting dissonance in her marriage.

Nico ran back toward Jorie and pointed at her pack.

"Do you have any bread?" he asked.

"Sorry," she said.

He bolted away from her toward the tall man at the railing again. The man held the heel of a baguette, which he gave to Nico.

"Nico," Jorie called to him—he was too far away. "Come back."

He had dropped his hat, which Jorie retrieved from the pavement.

"You dropped your casquette," she yelled.

The drizzle seemed to pick up and abate according to a weird pulse, as if someone on high were wringing out a washcloth.

"You didn't ask who," Will said. "Who I'm visiting."

Jorie turned toward him.

"My ex-lover Pedro. I came to see him and now I want to run off with him."

Jorie blinked. "That sounds romantic. His name is Pedro?"

"Pedro Douglas. He's an art historian."

"And how ex is ex?"

Will didn't get a chance to answer her. Jorie had turned away from Nico briefly, but Will was watching him, and so he also could see the approaching gang. Another roaming pack in their ripped dungarees and their steel chains and their spit-polished shit-kickers. This time they were hooting and moving fast, ten boys strong. This time they would strike, and everyone on the bridge was getting out of the way, pushing toward the railings.

Except Nico.

Who stood frozen in the middle of the road, his mouth agape, staring at the swarm of big boys accelerating toward him.

Jorie pivoted and must have seen what Will did, but unlike him, she moved immediately, removing her backpack and letting it drop and tip over. She ran toward Nico.

Will didn't move at all at first and frankly misread the scene—he didn't know, he hadn't heard about this new form of terrorism—and with some difficulty, he hoisted Jorie's backpack over his right shoulder, without loosening the strap to fit his arm, all the while still grasping the small plaid suitcase.

Jorie ran toward Nico and reached out both her hands.

Nico stared at her and let go of his piece of bread. His arms dropped to his sides. He looked addled, startled—caught in that frame between the moment when a child falls and bangs his head and the moment when he begins to cry.

Jorie yelled, "Nico."

But the gang reached him first.

She screamed—all the people around her screamed.

One of the gang boys had grabbed Nico by his waist. The other boys fell into a ring around him. Then they ran.

"Put him down," Jorie yelled.

The gang ran back the way they had come, back to the quay on the Left Bank.

Will could see Nico's green sneakers, the hood of his jacket.

"Nico," Jorie shouted.

Then Will couldn't see the boy at all.

"Stop them," Jorie screamed, "stop them."

But anyone in the gang's path made sure to get out of its way. They knocked over a kid on a bike. They took out a man selling flowers.

Jorie ran, both hands out in front of her.

Stop, she was yelling—or Will was yelling stop now, too. Yes, he was shouting stop. There was a buzz in his ears, wind in his gut, and the luggage weighed him down.

He lost sight of Jorie.

He dropped her backpack and the small plaid suitcase on the road and jogged on ahead. He heard Jorie yelling but couldn't locate her.

By the time he made it to the quay, the gang had escaped with the boy—later he was told that they drove off in a getaway van—and when Will finally spotted her, Jorie was surprisingly far away. She had run several hundred yards after the van and then, in the distance, fallen to her knees in the middle of the street. She was hurling something—what? rocks?—down the empty road in front of her.

Will tried to be smart, to act fast. First he needed to retrieve Jorie's luggage, and so he doubled back to grab the backpack and plaid bag—he moved as quickly as he could, but the crowd was in his way—and then after he had turned around and made it back to the quay, the police had arrived, the police swarmed everywhere. He pushed his way over to the spot where he'd last sighted Jorie and nearly tripped on something. A chestnut—Jorie had been throwing Nico's chestnuts at the gang as it sped off with the boy. Will put the nut in his pocket.

He couldn't find her. The crowd filled in the space it had evacuated, and the police made themselves busy, promising order, but Will couldn't find Jorie anywhere.

He spun around. He stepped toward the bridge. He turned back.

Then he noticed a police squad car a half-block up the street with a woman in the back, its lights a-strobe. The squad car pulled away and disappeared fast up a hill.

The drizzle became rain. Will did not know what he should do. He adjusted the straps of the heavy pack on his back, and he wrapped his arms around the small plaid suitcase, holding it securely against his chest.

HE CONSIDERED HIMSELF in reasonable shape but discovered that he was unprepared for the heft of Jorie's backpack, which became heavier and heavier as he made his way up the steeper twists of the Latin Quarter. He had asked a cop for directions to the nearest police station but couldn't believe it was this far. Some streets were overrun with Parisians either returning from or still working their way down to the river; and then some squares were as empty as they might be on a religious holiday. For all Will knew, it was in fact a religious holiday; he could never keep track of them all, the virgin visions, the archangel whisperings. He became very disoriented. Twice he took a wrong turn and had to consult the worn *Paris par Arrondissement* that he'd borrowed from me, and twice he had to set the pack down and rest. The drizzle thickened and it became colder out, but he was a sweaty mess when he finally reached the precinct house.

Quickly he regained his bearings. For me, when I traveled to a new city and suffered some measure of alienation, all I had to do was find a museum and linger in its galleries to relax myself and feel more at ease. All Will had to do, however, was walk around any local government office, any maze of civil administration, and his confidence would be restored. As far as he was concerned, they were all the same. The antechamber receptionists. The halls of overflow cabinets. The ceiling fans spinning no matter the weather. All the closed, nameplated doors and open transoms.

A guard waved him through a metal detector and then made a visual inspection of Jorie's luggage, which Will half-wanted to inspect himself. Then a woman in civilian attire seated at a high desk refused to acknowledge or deny the presence of anyone named Jorie Cole.

"Vous êtes avocat, Monsieur?" the woman asked.

For a moment he considered claiming he was indeed Jorie's attorney—or possibly her husband or brother—but instead he opted for the truth: "I'm just here to return her luggage. Which she dropped in the street."

That was a no-go. The receptionist returned her attention to a computer screen and said she couldn't help him.

"You return her luggage," she said and appeared to snicker as if, please, that trick had been attempted a hundred times before. Returning her luggage—you'll have to do better than that.

Plan B.

"Madame Cole is an American citizen," Will said.

He removed his wallet from his jacket, and from his wallet, a plastic badge graced with the seal of the United States Department of State. If the policewoman asked to examine it, he would have to huff and flap, because all she would have to do would be to take one look at the card and note its expiration and/or call the embassy to determine that Will had forfeited his various privileges.

The woman eyed the card and sniffed as though she'd seen the ID with its imperial seal before and frankly did not enjoy being bullied.

"I need to see Madame Cole immediately. As her representative." Will held the plaid suitcase in the air. "And as I said, I have her luggage."

"Attendez, s'il vous plaît," the woman said, although she neither picked up a phone nor flagged down a colleague. Instead she officiously typed a few keystrokes and stared at her monitor. Then she appeared to return to the work that Will had interrupted.

He knew better than to push his luck and took a seat on a wooden bench. He waited a quarter hour—and well over an hour had gone by since Nico had been taken. He had no reason to believe that Jorie was even in the precinct house; that had not been confirmed. Then a man tapped his shoulder. He, too, was not wearing a uniform, although his unstructured, safe-gray suit was a uniform of a sort. Will was led into a vast room sectioned into a matrix of half-walled offices and told to leave the bags by the detective's desk. Then he was ushered into a long and narrow chamber with an almost equally long metal table—an interrogation room?—at one end of which a uniformed cop sat with Jorie, speaking to her in a soft voice.

She had been swaddled in a heavy wool blanket and given a cup of something warm to drink, although it didn't look as if she had taken a sip. Her eyes were red-rimmed; already she looked cried out. And yet when she noticed Will, she actually appeared to smile.

He felt as though he had known her for a very long while. He smiled back.

"I've got your luggage," he said and then felt a little stupid; at this point, the poor woman probably didn't care one way or another about her possessions.

"Thank you," she said. And then, signaling him closer, waiting until he had crossed the room: "I need your help."

The uniformed cop offered Will his chair and took another.

"You are with the United States government," the detective stated.

Will didn't hesitate to nod.

"My French," Jorie said. "I've lost my ability to speak fluent French."

"That's understandable," Will said.

"I can't express myself at all. I can't say what I want to say."

"Let me try," Will said.

"We are trying to help the Madame," the detective said, pacing the length of the room. "Yet she will not cooperate."

To Will, Jorie said: "They're running me around. They're questioning me like I'm a criminal."

Will sat up straight.

"Please," she said to the detective, in French. "Please. We're wasting time." Each sentence seemed like a struggle. "We don't have much time."

Will knew that to be taken seriously, you had to remain

calm, appear reasonable. He could do that for her now. He could help.

"Could you catch me up?" he asked the detective, his French slow and deliberate.

"We shouldn't be sitting here," Jorie said, breaking into English. "We need to find him right now, right now. Please. I don't see how calling Luc will help you."

"They want to call Luc?" Will asked.

"Not that he'd be able to do anything except worry," she said.

Now the detective spoke in English as well: "First we asked Madame for a photo of her son to circulate among all the bureaux around the city and to the banlieue. Which she did not have with her at this moment."

"Now he speaks English," Jorie muttered.

"So we had to dispatch a man to her apartment to retrieve the photograph, which of course has taken some time with all the traffic today," the detective said.

"And they insisted on keeping me here," Jorie said. "They wouldn't take me home to get it. I had to phone the building superintendent and ask him to let them in."

The detective removed a folded page from his pocket and placed it on the table. Will examined the fax: a poor transmission of a photograph, but clearly a blurry and out-of-date snapshot of Nico. He was holding a kite. The boy and the kite looked roughly the same size.

"We have just received this," the detective said, "and so now we send it out."

"Good," Will said.

Jorie studied the faxed photo and written description of Nico. She smoothed out the creases in the paper.

"But may I point out that most mothers carry with them in their wallets a photo of each of their children," the detective said.

Jorie shook her head. "We're wasting time. He must be so scared. He must be..." A single tear raced down her cheek.

Will tried to warm her icy hand in his.

Again, the detective addressed Will: "She does not carry these photos, you see, but then again, she is not the mother."

Will glared at the cop, wondering how he could be so mean. Then he looked back at Jorie, who had not flinched at the statement.

"I've never been a big picture-taker, that's all," Jorie said.

"You're not his mother?" Will asked.

She pulled the blanket more tightly around her shoulders and took a sip of her cooled tea.

Will placed his hands in his lap.

"Mais où est la mère?" the uniform asked—clearly not the first time he'd put the question to her.

"I told you. Nico's mother died," Jorie said. "When he was six months old. His mother was hit by a taxi. Elle est morte il y a quatre ans."

"Où est le père?"

Will felt as though he had stumbled into a language tutorial.

"Comme je vous ai déja dit. En Afrique," Jorie answered. And then she exploded in English: "Where do you think they took him—do you have any idea? He must be so scared. And you don't know him, but he's so sweet and so good-natured about everything and he's not had an easy life at all— He must be so scared—"

"Madame," the detective said. "S'il vous plaît. Ces questions doivent être posées."

The detective told Will that they wanted to call Luc, since he was the boy's father and Jorie, as far as they knew, was merely a nanny or maybe even a complete stranger. She had called a building superintendent and knew where the police could find a photograph in an apartment, true. But how could they be certain what her connection was to the boy? Making claims, needing attention. She didn't have a photo of the boy on her. Now she would not surrender a number where the father could be reached.

"Why are you making this so difficult?" she asked. "Just find the boy—that's all you have to do. Just find him."

"Calm down," Will said.

"They're not doing enough. They should be out in the streets—"

"Jorie," Will said.

He didn't like his tone of voice. He didn't want to appear to be switching sides, although he could see the police point of view. A distraught woman makes certain assertions on the street, which at first seem legitimate. But then you start talking to her, and suddenly the facts are not so clear. When Will looked at Jorie, he had to admit to himself that despite his earlier affinity for her, she remained a stranger to him. In the café, Nico appeared to have an established rapport with her, yes. However. Perhaps he did not know her at all.

She took a series of deep breaths. She stared at Will.

She said, "Luc and I never married. So I haven't adopted Nico. But I am the only mother he's ever really known."

Will sat back in his chair. He had brought the woman her luggage, fulfilled his samaritan duties, and he was tempted to get up and leave. But he could not dismiss Jorie so easily.

He turned to the detective: "Could you give us a moment alone?"

The detective shrugged. He and the uniformed officer left the room but did not close the door all the way.

"I'm trying to understand," Will said. "Nico's father is in Africa. You're carrying around all this luggage. You were heading out somewhere with the boy."

"You don't trust me either," Jorie said.

"You were, what, on your way to join Luc?"

Jorie swallowed. "No," she said.

"Don't you have a number where he can be reached?"

"Don't trust the woman. Call the man," she said.

"Call the blood relative—that's protocol anywhere."

Jorie sighed. "I'm so scared. I don't do well when I'm scared."

"No one does."

"They should be out there looking for him."

"They are," Will said. "They faxed around the photo."

He pulled his chair closer to her.

He whispered, "Let me be honest. This is what it looks like to me. You were taking the boy somewhere—where? Out of the country?"

Jorie's eyes widened. She hesitated but nodded yes.

"Without his father knowing it," Will said.

Again a nod yes.

"How long have you been with Luc?" he asked.

"Four years," she said.

"You were leaving him," Will stated in a flat voice.

Jorie moistened her chapped lips.

"He's abroad," Will said, "and you were leaving him and taking the boy. His son. I take it you were not going to leave a forwarding address."

"Just this morning, we were sitting in the park, and I decided," she said. "I decided to leave, and Nico didn't want to go, because on some level he understands more than we think, and he just wanted me to take him to the zoo in the Jardin, but I said no, and..."

Jorie squeezed her eyes shut. She released a soft *oh*. She was shivering but she loosened the blanket around her and reached into her pocket and produced a slender palm-sized, cordovan-covered book with a red-ribbon marker—an address book—its pages softened by years of ink cross-outs and new scribbling.

"Luc is short for Lucien. Lucien Chamoun," she said. "You can look him up, but you'll only find his Paris office number, and an old one at that. The number for his bureau in Nigeria is back home."

Will nodded.

"You're afraid that if the police call him, they'll start asking him questions, and they might tip him off in some way that you and Nico were traveling somewhere," he said.

Jorie shrugged.

"Or you're afraid that he'll come back to Paris. And if—when the boy is found, you won't be able to continue on your way," he said.

Jorie cleared her throat. "There's no way I can explain it to you," she whispered.

Will examined the address book, and he may have chuckled.

"What?" Jorie asked.

He had one just like it. It was a little larger than Jorie's, in better shape, but antique just the same. Look me up under D—I'd be in it with all my various addresses across the years; I inhabited a page. Will removed his book from his jacket and placed it on the table next to Jorie's, and to anyone—to the detective and uniformed cop certainly—this would have appeared to be a strange mating, an alien ritual. This kind of object would have meant nothing to me if I had not spent so much time around people who had moved frequently in their youth. They might lose scarves or sunglasses or car keys, but they never lost their address books. They were totems of nomadhood. It was the way Will and Jorie kept track of their own private diasporas. Move to a new city. Meet new kids. Move on, and keep in touch with some, lose some. Make new friends. Lose them. And then, after a while, when you were older, you became selective about whose information you admitted into your alphabetic album. You ran out of space, that was the rationale, you had to be choosy, either that or start a new address book, which would mean losing the useless addresses you could still read through single-stroke deletions. Deeper than that, however, you considered it a privilege not worthy of every acquaintance, the honor of, say, a casual friend or a neighbor in your building, sharing a line with a lost childhood friend.

Jorie looked at Will.

"We've both been traveling a long time," she said.

He returned his address book to his pocket.

"I should tell them Luc's company name and let them make their call," she said.

"Yes," he said and stood.

"Please, Will. Just tell them to find Nico. Forget about me. He's a little boy. They don't need to know the rest. Please. Just make them find him."

She could barely speak.

"Please," she said.

Will did not like the way Jorie looked at him now. No, no, no—she had him all wrong.

"They don't need to know about me," she said, she begged.

She feared him. He had figured her out, and she worried that he would betray her confidence. He had no reason to back her. He had no reason to risk withholding what he knew.

"Please," she said.

He noticed a clock on the wall; the ceaseless sweep of its second hand became menacing. He did not want to be a stranger to her. He did not want her to be afraid of him. On top of everything else today—this was too much to bear.

He stepped into the hallway and spoke with the detective and uniformed officer, who were hovering nearby.

"I understand why you are reluctant to trust her," Will said, "but the bottom line is that a boy was taken. It was a gang. I saw it happen. A hundred people saw it happen."

The detective rubbed his nose.

"You know how it is. You must see it every day," Will said. "People get upset, they aren't themselves."

"Do you trust her?" the detective asked point-blank.

Will could picture Nico's brown eyes, round, dilated. The boy would be unable to blink. He would be too frightened.

"We would like to be on her side, Monsieur," the detective said.

"You have your procedures to follow."

"We have been through this sadly very much of late. And we do know. We need to find this child before something happens."

"Something has already happened," Will said. "I don't think she's lying to you about anything."

"Oui?"

"I trust her," he said, although in truth he remained foggy with doubt.

The men reentered the interrogation room. Jorie had shed the blanket and was standing beneath the wall clock. She wiped her face with her palms.

"We will take you home soon," the detective said.

"Merci," Jorie said. She named Luc's firm.

The uniform left the room to place the call.

"Just a few more questions," the detective said.

"Standard procedure," Will said.

Jorie looked ready to protest but said nothing.

The police wanted to rule out the possibility that the kidnapping was a premeditated act of vengeance inspired by something that either she or Luc had done to someone.

"As I mentioned to you," Jorie said, "one of the gang boys looked familiar to me."

One of the boys at the fringe of the pack was skinnier and smoother-cheeked than the rest, shorter, younger—he hadn't shorn his head, which was why he stood out to Jorie, even though he wore the same faded, fraying uniform; his hair was longer and red. That was the description she offered.

"Did you notice him?" she asked Will.

He could not say that he had.

"Obviously I only caught a glimpse of him," she said, "but I know that I've seen him around my neighborhood. They hang out in the place de Stalingrad."

"That is not what we mean," the detective said. "We are wondering if there is anyone in your life, someone you know with whom you have regular dealings—someone who might bear a grudge—"

"No, there's no one. But don't you think there could be a connection?" she asked.

"Non, Madame," the detective said. "If it was one of the routine gang kidnappings, as I think we are inclined to agree, it would have been a hatefully random act."

"I'm sure I saw this kid on the avenue Jean-Jaurès, and he runs with that gang that's taken over the place de Stalingrad."

Jorie looked at Will and shrugged; he could tell that she herself did not entirely believe that these were useful clues.

Nevertheless, it was all she had. She pursued her scenario: "Maybe the gang saw Nico with his father. And they happened to wander down to the pont de Sully this morning. And then they recognized Nico—"

"But you say the boy is dark," the detective said.

Dark. Brown, butter-skinned. Il est beurre. These were the slurs one heard around Paris these days. To be dark was dangerous, a liability—Will understood what the detective was implying.

"Yes, but I was with him, and I hardly look Middle Eastern, I hardly look North African," Jorie said. "They had to have recognized Nico from seeing him with his father. How else would they know to abduct him in a part of town that isn't remotely Arab-French—"

"Madame," the detective interrupted. "We will send our men to the place de Stalingrad immediately, rest assured. However, it is unlikely that this boy was targeted in advance of the crime. That is not how these gangs work."

"I see," Jorie said, defeated. Her shoulders sagged, her head dropped; the idea of a random act knocked her hard; it was too cruel.

"They took him because they knew. They saw him, he was brown. He could be American like you; it would not matter as long as his skin was dark. They have a pattern, these gangs."

"Will there be a ransom?" Will asked.

"It is unlikely," the detective said.

"But you'll send some men out to the place de Stalingrad," Jorie said.

"We will find the little boy," he said. "Or even more likely, before you know it, a good citizen of our city will find him and bring him home."

"Someone will find him?" Will asked. "Where?"

"That is the way these gangs make these abductions," the detective said. "They take the children and drive off to the edge of the city or to the banlieue sometimes. Then they let the children out of the cars and make them find their own way home. That is the way this new terrorism works, you see. More than the children, they want to scare the parents. But they do let the children off and someone finds them always. They are home within hours. That is the pattern. Have faith."

"Wait, I don't follow," Will said. "They pick them up and just drop them off anywhere?"

"Oui, Monsieur, this is what I am saying. It has been happening more and more. It is—how do you call it? The fad."

"A sick fad," Will said.

"What if they're not doing that anymore?" Jorie asked. "What if they used to do that but now they're holding the children somewhere?"

There was nothing the police could say to rule out that possibility. They were done with their questions; they were ready to take Jorie home.

The uniformed officer returned. He was relayed a number by Luc's Paris office, but then Luc could not be reached in Africa. He was out in the field, apparently incommunicado. A message was left to call the Paris police.

Will was disappointed that the connection had not been made. He was uncomfortable being the only one (besides Jorie) who truly fathomed the day's blunt irony: The boy had been kidnapped while he was in the process of being kidnapped.

"Let me get you your bags," he said.

They followed a hall to an interior courtyard, to a squad car.

"You will wish to accompany us?" the detective asked Will.

Will remembered the pretense of his intervention in Jorie's affairs, as a representative of her government. And he had, after all, vouched for her, claimed her trustworthy. He could not decide: Should he tell the police the truth about her? Or should he merely mind his own business and make his way back to my apartment?

"That won't be necessary," Jorie said. "Thank you, Will, for all your help."

And she looked at him the way she did after he had deduced the true nature of her exodus, without blinking, with a pleading, breaking grin.

He remembered her back in the bistro, waving a banana in the air, and the way the boy performed his monkey-chicken shtick.

He did not want to be feared—he never wanted to be feared.

The uniformed cop climbed behind the wheel of the squad car, and the detective rode shotgun. Jorie slid in across the back-seat. Will placed the backpack next to her. Then he climbed in as well, set the plaid suitcase on his lap, and slammed the door shut.

THE RAIN CAME DOWN harder, inking the streets. Will was unfamiliar with Jorie's part of Paris, all the way north in the Nineteenth. Every shop along the main boulevard appeared to be closed, even the supermarket, and then some stores on some avenues looked as if they had been boarded up for good. A florist's window had been covered with neon scrawl: *France for the French,* written three times, in red, then white, then blue. Over it and beneath it was a response in Arabic curves. Below the Arabic, there was more French: *Go home or die.* The plywood fencing around a construction site had been plastered with posters of the high-browed, narrow-billed French Front leader; soot-smeared graffiti ran across his face. More than one building had been gutted. Legible scraps of signs remained. A glass blower, a cheese shop, a butcher—each surrendered to fast flames. They came close enough to the périphérique for Will to hear the constant murmur of highway traffic, a gnawing hum punctuated only by the screech of train wheels braking against the tracks on the approach into a station. The few pedestrians out and about shuffled along quickly, hugging the storefronts, anonymous behind upturned collars and umbrellas.

Jorie lived in a housing complex set back from the street. The police followed her and Will up an escalator that carried them above the street-level stores and delivered them to a blank plaza embraced by a horseshoe of squat concrete towers. The buildings trapped a mild cyclone. A shallow pool, emptied of water, fountains off—this was where Nico must have wanted to sail his cat boat—was layered in brown leaves, although there were no trees in sight. A distorted rock and roll emanated from a high window, an electrified oud backed by a tinny jangle, cymbals, and a voice of a certain legato, playfully ascendant.

They entered one of the buildings. They passed a wall of mailboxes and a bank of elevators. They took the stairs two flights up. Identical doors on a long hallway were not numbered. Jorie let them in and immediately checked the answering machine; the only message, however, was from a man whom Jorie taught English, who was furious she'd not shown up for his tutorial.

Will set the luggage down. The flat consisted of only two rooms, three if you counted the galley kitchen. There was a bedroom and then the main room, which had a nook, if you could call it that, what looked like a leftover square from an architectural miscalculation. Clearly Nico's space: A toy truck was parked in the ravine of a blanket fold. Posters were thumbtacked over the unmade cot: a map of Lebanon and, beneath it, one of the U.S., along with a poster of a French-Algerian soccer hero who did not appear to be hindered by any laws of gravity.

Sliding glass doors banked one side of the main room; they opened onto an ornamental balcony that was only a foot deep. The apartment was in the back of the building and the view in the distance was a field of train tracks; more immediately, Will could look down at the canal de l'Ourcq, a stagnant, barge-less strait of muck. He stepped into the kitchen and took the liberty of filling a kettle with tap water and setting it on the stove. The kitchen was lined with shelves of grains and spices, and one glass canister clearly contained dried mint—he opened it and sniffed— but he wasn't sure if he should use it for tea.

The police stood in the threshold and repeated their tired assurances. The detective reminded Jorie once more to bear in mind an important fact: None of the children who previously had been taken by a gang during a daylight raid, not a single one of them, had been harmed—not physically, at any rate.

"I'd like to believe you," Jorie said, "but you know that's not true."

There was the one boy who did break a leg, but that was because he fell in the sewer, silly child; that could have happened any day of the week. And yes, oh yes, there was the one girl, who went missing for a week.

"But in the end, you will recall, she was found," the detective said. "All of them have been found."

He tried to leave.

"But what should I do? There must be something I can do," Jorie said.

"As I have said, Madame, the best way you can help the

search effort would be to stay at home and wait by the phone because there are more good citizens out there than you realize," the detective said. "He will be dropped off in another arrondissement. He will sit down on the curb and cry awhile. A shopkeeper will see him and ask him what is wrong, where do you live, and so forth. This person will call you and bring the boy home."

"Shouldn't we drive around together and look for him?" she asked. "The photo I gave you is old. You don't really know what he looks like. Don't you need me to drive around and help you find him?"

What if the stranger who found Nico wanted her to come and pick him up? She should wait for the call.

"You could have an officer stay here," she said.

"Madame. You will remember the day as a horrible day," the detective said. "But you will have the boy back soon. Have faith in the pattern." And he and his colleague retreated down the hall.

Jorie shut the door and leaned against it and looked at Will.

"Have faith," she said. "Faith in what—faith in evil?"

There was a couch pushed against one wall, and a phone on the table next to the couch, which was where she positioned herself.

"Can I make you some tea?" Will asked.

Jorie didn't respond. When she did speak, she said, "I always know where he is when he's not with me. If he's at his nursery school, I can see him constructing a skyscraper from blocks. If he's running errands with his father, if I think about it, I know where they are. At the dry cleaners or the bakery or the barber."

And what was Will supposed to say? I'm sure the cops are

right, someone will call. You wait right there by the phone. Any minute, just you see. He'll turn up before dark. Everything will be fine, I know this to be true.

He did not want to administer placebo platitudes.

"You don't need to stay with me," Jorie said.

Will was holding the kettle.

"I can stay a little while," he said.

"I can manage," Jorie said.

"I didn't tell them what you told me."

Jorie nodded.

"I know," she said. "I would like some tea, thanks."

Will found a teapot, cups, and a tea ball, in which he jammed what he thought was a reasonable quantity of mint. Before long, a humid grassiness drenched the small apartment.

He noticed a yellow magnetic L holding a scrap of paper on the refrigerator. A foreign phone number.

"Do you want to call Luc yourself?" Will asked.

Jorie let the tea steam warm her face.

"Usually we use those little gold-rimmed glasses for tea," she said. "These cups are for coffee," she added.

"Sorry," Will said.

"No, don't be sorry. That's just another one of Luc's rules. Cups are for coffee, and the mint tea goes in the glasses."

The tea was weak; he hadn't let it steep long enough. He apologized.

Jorie didn't seem to hear him. She said, "Luc's mother sends the mint from Lebanon."

"That's sweet," Will said.

"When Luc used to come home from his business trips, I

would make him tea, hoping like his mother that it would make him homesick for Byblos. Of course, it had the opposite effect."

"You mentioned wanting to travel there," Will said.

"Not travel, live. I wanted to live there—I thought it would be better than this. This," Jorie said and indicated that she meant the apartment. Or perhaps she meant France.

"What does Luc do for his company?" Will asked.

"But, you see, Luc can't stand his family. He didn't stay and run the family business. He won't go home and work with his brother, who's doing pretty well, all things relative. He's a contractor in Beirut and there's a lot of construction now. Luc makes an okay salary, but he sends a lot of money home—guilt—and he keeps promising we'll move soon to a bigger flat. But."

"Jorie—"

"And he doesn't want Nico to grow up in Lebanon, but he won't go to the States either, or anywhere—so we're stuck here. Where people call Nico names. Where all these new laws say that even though he was born in France, he isn't a French citizen. Nico could be kicked out of his crèche or school eventually or a hospital. If I take him anywhere for any length of time outside of Paris, do you know what I have to do? I have to notify the local mairie."

She glared at Will. Anger elongated her face.

"Why would you want your son to grow up in this climate? I ask Luc. And he says, I do not want my son to grow up in this climate, but times will change. He says, The laws, they cannot last. He says, You know these laws affect me, too, Jorie. Or he says, We will talk about it when I am home. Which is not too often anymore."

Rain ran down the sliding glass doors.

Jorie's eyes reddened although she didn't cry and once again she winced a soft *oh* of anguish.

"Nico," she said. "Nico, Nico, Nicolas."

Will was sitting next to her on the couch as if they were fellow passengers on a plane. Her crying—or not so much crying as tearless shivering—seemed to come and go in counterpoint to the rain. She calmed somewhat and the storm resumed; the storm relaxed and she broke down.

"He started out in engineering, but now he's really a salesman," Jorie said. "The company builds entire cities in the desert. In the jungle. They put up a lot of oil platforms, which is why he went to Nigeria," she explained. "He's been gone for three days so far. I've been sleeping late. It would make Luc crazy, if he knew."

Jorie set her tea down and crossed the room to look out at the canal.

"What would I tell him? He's far away, there's nothing he can do. I'd just scare him," she said. "I don't want to call him."

She removed a pomegranate from a mostly empty bowl on a round, teak-veneered dining table by the window and nervously began to pass it from palm to palm. She paced in short laps in front of the couch. She took off her sweater, and Will noticed that her T-shirt beneath was soaked with sweat. She slipped into the bedroom and shut the door but returned to the main room for her luggage. When she emerged from the bedroom again, she wore an oversized gray flannel shirt.

The plaid suitcase remained alone by the door. Jorie eyed it and cupped her hand over her mouth. She straightened her back.

She picked up the little bag and carried it over to the cot in the nook, to a wall cabinet adjacent to the nook; she unzipped the suitcase and returned the boy's clothes to various shelves.

Will watched her perform this task and he said nothing.

When Jorie was done, she placed the toy truck on a shelf along with some other toys, and she began to straighten the bedding.

"Jorie," Will said.

She must have known what he would say, what he wanted to ask. She didn't interrupt her chore.

"I want to help you," he said. "Truly. I feel miserable, and I'd like to help—"

"What do you want me to say?" she snapped. "Yes, I was leaving Luc."

She fluffed a pillow.

"Taking his son with you," Will said.

"Kidnapping. Officially, legally, technically. Yes, you could say that I was kidnapping the boy."

Will tried to arrange his questions. To construct careful wording. But all he could do was frown and ask, "Why?"

"You've been very kind. And if you want to leave...If you need to go," Jorie said.

Will stood. Fine, he thought, enough—I've done my part. He put on his coat.

"I'm the only mother the boy has known," Jorie said.

Will waited.

"Can I tell you how I met Luc?"

Will leaned against the door. An unexpected thought surfaced. He wanted to say, My own mother died when I was young.

Jorie described how she had been unhappy for a good part of

her life. She didn't make it through college. She had absolutely no desire to pursue a career in foreign affairs. She moved around as an adult much the way she had as a child, finding work where she could. Mostly she found jobs on archaeological digs. She was paid to go at stones with a pastry brush under a very hot sun, which sounded reasonably romantic to Will, a life as an itinerant sifter of dirt.

He remained standing by the door with his coat on.

Often between the excavation gigs, she ended up in France. She had always liked Paris. In some ways it felt like home, although it didn't occur to her that she could settle here.

"I was, as I said, very unhappy. Lonely. Have you ever reached a point where you don't think you'll ever be with anyone?" she asked.

Jorie sat down at the dining table, which in turn drew Will back to the couch.

One day, four and a half years ago, at the beginning of what she somehow knew was going to be a good summer, a better summer, she went walking in the Jardins du Luxembourg. It was the end of the afternoon and the park was empty. She strolled past a man sitting on a bench—he held an infant in his arms.

Jorie could not curb her grin. She smiled broadly.

"The man was sobbing, tears just streaming down his face, but curiously, I noticed, the baby was not crying at all. I asked him if he was okay—"

Will had to smile.

"What?"

"Do you do that often? You see men who looked distressed and you stop and ask them if they're okay?"

"Oh," Jorie said and managed a wink. "Maybe it's a habit and I don't realize it."

Will took off his coat. "I interrupted," he said.

She asked the man if he was okay, and the man didn't answer her but instead handed her the child and dashed off out of view behind some shrubs. He was gone a long time. Jorie thought that it was possible the man was deserting the kid—he was gone a good half hour. She considered calling the police, but the baby looked so content, sleeping in her arms. Finally the man did return—he had stopped crying—and he sat back down on the bench and took the baby and thanked Jorie and gave her his life story. The facts were these: The baby was six months old. The man's wife had been dead for two months. That was the first time he had truly been able to cry.

"Luc introduced himself and asked if he could repay me for my kindness, and I said, you know, It was nothing, you've been through a lot, and Luc insisted and…"

Will waited. Jorie wasn't looking at him. She was gazing at the dining table and, Will imagined, considering that moment in her life with some nostalgia.

"I thought there was something wrong with me," she said. "His wife had been dead for only two months, and I wanted him."

Lucien Chamoun, who was wearing a crisp white shirt, beneath which she could see the rock-face of his body. He was lithe; once upon a time he ran marathons.

"I wanted him, I didn't care why," Jorie said.

There was the promised dinner at Luc's place here in the Nineteenth—he made a narcotically garlicky stuffed cabbage—and another meal, after which there was a twilight swim; the single amenity of the housing complex was a top-floor pool. And then another supper and swim—a neighbor-girl in Luc's building would baby-sit—and then Jorie found herself spending the night, and they enjoyed a sweet sort of heartache during their lovemaking, an urgency, cries of joy, yes, but backed by a chorus of grief. He let her hold him.

"And I hadn't experienced that before," Jorie said. "A man letting me hold him, truly hold him."

"He allowed you to be strong," Will said.

Jorie looked up with a start, as if she'd forgotten he was in the room. Her face went pink. She described how during the night, Nico would cry, and she would be the one who got up to coax him back to sleep. One night she came over and she never left.

"I'm supposed to tell you now about how I wiped the kid's nose and treated his fevers and bought him sneakers and taught him how to tie them. I'm supposed to tell you that I made up a game when he didn't like to get dressed or eat anything in the morning and that I read to him and took him to the park and came to know him, Nico, Nicolas, as a very clever boy. I'm supposed to prove to you what a good mother I've been. The role I've played and played well."

"I saw for myself," Will said.

"The women in the park, the people in the supermarket, in bookstores—anywhere we go. They say, Your son is a bright boy. Your son is a strong sprinter. Your son is polite beyond his years."

"Your son," Will said.

"You'd think they'd ask questions, especially these days—I'm so fair and he's darker—but they never do. They just assume. Votre fils, votre fils, votre fils."

Jorie stood and paced again.

"I call him mon mignon. I call him my boy. I never say my son. I can't say my son. I say my Nico. I say mon petit. It makes me very sad. I don't know why I don't just say my son, but I can't. If he called me Maman, Mom—maybe I would. You heard, he calls me Jorie."

"Did you and Luc ever discuss marriage?" Will asked.

Jorie picked up the phone to make sure it had a dial tone. It did. She set the receiver down hard.

"You and the man you mentioned," she said.

"Pedro," Will said.

"You say he was your ex."

"We were together for five years and apart for seven," Will said. Our math.

"So you know," she said. "Things don't go as you expect. Please don't ask me when we started having problems. I don't know. I just don't recall."

There was a time when they couldn't bear to be apart, not for an hour; it was painful when Luc started working again after a long leave of absence, quite painful when he began to travel for weeks at a time. Was it two years along? Right after they got back from a summer trip to Lebanon. Luc did not get along with his father, and he was in a bad mood, a nasty funk, and started fighting with Jorie—but was that what they were actually fighting about? Maybe their problems began later when Jorie wanted to work and Luc didn't think she should—caring for Nico was her job and he claimed he could make enough money for all of them and his extended family, which he couldn't—and he objected when despite his edict, she worked anyway, albeit less than part-time as a freelance tutor, helping a student prepare for the history part of his bac or teaching English to a Syrian businessman. How did the arguments begin? She tried to make dinners he liked, recipes she got from Luc's mother, and Luc became hostile, always correcting her.

Jorie lowered her voice: "If you are going to make the lamb correctly, Jorie, you should marinate it for at least two days. Use green olives, never black."

She sat down next to Will on the couch.

"Sometimes I think, I try to think, I can turn it around. We'll take a drive in the country in a rented car, and we'll drink picnic wine, and we'll watch Nico chase a rabbit. Don't we all have it in us to turn our lives around? Luc will come home some night and we'll take a swim like old times, just the two of us, and we'll get all hot and bothered and..."

Will realized that his hands had formed tight fists.

"I barely know you. I don't why I'm telling you all this," Jorie said.

"You're all alone," he said.

"I've been all alone for a long time," she answered.

"Nico is missing," he said softly.

The rain again. The hiss of heating vents. The steeped mint still hanging in the air.

"I can't turn it around," she said, "because to turn it around, I would want to have to love Luc again, and the fact is... The fact is I don't want to love him."

"You have no legal standing," Will said.

"I can't make a claim for custody, no."

Your son is a strong swimmer, mothers would tell her up in

the pool. You know it is a sign of intelligence, the way your son can play by himself. Your son has your eyes. Your son has your smile. Votre fils, votre fils, votre fils.

"I want to be able to say my son," she said.

"Today you decided to leave."

"I got a train schedule and figured we'd head for the South, leave the country by train. I told Nico we were taking a trip. He didn't want to go. I made him. I packed his bag, promised we'd have fun. Where are we going? he wanted to know. I couldn't tell him. Will Baba be there? he asked, and I had to say I didn't think so. And the reason you met us where you did was because I had just been to the bank. I'd withdrawn all the money I had in my own account and from my joint account with Luc."

"You have all that cash with you now?"

"Oh, Will. I'm evil, I know. And I'm to blame."

"To blame? For the kidnapping?"

"Yes, I kept him out of his crèche today and I took him to the park and decided we had to leave. Yes, I took him home and packed our bags, and I took him down to the river. Yes, I was running away with him—and then look, look what happened. Don't tell me I'm not to blame."

She cried awhile—her tears looked waxy and hot—and Will reached an arm around her and tried to comfort her; she eased herself from his grasp and crossed her arms and legs, as if she had exposed way too much, and now she had to shutter herself and guard what misery was still hers and hers alone.

"Can I make you something to eat?" Will asked.

Jorie gave him an indifferent blink.

"You should probably be going," she said.

He ignored her. "You should eat something," he insisted and went into the kitchen.

"What time is it?" she asked.

The afternoon had wasted away. There hadn't been any calls. None from the police, none from the mythical good citizens.

Will examined various plastic containers in the refrigerator. Most of the contents looked as if they contained overdue beef and expired green beans.

"A sandwich?" he asked.

"No bread," Jorie said.

She pulled her hair back and rolled up her sleeves.

"I'm going to call the police," she said.

She had a number for the detective. She didn't reach him but was able to determine that no one had any news for her.

Will arranged some cold chicken on a plate. He found some roasted peppers, some roasted garlic. He made a platter of food and set it on the table. Some Camembert, an apple. It was a modest feast.

Jorie feigned interest. She sat at the table with Will and placed some food on her own plate, but she didn't eat anything.

The chicken turned out to be quite moist. Will was hungry now, his stomach restored, and he surprised himself with his own appetite. Then he became embarrassed, eating so well. He felt a lump in his pocket, the chestnut. He considered showing it to Jorie but decided against it.

She said, "You don't have to stay with me. Nico's baby-sitter is a pleasant kid, very sweet, and I can get her to come down here and"—she chuckled—"baby-sit me."

"Why do you keep telling me to go?" Will asked.

Jorie stared out the window.

"Please, just don't be afraid of me," he said. "Please."

He decided to wait another half hour to see if anyone called. Then that half hour was up and he waited another. Another. He couldn't leave her.

Three hours went by. They watched the rain. There were no calls. Will tried to phone me twice, but I wasn't home yet and I'd forgotten to turn my answering machine back on; I had turned it off when Will showed up. Now and then they talked about nothing in particular.

"I remember that whenever my family moved," Will said, "and we were living in a new city, walking home from school became an adventure."

Jorie hummed.

"The way the streets ran. The alleys that became staircases, and then suddenly you found yourself in a plaza. The men hanging out in cafés. The women talking to each other from high windows."

"I'd always wander through the market," Jorie said. "It would be the end of the day, and the vendors would be closing up, giving away figs, free glasses of lemonade."

"The empty bookstores. I could lose myself for a very long time in bookstores where I didn't even know the language."

"You know a city when you can ride the buses," Jorie said.

"True."

"I'd always see how long it took to master the bus routes. I'd test myself. I'm consequently very handy with maps."

A few names surfaced, people they might know in common, and some names were familiar to Jorie, some to Will, although neither one of them could relay recent gossip.

"Tell me something," Jorie said. "Although it's none of my business."

He had no idea what she would ask him, but if any topic could distract her however briefly from the crisis at hand, he would happily pursue it.

"When you started dating—"

"Did I go out with girls?" Will asked.

"No, that wasn't what I was going to ask. I'm wondering, you know, living where we did, at our age, not entirely sure who we were, where we belonged…"

Will understood the question: With whom did he have his first real romance, a fellow student at school or a local kid? It was one way the international-school crowd separated themselves. There were those who exclusively dated their peers, and those who exclusively did not.

"A Turkish kid, older, a philosophy student. He said that one day he would write novels," Will said.

"Did he?"

Will didn't know. "And you?" he asked.

"I started out with boys from school," Jorie said, "but then not. In a big way not."

"No doubt you lured them with your country music," he said.

Jorie flashed a smile. "No doubt," she said.

They meandered through their respective adolescences, although their reminiscing was woven with long lulls, and Will didn't fool himself: He knew that Nico was never very far from the surface of their conversation.

At one point toward the end of the afternoon, Jorie said, "I keep thinking that I should lie to you."

"Lie to me? Why would you need to lie to me?"

"Tell you that Luc was leaving me for another woman. So I had no choice, right? I had to run off with Nico because Luc was involved with this other woman and I'd be out of the picture soon with no claims to the boy."

Will didn't know how to respond.

"Was that what you wanted to happen?" he asked.

"Then you would see the corner I was in," she said. "And it would be terrible, it would be torture for Nico to lose me, right?"

Will made a grand gesture out of checking his watch.

"You should go," Jorie said, although with much less conviction than earlier.

"You could call the baby-sitter?"

"Yes," she said.

"Then I should probably go, yes."

But did she want him to stay? Did his company make her waiting any easier? He didn't get up from the couch.

Jorie was shivering again.

"The boy is smart," Will said.

"He is," Jorie said, "yes."

"It's in his eyes. I know he's bright, and he'll be smart when he needs to be smart."

"Okay," she said.

"I've done some things," he said. "I've made mistakes, tragic mistakes."

Jorie squinted at him.

"I'm not one to judge," he added. "That's what I'm trying to say. I'm not one to judge."

Will phoned the detective and did speak to him but discovered nothing new. He called me once again as well, but I still had not made it home.

A full fleet of clouds had traveled the sky; it had rained and stopped and rained again a dozen times. Will turned on the radio in Jorie's kitchen, which proved a major miscalculation. The news could not have been worse for her to hear: He expected some report about the boycott of bakeries, how it had spread throughout the hexagone, and instead the top story was about children at risk in Paris.

Apparently Nico was not alone. The gangs had either planned or inspired one another to take dark-skinned children all over the city that afternoon—perhaps it was their response to everyone throwing bread in the river—and although the number went unconfirmed, it was reported that five children had been grabbed in broad daylight. None as yet had made it home.

Jorie became a dog in a run, back and forth, back and forth across the room.

"I saw that kid with the red hair," she said. "I know I saw him."

"Jorie," Will said.

"Five children now," she said. "And today might be the day that they aren't merely dropped off. Today might be the day—"

The phone.

Will answered. It was the uniformed officer, not the detective. He was unaware that Will had recently spoken to the detective and was wondering if anyone had contacted Jorie.

She grabbed the phone. "You're calling me to find out what's going on? You are calling me?"

Will eased the phone away from her and concluded the conversation.

Jorie went into her bedroom and returned wearing her coat.

"It's almost dark," she said.

Before Will knew it, she was out the door. He trailed after her down the hall, down the stairs.

"Jorie, wait. We need to stay here—"

He caught up to her outside.

"I shouldn't have waited this long. I'm going to find him," she said.

They were standing by the drained fountain in the courtyard and the wind slapped at them every which way.

"Okay, but wait," Will said. "Let's think it out."

He buried his hands in his pockets.

"Think it out? Fine, you think it out. I got a look at that gang boy this morning," Jorie said. "I know where he hangs out, and I've been a fool to sit around— I've been a fool."

She skipped steps down a broken escalator to the street.

The cold wind made it difficult to breathe, but Will matched her step. They followed a series of side streets until they reached the avenue and then headed toward a square in the distance. They were walking parallel to the canal, which stirred with a gentle wave, or so it seemed, the wake of their stride. They reached the place de Stalingrad. An elegant structure stood at the center of the square.

This was the Rotonde de la Villette, designed by the architect Claude-Nicolas Ledoux in 1784. He was the subject of my dissertation. I could draw the building in my sleep: a solid cylinder riding a solid square. A low pediment ran along the base of the structure, the pediment supported by evenly metered square columns. The second-floor cylinder sported pairs of round columns and arches and recessed windows in the arches. And then, linking the two pieces, was a neat tiara, a clerestory of small square windows. You could understand the design in a glance, and yet every time I looked at the building, I saw something new—the plain lintels over the second-floor windows or the way the stones around each arch were arranged in triangles echoing the triangle of the pediment. I had gone inside all the other remaining Ledoux structures, but I had never entered this one. The Rotonde was built as a toll house and more recently housed a museum of the city; after that its hall was rented out for special events; and then it was abandoned, landmarked yet neglected. It was scarred with graffiti, with the soot from years of exhaust; city caretakers had stopped trying to keep it clean.

The clouds had receded into the distance, and although the sky looked smeared with ash, the sun in its autumn yawn still managed to light the structure from behind and give the stone an amber cast. Close up, this stone would look fossilized and rough, but on the approach, the lines were as neat as the way the architect first drew them, sharp, pure in form. The square base was a true square, the cylinder story perfectly round. And there were pockets of darkness, the deep shadows beneath the pediment hiding the full sweep of the stairs, sheltering dark figures shifting and shuffling about.

A loitering gang. The troublemakers in repose. All of us yearned for a little rest at the end of the day, especially when the night ahead promised danger.

"Jorie, stop. You don't want to mess with them," Will said.

He could see that they now occupied the building, which was

the reason I had never gone inside; he saw figures moving past the windows of the upper floor.

Jorie stepped closer and closer still, with Will right behind her.

"Stop," he said. "Wait."

"The boy with red hair," she said. "If we find that boy..."

The gang boys smoked cigarettes and talked slang to the gang girls, who were dancing in place to the beat of the music they played, and over by one particularly graffitied pillar, Will spotted a couple making out, hip to hip, serious, quite possibly in love.

Jorie was checking out each and every kid, all the buzzed heads, but no one's hair was red, no one's long. She kept steering back toward the lovers making out—the boy had his coat pulled back and was wearing only a white tank top, and his skinny arms were bruised with blue-black tattoos that, when Will squinted, blended in with the graffiti on the pillar. The boy didn't appear cold at all and the girl—how old was she?—was equally ill-prepared for the hour and the climate, her shirt mostly unbuttoned. These two must have held some rank, Will decided, because there were other boys, boys without girls, who moved in now, protecting them as Jorie insisted on getting closer.

Will pulled her back. "I don't think the kid you saw is here," he said.

Jorie made them circle the entire building twice. Will couldn't keep her from moving up and down the stairs beneath the pediment. Finally someone called out at them. A pack of boys tailed them now.

Someone yelled: "Get out of here. We don't want you here. Get lost."

"Let's go," Will said. He had his arm linked with Jorie's, but she wiggled free.

"That boy is here," Jorie said.

"Let's go."

"He's here," Jorie insisted.

A métro train screeched across the nearby elevated tracks. The iron trestle vibrated when the train pulled away.

Jorie marched back up the steps toward the main door of the Rotonde, and when she tried to go inside, the boy whom Will had pegged as the leader appeared, his girlfriend a few steps to his right.

"Get lost," the gang boy said.

His nose was broad and flat; a raw scar ran from the bridge down to his left nostril.

"You've got that redheaded boy in there, don't you?" Jorie said.

Which sounded absurd to Will; he knew he had to take charge somehow.

But then Jorie screamed.

"Nico."

Because it must have occurred to her that maybe, just maybe they had the boy inside. She called out his name with such volume that the gang boy had to step back, and Will grabbed hold of both her arms.

Jorie screamed his name a third time, and Will managed to ease her down the low steps and back to the plaza. But she broke free from his grasp and she ran toward the Rotonde again, although she didn't make it very far. She ended up face-to-face with the top dog, the boy who stood on the lowest step and rocked back and forth, his hands at his waist and pulling back his jacket to reveal a square-handled black gun shoved into his belt, its barrel angled toward his crotch.

Other gang boys and girls formed a semicircle behind him.

Will said, "Jorie. Nico is not here. Listen to me. He's not here."

The gang boy with the gun glared at her and Jorie stared back.

"Nico's in there," Jorie said to Will.

"He's not," Will answered as firmly, as definitively as he could.

"Get the fuck out of here," the boy said again, stepping onto the square and closer to Jorie.

She held her ground.

The boy was in her face.

"Tell me where," she said.

"Where what?" the boy asked.

Will could smell the kid. He smelled like rotten cabbage.

"Where what?" the boy yelled. The scar on his nose reddened.

Will said, "Let's go, Jorie."

"Where you took my little boy," she said.

The gang boy snarled.

"Your little boy is missing?" His snarl blossomed into a wicked grin.

That made Will want to slug him. Forget that he'd get shot in the gut, he wanted to slug the punk.

In a small voice, Jorie said, "I just want him back."

"But you won't get him back," the gang boy said.

Jorie closed her eyes.

"He's probably dead by now," the gang boy said and snickered. He cackled and everyone around him laughed.

The boy went up the stairs into the building, and Will thought he would have to hold on to Jorie now to keep her from charging after this asshole because who knew what her anger would make her do now. However, Jorie didn't charge up the stairs, and instead she started to breathe fast, and she looked up at the ash-sky—and it was easy for Will to read her mind: What the gang boy told her could be fact.

"No," Will said. "He's still with us," he said.

Will ushered her back across the square toward the canal. He looked back over his shoulder at the Rotonde. It wouldn't take much to bring it down, the tired stone.

Back in her apartment, Jorie listened to the radio and then had to lie down on the couch. The news came on, another grim bulletin: The gangs had taken more children than originally reported. Seven were missing.

Jorie stared blankly at the ceiling.

Will stood at the window and peered out at the dark canal. There was nothing he could do, no way for him to help. It was time for his watch to end, time for him to retrieve the baby-sitter and then at last make his exit. In truth, he was a little shaken by the events in front of the Rotonde. Here was evil embodied in the form of teenagers, and maybe in the end they would win. He didn't want to admit it, but that could be the way of the world, that they would win.

He picked up the phone and dialed my number. This time I was home.

"Pedro," Will said. "There you are."

"And there you are," I said.

"I tried calling you before—"

"Yes," I said, I exploded. "I've thought about it all afternoon: Yes. I'll go wherever you want to go. Tonight. Yes. Let's leave as soon as we can."

I listened to Will breathe.

"What's wrong?" I asked.

He didn't answer me.

At that moment, I suspect, Will was standing next to the couch in Jorie Cole's apartment and looking down at her. And she in turn shifted her eyes toward him and met his gaze with such a sorrowful, trenched look of defeat that he placed his palm across her forehead, as if to cool her fever.

"Will, where are you?" I asked.

He still didn't respond.

"Will?"

And what, what—what was he thinking then?

Jencks had asked him, What's the best thing you ever did for someone?

Jorie had said, Don't we all have it in us to turn our lives around?

And now, in Paris, in the dim apartment of a woman whom he had known only for an afternoon, it occurred to him that maybe all it took was one good act to right oneself. One good act—one seed cast into a hard fallow field, from which a new good life would inevitably flower. One good act. He knew what he had to do.

3

AFTER WILL LEFT ME at the river, I wandered through the crowd on the quay for a while until I awoke from a state of mild amnesia and remembered the day of the week, the date itself, and the appointment for which I was an hour late. I jogged all the way up into and across the Eighth, where, as the day darkened, the faded stone of the domed circular pavilion at the edge of the Parc Monceau appeared to brighten, which was the effect everywhere in Paris—the architecture came into its own under a nimbus-filtered sun.

Ledoux's Rotonde was a handsome structure, easily my favorite of his four remaining custom houses. It looked to me as though the pure-form cylinder was wearing a perfectly round pearl-strand of doric columns. Above the peristyle, there was a band of sparsely metered, modestly arched windows, and frankly there was something erotic about the dome itself, with its yawn-

ing curve, the wrought-iron vane. This building made you want
to sigh. Most architects preferred the symphonic composition of
the structure in the place de Stalingrad, and I would have to
agree that the Rotonde de Monceau was more of a chamber
piece; yet the massing was just as formidable, and all of Ledoux's
visionary notions were equally in evidence here.

The photographer whom I was supposed to meet was clearly
in a foul mood, having trouble adjusting his tripod, snapping
orders at an assistant, who in turn shifted a white screen in vain.
The photographer saw me and waved me over. He shrugged at
the sky. How was he supposed to work with this cloud-cover?

"You might get some great mood shots," I said to him.

"That is not my style," he complained. "I was not hired for
my moods."

"I know," I said.

The assistant set down his white screen to light a cigarette and
the photographer barked at him to do his job.

"We must be ready. The clouds may shift," he said.

"Is Didier here?" I asked.

Didier was an exhibition designer retained by a museum in
New York mounting a show on Ledoux. I had known about the
exhibit but originally had nothing to do with it; I had simply
come to Paris on a research grant and met Didier when we were
both trying to examine the same rare Ledoux folio in the Biblio-
thèque archives. Rather than compete for time, we studied the
intricate engravings together, and then one thing led to another
and Didier hooked me up with the museum; I became a con-
sultant on the catalog, and the two of us ended up traveling the
French countryside together to look at and photograph all of the

extant Ledoux houses and public works. In the process, we had become good friends.

"Somewhere," the photographer said. He looked at his camera, at the sky again. "This weather?"

"I'll work on it," I said.

The photographer adjusted his aperture. He was trying to take a head-on shot, the entire Rotonde in the frame, which would capture the confident proportions and—Ledoux's greatest talent—the way he could balance separate, self-sufficient forms, the circle of columns with the cylinder they belted, to achieve a harmonious whole. He was the kind of artist whom I admired most, one who could find countless ways to express himself within an economic idiom. During my season in France, I had made dozens of drawings of his buildings with my untrained hand because I thought that if I gave into my obsession, I would get inside his head. I would see the way he saw.

Ledoux designed forty-seven of these city gates or custom-houses as part of a royal commission that also included some thirty additional observation posts and fifteen miles of wall. They went up between 1784 and 1789, which was ironic because Ledoux was something of an anti-baroque visionary, yet these buildings served the needs of the Ancien Régime to streamline the collection of taxes. He had practiced a new architecture that eschewed the old guard's rococo ornament—he believed that an edifice should nakedly reveal its function, and so he was ahead of his time—yet because he had built the city gates in the service of an overthrown government—and they were merely commissions as far as he was concerned, a chance to show off his range since no two barrières were alike—he was nearly guillotined and instead thrown in jail during the Revolution. He never made any other buildings and devoted his later years to publishing the folio of his work; his seat in the pantheon wasn't secured for another century, and even now I didn't think that Ledoux had received the attention he deserved. The working title of the exhibit back in New York was "Ledoux and His Legacy."

"Merde," the photographer said. It had begun to drizzle.

"Maybe we'll have to reschedule the shoot," I said. "I'll find Didier."

I walked around the building. A sparrow tried to scale the curve of the dome and then gave up and flapped off. Another bird circled the vane. The park was empty. The various marble statues of orators and poets began to sweat in the mist.

When Will and I came to Paris after college, I saw the bar-rières for the first time. We were on our way to check out the famous folly of ruins amid a garden in this very park when we walked passed the Rotonde and I made us stop and sit on a bench across the path from the pavilion. At that point I knew very little, if anything, about Claude-Nicolas Ledoux, and all I took in was the surface, the sheer face of the form. I was fond of symmetry—there was that. I had an unabashed, romantic affinity for ruins, which was why Will was taking me to see the garden folly, and which was, I admit, a trifle adolescent, this fascination with decay. And there was something else, a deeper suspicion that what I was looking at in the pavilion was somehow— what?—enlightenment and reason and good taste all embodied in one classical gesture. As I said, I knew nothing about the architect or his break with conventions in design, nothing about the complexity of his character, Ledoux the progressive utopian in the employ of the king—all I had was the architecture itself, and just the exterior at that. Can a building seduce us? I think so.

On that first excursion, I sat on the bench with Will and studied him in turn studying the pavilion, and then I surprised him with a kiss on the cheek. I took his hand. I led him across the path to the monument, onto the peristyle porch, into the shadow of a column. And I remember kissing him and untucking his shirt and muttering, Thank you, thank you, while he said, Pedro, wait, while he asked, For what? For all of this, I said, and we were making out and getting hard and I think we would have made love right then and there if a custodian hadn't emerged from the main door of the pavilion and begun mopping the stone with a tart solvent. All of these memories came back to me now.

"Didier?" I called.

I noticed that the door was slightly ajar and stepped inside.

"Didier?" My voice echoed. The building was empty, a damp catacomb.

I headed up the turn of stairs and didn't find him on the second floor. Up another flight, I stepped into the round domed room, its must cut by a vanilla cologne that I associated with my colleague. Didier stood at a window overlooking the spot where the photographer, who had draped his equipment, still waited for the clouds to part.

"There are many places in Paris for an assassin to get a good aim," he said.

He was my height, not tall, but he looked tall standing beneath the arch of the window. Old buildings will do that to us, add stature.

"This rain will ruin the photo shoot," I said.

Didier turned and looked at me and rolled his eyes: What will I do with you?

"I have called you for three days," he said. "We speak every day, and then suddenly you are nowhere."

"Sorry," I said.

We double-kissed.

"There was today and there were other things I needed to pose to you," he scolded.

"I've had a friend visiting," I said.

A friend?

"I turned off my machine—Didier, I'm sorry."

"Oui, oui," he said.

He walked the circumference of the room while I stood in one place.

"So we're going to have to reschedule this shoot," I said.

"The photographer will want money for today," Didier said.

"Of course," I said.

"And we do not have all the time in the world, you know, with the special processing I would like to do."

"Yes. I agree. I still don't know what images we should push for the catalog, not to mention the fact that I've barely looked at the text the museum faxed me. And then I've been awol for three days—"

"What is awol?"

"A bad boy to you," I said.

"Yes, you have said you are sorry," Didier said.

He grinned; the room was dark, but he had a proud smile of

fine white teeth. He was not someone of effortless style—you could see the way he trained his hair with gel, the perfect match of belt leather with shoe leather—yet I admit that I was attracted to him and suspected in turn that he was fond of me. Even when we had shared hotel rooms in various châteaux hamlets, however, we had maintained a professional distance.

I followed Didier down the stairs and let him manage all dealings with the frustrated photographer. I stood beneath the peristyle and watched the men gesturing in the rain. The photographer shook his fist at the sky one last time and then finished packing up and departed.

"À quoi penses-tu?" Didier asked.

That I liked this life. That these months of combing through the Ledoux engravings and inspecting the architecture and attending photo shoots and redacting catalog copy had challenged me completely. The exhibit was the first that I had worked on at this level. It would be the first devoted exclusively to this architect in the United States and therefore receive critical attention. I had gained an entrée into the low-vaulted cloister of the museum world, and if I wanted to, I could maintain contacts, maybe even evolve a career as a bona fide curator. I had spent far too long in the purgatory of doctoral candidacy, and this kind of ambition had hitherto eluded me. Yes, I liked this life very much—it was what I desired for myself.

"Nothing," I answered.

"You know one message I wanted to leave you was about the maquette."

"Oh dear. What now?"

"No, Pedro. It is good news. It is finished."

I checked my watch. I hadn't actually agreed on a time to meet Will back at the flat.

"I have my car," Didier said.

"Great," I said. "Allons-y."

The drive south from the Parc Monceau to the model shop in the Fourteenth took the better part of an hour—most of which was spent finding an open bridge to cross the Seine—and our ride was silent. At first I thought that Didier was still steamed at me for stranding him for three busy days, but then I remembered our road trips into the countryside and how on those excursions we tended to cover great stretches without uttering a word. I could take this as testimony that we were comfortable with each other in the way that old friends but rarely new friends can be.

Didier ably manipulated his cramped European city-car through the heart of Paris. I've always thought that you could learn a great deal about a person when you watched him drive a car, that some naked character surfaced, and in Didier's case, the way his right hand remained steady while shifting gears and the way his left foot smoothly danced from brake to clutch signaled an existential steadiness, as it were. His left hand barely gripped the bottom of the steering wheel, releasing it completely when making a turn. He drove this tiny no-frills engine-plus-seats the way one drives a steel-reinforced, rack-and-pinion big sedan. He drove his petite voiture like a yachtsman. What I am trying to say is that Didier was handsome.

We pulled down a narrow mews in the Fourteenth and parked in front of a carriage house that had been converted into a studio. Didier tapped on a frosted-glass door, and no one answered.

"He's probably down at the river tossing his bread," I said.

Didier removed a key from his pocket and looked around sheepishly.

"You have his key?"

"It is a story. Once we knew each other better," Didier said.

"I see," I said. "You never mentioned that."

"And you never mentioned this friend who has visited you," Didier said.

The model shop did not occupy a large space, and yet the workshop with its unfinished ceiling and cement floor looked spacious relative to the maquettes arranged on a series of tables pushed together in the center of the room, an entire eighteenth-century city laid out one-centimeter-for-a-meter. All of the machinery, the lathes and planers and table-saws and complicated vise contraptions, were pushed to the perimeter of the room. A piquant arboreal dustiness hung in the air.

We circled the models, bending down to examine the carpenter's work at eye level, and even though I had seen the project in the making, I couldn't help but shake my head in awe. Here before me was Ledoux's unbuilt utopia, the Ideal City of Chaux, transposed from engravings into wood, not realized yet made tactile. The chief curator had talked about rendering Ledoux's Neoclassicism in the traditional white foam, but Didier had sold him on wood. This was the trademark of the French carpenter Didier worked with, that he didn't limit himself to balsa but that he worked in cherry and added details in walnut and wenge and a whole range of other woods that remained a mystery to me because Didier knew only the French tree names. The expanses of lightly varnished wood endowed Ledoux's simple shapes with a delicate elegance, and the way the carpenter used darker lines around doors and windows, in column capitals and pediments, the way he slipped in lighter grains where certain stones were rusticated, left rough, somehow did not violate Ledoux's program and instead reinforced the rhythms and patterns achieved from the structural components themselves.

"Ça va?" Didier asked. He put his arm around me.

"This is magnificent," I said.

He kept his hand on my shoulder for a moment until it became awkward and then he stepped aside.

"The first room will be beautiful," he said, "but then there will be this. The knockout."

Three gallery rooms had been allotted to mount "Ledoux and His Legacy," and the first would focus on Ledoux's houses and his customhouses, the king's city wall. The second room would focus on the Ideal City of Chaux. In the first room, photographs would hang on the walls and there would be glass cases with open folios—a standard treatment—but in the next space, the curator was executing a suggestion that I had made. The idea was not to offer any of Ledoux's engravings and no photographs (none, after all, could be exhibited of an unbuilt project); the model itself would stand for what was, in the end, merely reverie. A wood model spot-lit from above in a black room.

Here was what fascinated me about Ledoux: On the one hand, he was eager to assist the Ancien Régime in its lubrication of tax collection, in realizing its traditional desire that a city be walled. Yet even before that royal commission, Ledoux had convinced the court to support another kind of vision, the design of a nonhierarchical industrial community devoted to the production of salt in Chaux. At the center of this community was an ellipse of structures, buildings with strange names like the Temple of Memory (with inscribed minarets), the House of Union, the Palace of Concord—even the Temple Dedicated to Love— and the sun in the center of these planets was the salt factory itself. And what was radical at the time was that the factory was treated with the same sense of refined high design as the house for the director of the salt refinery. A factory with columns—this was unheard of. As was the attempt to eliminate differentiation among the homes of the factory laborers and the merchants and the cabinetmakers and the stockbrokers and the other professionals. Granted the latter received more space than the former, but still, the democracy, the social romanticism of Ledoux's city plan, was measurable and new—and ultimately never achieved.

Claude-Nicolas Ledoux was a man who both built a wall around Paris and imagined a city with no wall at all. That paradox alone kept him immune from any easy reading.

In the tract that accompanied his folio, Ledoux wrote: *The character of monuments, like their nature, serves the propagation and purification of morals.* This was his oft-quoted principle, his maxim—call it his motto. Although to be honest, whenever I paged through *L'Architecture,* I always skimmed the brief text so that I could hurry up and get to the drawings. I'd studied the prose long ago—it was what it was—and any architect, any artist's manifesto interested me less than his buildings, the art itself. I invested myself less in Ledoux's content than in his form.

The maquette carpenter had captured the essence of the wall-less utopia by fabricating a band of mock trees around the edge of the tables; he had used wood shavings for foliage, suggesting the blur of a dense forest. The Ideal City of Chaux had its planned center, but once you moved beyond the concentric rings of dwellings, the city went without demarcation, the built world spilling into, becoming one with arcadia. With my pinky, I touched the soft curls of wood.

"After all this, you still love this architect?" Didier asked.

I made my way around the models again.

"In the end, the biographer must murder his subject," I said.

"This is true? Will you murder?"

"Not yet," I said. "I can't afford to."

Didier frowned.

"What?"

"I didn't know much about this Ledoux before I was asked to make him my obsession," Didier said, "and now..."

"And now what?"

"Now he is, well, seulement un homme comme tous les hommes. Just a man."

Now I was the one who frowned.

"He was complex," I said.

"He was—how do you say?—full of compromise."

"Yes," I said.

"He is still your hero? With as much as you know?"

I didn't like the way I felt just then, as if my associate, my junior by five years, had intellectually leapfrogged me, although I wasn't sure how exactly.

"I need a phone," I said.

Didier's office was a two-minute walk away, near Denfert-

Rochereau. We cut through an idle market. The rain had thinned, but I stepped in several puddles and ended up with soaked trouser cuffs. His firm had a staff of ten, yet only one of his peers was there, working under a crane lamp in his cubicle, hunched over his drafting table and too involved in his drawing to notice us when we came in. Didier showed me his phone, and I called my apartment. Will didn't answer.

I swiveled on a chrome stool. A rough layout of the third gallery room was taped to the drafting table, and Didier's own diorama of the exhibit sat atop a credenza.

"I should tell you that the American architects have egos that are larger than the egos of the French architects," Didier said. "Although that would seem impossible."

"You're having trouble with the releases," I said.

The third room would be devoted to Ledoux's legacy, using photographs and models of works by the architects whom he had directly influenced. In my own dissertation, I wanted to draw a line between Ledoux and the modernists: What enabled the form-function marriage was his divorce from the baroque facade. I wanted to connect Ledoux with the postmodernists, who in making grand gestures out of historical references were not so much drawing upon Palladio or other neoclassicists as much as they were relying on my guy, who himself had a habit of appropriating classical elements and then exaggerating them, expanding the scale. Ledoux made possible the architectural hyperbole.

"I told you that I'd call their offices for you," I said.

"Yes, and where you were then?"

Didier left me so he could chat with his colleague. Some time passed. I tried my apartment again, and still no Will. I moved toy benches around the exhibit diorama. I flipped through other drawings on Didier's desk. He startled me when he started massaging my shoulders.

"So tense," he said.

I didn't say anything so he would keep going.

"Why so tense?"

"My friend isn't back yet," I said. "He should be at my place, and he's not."

Didier applied his fingertips to the back of my neck.

"You say friend. Stop saying friend."

"Will," I said.

"Will what?"

"That's his name," I said. "Will Law."

And I swiveled around so that I was facing Didier, and I gave it to him straight, the short history of my life with William Law, which was neither brief nor linear the way I told it. Didier was not so pretty when his feelings were hurt; he had elastic lips that tended to flatten and pale when he became uneasy. But I couldn't stop narrating my saga, I laid it all out, and when I was done, thinking myself frank, Didier said nothing.

"What?" I asked.

"What am I thinking, you would like to know," he said.

"Yes," I said.

"I have not known you a long time, but I thought I did, you know, know you."

He looked as if he might cry.

"There is a very big part which I don't know, no?"

"Maybe that's why I told you about him," I said.

"And not before now," Didier said.

I felt as though I were confessing an adultery to the man I had cuckolded.

"He wasn't around before." Although he was, he was—his stream of letters. All the letters I wrote back—he was around.

"I am supposed to kiss you now and tell you what?"

"Didier," I said. He waited for me to continue, but I couldn't explain myself.

"I do kiss you, Pedro," he said, although he didn't move toward me.

"I kiss you, too," I said and also stayed put.

"Sadly I will still be around when it is all over," he said and began to make himself busy by shuffling papers and tidying an already-neat work space. He rearranged a fasces of pencils in a mug.

"I don't think it will be over this time," I said.

"Toujours optimiste," he said. "How do you say? Whatever."

He needed to be mad at me for not making a move. All these months of traveling around, dedicating ourselves to our work. I should have made a move, and it was mine to make, I suppose; and yet he couldn't be mad at me, which perversely drew me to him, Didier who was too generous for his own good.

"I want to go away with him for a few days. Or he wants to go away," I said, "and I was thinking, your family has that cottage. Is anyone there?"

Didier laid both hands flat on his drafting table and paused. He blinked. He opened a drawer and found a key, which he set on the table.

"No one will be there this time of year, no," he said.

He shuffled the papers he had just neatened.

"Didier," I said.

He didn't look at me.

"Didier."

"Alors," he said. "If you are so in love, as you say, then you don't need my permission, n'est-ce pas?"

His permission?

"So go, Pedro. There is the weekend. Then we work on Monday or Tuesday, whenever you emerge again?"

"Yes," I said. "Thanks for the key."

I placed my hand on his shoulder briefly and left.

Didier said something in French to my back which I didn't quite hear but which I thought sounded like, Tu me manques. I miss you.

I turned back: "What, Didier?"

"Nothing," he said. "Nothing at all."

I HEADED HOME ON FOOT, and whenever I passed a pay phone, I checked my apartment. I convinced myself that the simple reason Will had not yet answered was that his lunch had run long, which was not so odd, was it? And yet it did seem curious to me by three, by three-thirty, by four. For some reason, I didn't want to arrive home and still find him missing. I was hungry but didn't want to dine without him; we'd collect ourselves and go out soon enough. Even so, I passed a brasserie on the boulevard Montparnasse and began to feel weak-legged. I went inside. I ordered steak frites. The fries came with too much salt, and the steak with a béarnaise sauce that I knew would shorten my time on earth. I ended up feeling miserable. Eating alone. Calling the apartment again and still no answer. Drinking coffee, more coffee. I didn't feel like a loved man, someone who had someone; I became a loner in the big city, simple as that, jittery with caffeine, ugly in my self-pity yet unable to stop wallowing.

Dear Pedro: I've been trying to remember and having trouble, Will wrote in his first out-of-the-blue letter. *Do you recall anything about that course, the one we took together, the one where we met?*

I remembered spotting a slender-wristed blond boy sitting in the back of the lecture hall. My first observation: He always unbuttoned but never rolled up his sleeves; I don't know why, I thought this was charming. The course was on Latin American literature and taught by a Peruvian novelist and occasional diplomat whom I later learned was a friend of Will's family. Will sat with an identifiable group on campus, one which I'd hitherto only known from afar: These were the diplomats' children and military brats, the expatriate kids who all knew one another from various boarding schools in the States and abroad, and mixed among them, the scions of various Latin presidents and Asian oligarchs. It was rumored that they all had trust funds and vacationed in Hong Kong, and these were the years when coke was big; all of them, it was said, were major fiends. I saw Will in the middle of the group and craved the total plot of him. I wanted to be the eminent scholar of his history. I presumed that I would never get close. I didn't stand a chance; he was out of my league of nations.

I should explain that I had grown up in suburban New Jersey and never traveled anywhere. My mother's background remained a mystery; she had grown up in Chile, but I never heard her speak Spanish. In fact, when it came time for me to choose a foreign language to study, my parents insisted I take French. French, they claimed, was the language of diplomacy. Diplomacy signified sophistication and demi-nobility and solomonic mediation, and imagine my first encounter, then, with my peers who actually arrived from that sphere. They seemed worldly and hence weary, enviably exotic.

What in turn did they see in me? And how did I fall into that clique? Was it my mocha complexion? Or was it merely because Will—whose father's fame in turn made him a prince among his friends—started talking to me during section?

Because soon we started hanging out, just the two of us, taking afternoon walks along the Charles. He told me about all the places he had lived, never more than two years anywhere, usually less. He had a coin collection to prove it, which one afternoon he spilled out onto his dorm room bed. I examined the coins carefully as if each one would tell me something about him. There were faces pressed into these coins, the profiles of serious kings, the queen of the realm as a young woman. More often there were birds, the ancient ibises, the pelicans, sometimes an antelope, and phrases in dead tongues, the hopeful oaths of new republics. Crests on one side, draped goddesses on the other; heroes on horses and the laurel branches of peace. It was while I was looking at the coins that Will told me about how his mother had died when he was young. And so in this way, too, knowing grief at an early age, he had traveled to a place I'd never been.

All of the kids in Will's set had cars, and often on weekends or in the late afternoon on weekdays, we would go on drives to nowhere in particular. To other colleges in Boston, out of Boston to the Cape. Up to Maine, to the Law family summer house, way up the coast—sometimes a group of us stayed over. One afternoon, we were supposed to go to the Law-stead, as we called it, but for various reasons everyone but Will and me bailed out. Will said he wanted to go anyway. We arrived and made a fire and drank some wine and probably smoked some cigarettes. Then, early in the morning, the proximity of a shared afghan allowed Will to rest his arm on my leg, and the rest, an oneiric conversation of gestures—exactly the opposite of what I'd always anticipated—rolled on like a summer day, falling away from me slowly, so slowly. I remember looking at my hands in the morning and thinking they belonged to a man. With these hands, I could do anything—build a cabinet, cook a meal, write a book, and yes, make love.

Dear Will: I fell asleep in front of the fire, and when I woke up some hours later, you had made us something to eat—grilled cheddar-cheese sandwiches—and in between the slices of cheddar, you had inserted thin slivers of an overripe pear. It was about the most soothing yet luxurious thing I'd ever tasted. I asked for another sandwich. It was extremely sunny that morning, but also windy. I remember later we had lunch in a glassed-in porch of a room and that the wind outside was bending everything, the evergreens, the seagrass down at the cliff—the wind was violent. But we couldn't hear a thing. Inside your house—silence. Not even the windowpanes rattled. Silent and warm, while outside the world moved fast, the world was tearing apart.

Dear Pedro: Do you remember our Paris trip? I know it was only a month, but it seems like it was a year—

I often feel that my life, my true adult life, was launched that July. Just the two of us hanging out in an apartment that belonged to a friend of Will's family, oppressively ornate with its overpolished consoles and cabinets, the marquetry of which was invariably scarred by missing scrolls of pearwood. A maid came and went unnoticed. We drank champagne from delicate flutes. We were playing at the decadent life. We lounged on settees at dusk and then fooled around on a canopied bed and took hot showers and got dressed in the same uniform: a crisp white shirt and khakis and shoes sans socks. We would head down to the boulevard, a citrus scent washing over us, and pass an écailler outside a bistro and each slurp down a coppery oyster.

I remember one evening when we went to an organ recital in a small stone chapel. We slid into a pew in the back and at one point I reached out for Will's right hand and he allowed me to remove the pale gold signet from his fourth finger. I touched the tiny crest—three ravenlike birds and a single fleur-de-lis—and then put it on my own hand.

We lingered on bridges. We dined late on cold smoked trout and poulet rôti. We lolled around hotel bars and ordered drinks that looked like liquid gems. Sex was frequent and we slept with the windows open wide. We transformed Paris from Will's favorite city into our favorite city, and we vowed that one day we would live here.

Dear Pedro: When I look back now, I can see so clearly how my best times were spent with you. How did we drift?

We returned to New York and entered graduate programs at different universities, Will in international relations, and I in art history, and we did not spend as much time together and our lives became busy with what we imagined would be our futures. But we did have a good year, one great year in New York, which was followed by a difficult time, because certain destinies became impossible to ignore. Will was working at the UN while he was in school and he was preparing for the Foreign Service exam, which of course he did well on. Then the inevitable. He received his first posting: Jakarta.

He said, Come with me.

And I asked him, As what? You will introduce me as what?

He didn't answer me or he said something like, Times have changed. It's possible now for you to be there with me.

But what will I do with myself? I asked. Because I had my own life and my own glossy ambitions. In the end, we decided that I would stay in school in New York and we would call each other every other day, a lavish proposition. I would visit him, he would visit me. We would try to be bi-continental. But something happened, something shifted—what?

There was this: While he was still in New York, I had started to observe Will in action in a way I never had before, and I could not say that I liked this part of him, the affable Will, the prince, the heir apparent. People almost automatically trusted a tall blond man in a crowded room; he could wink at a waiter, get you a drink. He arrived late, you didn't care; there would be a good story behind his delay. After three months in Jakarta, he returned to New York on business. There were some receptions; he invited me to tag along, and I watched him operate. He was smooth. One cocktail, two cocktails. Say: Can I ask you something? I'm curious. Just between us. This goes no farther than this table. Three cocktails, four. Have you looked at the proposal? Have you checked out the potential numbers? Our two countries. Our maturing alliance. Our collateral interests.

He had fallen so fast and so easily into a life, it seemed, that had been patiently waiting for him. How could I have not seen it coming? Now he professionally executed the will of the American government. Privately—by which I mean when I pushed him—he might offer a line-item policy critique; but I would have liked to have witnessed some deeper crisis of faith on his part, even some minor welling-up of doubt. He said, Someday when I run my own desk. He said, I don't necessarily agree with everything we're doing, but the policy is the policy. And I thought, Who did I marry?

I saw these political differences between us as real and damaging; I do not want to diminish my newly emerging sense of disappointment in my lover. But I also need to recognize what I was doing for what it was, namely looking for ways to break him down, to achieve distance, for even after all these years, he remained mythic to me.

Dear Will: Your last night in New York, you asked me to go back with you to Indonesia, and we got into a big fight. I had been reading everything I could in the papers, studying up. You were bragging about some sort of team victory. Wage concessions, open elections—frankly I don't remember. I challenged you. I asked how you could collaborate with a corrupt regime whose documented violations were so egregious. In the past, you had allowed me my complaints, but that night you told me I didn't know what I was talking about. You told me that I was in over my head. You told me to be quiet. I said, Fuck you. And you went out to meet someone for drinks, came home after I was asleep, and although I was aware you were leaving the next morning, I pretended to be deep in a dream until after you were gone. We spoke less frequently. Occasionally we traded post-cards. Then nothing—that is how we drifted.

It seemed to me less like we had left each other than I had left him. I had left him—and this haunted me. I was a mess, full of regret. I took a long leave from my academic work. I lived alone. I fell into a nightly ritual: I mentioned the pale signet that Will wore, his father's ring, and how I would take it from his hand and put it on my own finger. One night during our New York years, Will gave it to me. I had it fitted. After we split up, I stopped wearing the ring and kept it in my night table drawer. Before I went to sleep, however, I would slip it on. Beneath my pillow, I would touch the crest. In the morning I would return the ring to the drawer.

One day I got on with my life. The air was clean after a storm. It was a Sunday and no one was out and about yet; I walked around lower Manhattan, and I read the paper in a café, and then in a snap, I had the epiphany: I was over Will. I announced it to all my friends, although in some remote way, I did know the inevitable truth: All of us chase someone. Will never left me, he simply became a part of me, the stealth witness to my every affair. For his part, I assumed, I was entirely absent; he rarely thought about me.

But I was wrong. Eventually his letters came to me, and I tried to absorb the facts of his new life: Will was touring the cities of his youth. He had left the Foreign Service. He was done being a diplomat—which would in effect trim back the high privet of conflict that had once grown between us, would it not? I wanted to believe that he had changed. He told me where to send my letters if I wanted to write back, to which American Express office in which city; I made sure he knew my address, when I would be in Paris.

Dear Pedro: I've missed you. I'd like to hang out with you again. I could meet you anywhere. Name the country, name the city.

He came bearing gifts. He remembered my fondness for dark chocolate; it made red wine peppery. Chase it with a d'anjou, and I was floating. But then the day came for us to go out into the city, and we made our way down to the river—

He said, Come with me.

I smiled but was speechless. What Will was asking of me was expensive: He was telling me to forget about my apartment in New York—would I arrange for someone to send me my cat, and what about quarantines?—about my friends, about my pursuit of a doctorate, about the track I was on to become a curator. Couldn't he see how, without him, I had renovated myself? Maybe he did see—that was just it—and my new, improved, independent, unneedy self made him want me all the more.

I didn't say yes or no—I merely said we would talk later back at my flat, but now I wondered what would have happened if I had said yes then and there by the river Seine, or if I'd at least made some pledge, even if that was all it was, a vow, an utterance: Yes, I'll go with you wherever you want to go. Tonight. You can tell me where the plane will land after it's taken off, or don't even tell me at all. Welcome to wherever, where the local time is the local time.

Will you come with me?

I hadn't answered him the way he wanted and so, as the day wore on, it was possible that he began to ruminate on my ambivalence. I knew Will well enough to know that despite his training in conflict arbitration, he was a man who had no proclivity for resolution in his nondiplomatic affairs. After he had returned to Indonesia and our correspondence withered, our dealings became a matter of bureaucracy, about where to send his books, his winter clothes; I was the one who wrote him a long letter and said, I guess this means we've broken up; I was the one who spelled it out, not him. Will could have gone on for years like that, never signing the official papers, as it were, at sea on the gray waters just far enough from any shore to know the news of the land.

I called my apartment one more time from the bistro; he didn't answer. I pictured him there, letting the phone ring while he collected his belongings, leaving the spare key I had loaned him next to the uneaten pears. I pictured him lifting his bag over his shoulder on the way out the door. Will making his way to the airport. Gone from my life again for another seven years or longer. The silence this time would destroy me. I started walking home again. I took my time.

Dusk. Some said twilight required a reckoning. Go to a café and order a glass of wine; consider the day before you take on the night. And there was a time when you couldn't find a free table at a corner café at sundown, but rituals evolve. Lately Parisians tended to hurry home, stopping only to buy some fish, some haricots, their evening chocolate. Any pause between night and day occurred in private. For my part now, I planned no accounting. I thought, Let the day die fast. Let the sun go down and stay down. My best hope was for early sleep.

The break in the rain had left a marine sky, and all at once, it seemed, the City of Lights came on: the government buildings, the fountains, the column monuments and arch monuments, all of the bridges and the quays washed with a reverent flame. I always felt at ease during the time when there was still some light in the sky after the sun vanished. Car headlights looked like jewels. The limestone looked clean. The day was lost, and it was not worth worrying about. The night had yet to be corrupted. The night was an open road. My mood improved.

Curtains remained undrawn, but lamps were switched on, so I could look inside apartments on lower floors of side streets. I could see Parisians unpacking their groceries. I could see them greeting one another, no doubt discussing the strangeness of the day. They loosened their ties, they unbuttoned their shirts. I could watch them pour their whiskey, pick up their cats. They were safe and they knew it, but they could not yet relax. They stared out their windows.

Halfway home, I was tired of walking and worked my way over to a boulevard. All of the taxis that sped by were taken. I ended up on a bus for a stretch; it ferried me a certain distance, but then I had to walk again, and I hurried because in a breath it became dark and I did not feel so safe. I remember that I walked past a row of embassies in the Sixteenth, the formidable mansions with flagless poles and robot-cameras mounted in place of finials on iron fences. Ten blocks from my building, I approached a mission that belonged to an emirate, and I noticed something impaled on a tine of its fence. A hat? Yes, a hat—a fez, its tassel flapping about like a dying fish.

I walked as fast as I could. And then, seven blocks from home, I heard the allegro beat of someone running behind me, closing in. When I heard shouting, I ducked into a doorway and waited. The shouting waned. I continued.

Five blocks was all I had left. It was damp and cold enough that I could see my breath, which for some reason was reassuring. Then the footsteps returned. This time when I looked behind me, I saw a trio of tall boys, and they didn't have to come any nearer for me to know who they were, their silhouettes sufficed. Three boys with fuzz-heads and heavy boots.

One of them shouted, "Bonsoir, Monsieur."

I should have run, but I continued walking at the same pace. I thought, I am safe in my own neighborhood. They wouldn't want anything with me. I had four blocks to go.

They moved fast, their boots like trotter-hooves.

Ignore them, I told myself. Don't even look their way.

"Hey, you. Hey."

Suddenly they were right behind me.

"Hey," the boy said.

I felt a weight on my shoulder. The boy's hand. I stopped but didn't look at him.

He asked, "Did you hear about the missing children?"

I didn't move.

"Where are you from?"

Vous venez d'où? You heard that question often these days. People wanted to scrutinize your heritage. And I knew that when I had been asked the question by strangers in cafés or shopkeepers, it was in part the curiosity that anyone native maintained about tourists. Then again, I also increasingly suspected that the question was posed because of my coloring. And that made me suspect—that made these gang boys wary of me.

Maybe I could have explicated my background in my best French, or maybe I should have declared myself an American; that very well might have ended the encounter. But what difference would it really make? My complexion was still brown, a darker nut in shadow, and that was enough.

"I asked you. Where are you from?"

I bolted.

"Hey," all three shouted.

I sprinted.

"Hey."

I slipped in a puddle—my ankle turned—and nearly fell. I ran and I ran, and I assumed that they were chasing me, I thought I heard their stampede. It was only when I reached the end of the street and turned the corner that I could see that there was in fact no one pursuing me. The boys were gone.

I limped the last half-block to my building, but my heart wouldn't slow down. I wound my way upstairs and heard the phone ringing. I nearly kicked in my door.

"Pedro. There you are."

I couldn't help but grin when I simultaneously heard Will's voice and saw his clothes still scattered around my bedroom.

"And there you are," I said.

"I tried calling you before—"

"Yes," I said. "I've thought about it all afternoon: Yes. I'll go wherever you want to go. Tonight. Yes. Let's leave as soon as we can."

Will sighed.

"What's wrong?"

Had he changed his mind?

"Will, where are you?"

Nothing.

"Will?"

Then he told me in brief and somewhat cryptic terms about a woman and an abducted boy. A tragedy in the making. He didn't elaborate, but he said that he was involved now. He wanted to start looking for the kid.

"Can you help me?" he asked.

Come with me.

"Yes," I said before grasping the scope of what he would propose.

"Do you think you could get a car somewhere?" he asked.

He told me where to meet him, he told me when.

Briefly I considered borrowing the grand old sedan parked in my courtyard, assuming its keys were still in the glove compartment, but decided against it and hurried instead to Didier's apartment. He appeared uncharacteristically disheveled, his shirt unbuttoned, revealing his general hairlessness; he was wearing no shoes and only one sock; he reeked of whiskey and cigarettes, as if he'd already spent an evening hopping sticky basement clubs. I had called ahead; he greeted me with the keys to his car.

"I appreciate this, Didier," I said.

He leaned against his door and did not invite me in. He looked as if he was trying to hide someone inside, but the door opened behind him and I could see into the depth of his studio and knew he was alone.

"Perhaps you will want this as well," he said.

He removed another key from his pocket and pressed it into my palm.

"What's this to?" I asked.

"My bike—well, actually it is my bike lock. Once I had a bike, but it was stolen. Now I have only the lock, you see."

He was loaded.

"Okay," I said and pocketed the key.

He handed me another much smaller silver key.

"This one is to my mailbox downstairs," he said.

"Didier, stop. If you don't want to lend me your car, you don't have to," I said.

He looked as if he was going to teeter over, so I grabbed his elbow and escorted him to a couch. He fell back and I lifted up his legs. He covered his eyes with his right forearm.

"Now I will sleep a little," he said. "I am sure you will have a very happy life."

"Thank you for the car," I said. "I'll bring it back later."

Didier shrugged and I bent down to kiss him on the forehead. He was cool, so I covered him with a chenille throw that matched the beige upholstery, and all that was left of him was his arm and chin; he looked like an infant marsupial tucked in its mother's pouch.

"À tout à l'heure," I said, but he was already snoring.

My knees were wedged beneath the steering wheel; the rearview mirror almost came off in my hand, and then I had trouble turning the ignition. After starting and stalling twice, I waited a few minutes, considered other options, and then tried the car one last time. At first the engine sounded out of breath, but then it ran. I headed for the river. The car drove low to the

ground. I felt as though I were skimming the avenue in a sled. I
had difficulty coordinating my gear-shifting with my clutch-
depressing—when I rented cars, I always opted for automatics—
and consequently came to a choking halt several times.

Fortunately I didn't have to worry about angry motorists
behind me since no one in Paris seemed to be out that Friday
night. This disturbed me. It was only eight o'clock, and yet the
streets looked thoroughly swept of pedestrians, as if it were three
in the morning. The few people I did see tended to move fast,
like the quartet of overcoats that scurried across the plaza in front
of les Invalides. Partly there was the wind—the rains had sub-
sided and made the evening cold and brittle, easily cracked—but
also I had to consider the day, freighted with news, quick-
changing news at that, and the possibility that more violence was
imminent. I could not shake free from my encounter with the
gang boys, however fleeting it may have been. I pressed my foot
hard against the gas pedal.

The radio news did not do much to foster my sense of safety:
A day that had begun with a symbolic march would more likely
be remembered as the day that the right-wing gangs seized dark-
skinned children. And it was not difficult to read the kidnappings
as some sort of coordinated effort, a rapid response to the morning demonstration, although the French Front party had repeatedly denied any formal connection to the gangs, claiming each
rogue band was its own independent organism. I was not alone,
however, in believing that the gang raids had to have been
planned—now the report was that the total number of children
taken was a dozen.

The heat in the car didn't work too well; the windows fogged up with my anxious breath. In the distance, I could see a bright flare just beyond the Tuileries, although I couldn't tell what if anything was on fire. I picked a bridge and crossed the Seine. I glided past the cathedral. I made it to the pont de Sully in good time, and there, as promised, stood the love of my life.

"Hey," Will said and climbed into the passenger seat.

He didn't comment on the car. He had neither gloves nor a scarf, and I felt foolish for not remembering how underdressed he would be for the hour; his jacket hardly looked warm.

I reached over to peck a kiss. His lips were chapped.

"Pedro, Pedro," he said.

Clearly his day had sobered him. When I turned on the light in the car, I could see that his eyes were red.

"Thanks for doing this," he said.

I nodded.

"Seriously. You could've stayed home and waited for me— I'm glad you're here."

He didn't smell like himself at all; in fact, it seemed to me that he'd arrived from a different season, namely spring; he smelled like a fresh-cut lawn.

"How old is the boy?" I asked.

"Four," he said and removed a snapshot from his jacket.

A boy in a striped shirt holding a bright kite—a photo from the same series as the one given to the police. Nico had guru eyes: dark, liquid, deep. He looked a little wily, very much the wag. He knew a few bad jokes. Every day he told you what he would be when he grew up, and every day he had conjured a new future for himself. A fireman, a lawyer.

"He's small for his age," Will said.

A priest, a thief.

"He's a good kid," he added.

"You were there when he was grabbed," I said.

A police van zoomed past us, lights flashing, its siren off.

Will nodded. We were parked beneath a street lamp, its sulfur burn flattering to neither one of us.

"I know that I owe you more of an explanation," he said. "For why we're helping this woman. But it will have to wait. I don't want to waste any more time."

Another police van zoomed past us across the bridge.

"I have to tell you, I'm a little scared," I said. "Where are all the people tonight?"

Will gripped my arm. "You're safe," he said.

I answered quickly: "I'm safe with you, I know."

"The police have been no help," he said.

"You said as much when you called."

"No one has found the kid, no one has phoned. Jorie feels a little better just knowing I'm out looking."

"I hear you," I said. "So. Let's look."

Will outlined his plan: He wanted to check out every possible place a child of four might hide—every place, that was to say, near what might be called personal landmarks. Jorie had scribbled a list of the buildings and locations where Nico might seek shelter if, after the gang dumped him, he recognized where he was. And then we had to take into account the direction in which the van had sped off and how far we thought they'd drive before unloading a passenger they didn't want to carry too far—it would not be prudent to be pulled over by the cops with your kidnapping victim on board—and with these approximations, then, we could fan out, also look down small streets and alleys and in parks.... In other words, we would pick a street according to rather skimpy criteria. We had little to go on, we were fishing a big lake. Too much was being taken for granted, and although I didn't want to sound contrary, I had to ask how we could assume that the child would find a place to hide and stay put.

"I think that's how a scared kid would behave," Will said. "You don't go roaming. You find a place where no one can see you and just stay there as long as you can. You wait. You cry and you wait."

Fine. What if strangers had in fact found him and carried him to a hospital, where he had not yet been identified because the ID, say, that was always in his jacket pocket had fallen out? What if the gang had actually driven quite far, deep into the banlieue? Hadn't they done that in the past with previous abductions, gone for miles before letting the kid off? How would we necessarily see Nico in the dark? Will had brought along only a weak kitchen flashlight; it brightened a shallow meter at best. How did we know that any number of conceivable gothic outcomes had not befallen this boy? We were fishing, we were entertaining amateur hunches, and I had an unpleasant sense of futility before we had even begun searching.

Will lost his patience with me.

"You can give me the keys and—"

"I'm sorry," I said.

"Don't you remember about how to find missing cats?" he asked.

"You picture them coming home to you," I said. "They appear."

"Exactly," he said. "Can you do that for me? Just try to imagine us driving along a street, and picture the boy stepping out into the open where we can see him."

I closed my eyes. I saw a small listless body lying in the street. I saw blood. Maybe it was best if I visualized nothing at all.

Will took out his (my) pocket city-plan and directed me to follow the quay along the Left Bank. He would tell me when to stop.

A cell phone rang in his pocket.

"Hi there," he said with pretend cheer. "I'm with Pedro now, we're heading away from the bridge— That's right. As we discussed."

I had trouble shifting again; we lurched back and forth. The car was forest green, reflecting little street light, and I worried that I'd stall out and a police van would round the corner, not see us, and we'd be flattened. Not to mention that I couldn't listen to Will talk on the phone and drive at the same time.

"Remember what we talked about," he said. "This boy loves you, and he wants to come home to you—trust me on that, Jorie, please. Quiet. You can't do that to yourself. You can't blame yourself like that."

His tone of voice irked me, so easy, so familiar, almost fraternal—and how long had he known this woman? She was a stranger, was she not? I felt at once jealous and petty in my envy.

"Whose cell phone is that?" I asked when he hung up.

It belonged to the mother of Nico's baby-sitter. The baby-sitter was now staying with Jorie.

"Good," I said. "So she's not alone."

"She's not alone, but she is alone," Will said. He dialed a number.

We passed the Salpêtrière hospital; at night it looked like a prison. Out of nowhere, a stream of cars traveled in our direction and passed us, rocking our little tuna can. We passed the Gare d'Austerlitz, a plain of tracks with a dormant herd of cargo cars.

"Who are you calling?" I asked.

"The embassy," he said. "Allô, oui. It's Will Law again. Is— Then I'm wondering, could you please connect me with—"

"Will," I said. "We'll hit the périphérique soon—"

"Turn right on the next big boulevard," he said to me, and then, to whomever at the embassy: "I can hold."

"You're working your contacts," I said.

"Such that they are. The police are overwhelmed," he said. "We need a consul to run interference, make Nico some kind of priority. Frankly I'm not sure what anyone—"

He returned to his phone call and from what I could tell made no progress; he slapped the cell phone shut.

"If you're out for a year, it's like you never played the game," he said. "I missed the rotation. I thought I had a friend here in Paris, but they're telling me he's in New Delhi now."

"You must have other contacts," I said.

"You'd think I would. I lied and claimed that it was an American child who was missing, but even then I was told that we had to wait until morning."

"How is that a lie?" I asked. "Isn't the son of a citizen automatically a citizen?"

"Nico isn't Jorie's son," Will said.

He explained the connections. Nico to Luc. Luc to Jorie. Jorie to Nico.

"I see," I said.

Next Will checked in with the detective in charge of the case and spoke briefly with someone who was clearly not the detective and who had done little more than follow the all-points-bulletins.

"The detective went home for the evening," he said and pocketed the phone. "I don't believe it. All these kids are lost, and he's sipping his whiskey now, watching soccer re-broadcasts."

I switched on the radio and eventually there was news, an unconfirmed report: Of the dozen missing children in Paris, two girls had been found, both alive; one was uninjured, but the other had a fractured wrist.

Will sat taller in the passenger seat.

"That's encouraging," he said. "It sounds like the gangs did drop off the kids."

"We don't know how they were found," I said.

"Take the rue Nationale," Will said. "Then right onto the rue de Tolbiac. Apparently Nico spends a lot of time around here. It's where his best friend from nursery school lives."

We had traveled a certain distance south into the arrondissement. All the apartment houses looked the same, the rooftops aligned, the high iron balconies forming a tidy band like a dark ribbon decorating an elegantly wrapped present.

"Turn there, and then a quick right again," Will said.

The side streets were darker, without depth. I could take my foot off the gas and let the car coast an entire block.

"His best friend lives here?" I asked.

"That's right. One more block. There, on the left."

"And Nico would know his way around," I said.

"Possibly."

"In the dark."

"Pedro," Will warned me.

We stopped in front of an emaciated apartment house braced by two broader-shouldered structures. Will examined himself in the side-view mirror and combed back his hair with his fingers as if he were about to go on an interview. He stepped out of the car, but I remained behind the steering wheel. He got back in the car.

"Pedro?" he asked.

"I know this isn't the time to talk about it," I said. "But I reached a point where I said yes."

"Yes," he echoed.

"I'll do whatever you want, go wherever you want to go," I said.

Initially I had made this pledge after my brush with the gang boys, and now my voice sounded strange to me; but I weighed my life in New York, as comfortable and busy and, of late, directed as it was, against a new life with Will, an unknown life since we would in effect both be making a fresh start, and passion tipped the scales. Passion, rare impulse—memory: Back when we were in college, we used to lie in bed and regularly redact a mutual fantasy about how someday we could run a café or a small hotel in some distant country—we never decided where exactly—an expatriate hangout to which the world-weary could return again and again and always feel at home. Tall drinks on the veranda at sundown; a piano man playing sweet-and-sour jazz into the morning. Travelers would come and go, but our outpost would always be there, a fixed star in an entropic galaxy.

Will let his shoulders slope. He stared at the glove compartment, then back at me. He reached over to me, grabbed a handful of my jacket, tugged me toward him, and gave me a deliberate, definitive kiss. Any jealousy I harbored toward the woman, the stranger whom we were aiding, at once evanesced.

"I picked up my friend's keys," I said. "My friend with the house in the country."

"When all this is over, we can go there," Will said.

"We can go anywhere," I said. And then, a guilty after-thought: "By the way, this is his car."

We surveyed the street. Patches of balding pavement revealed cobblestone beneath. A steady stream of rainwater rushed the gutter. Two women crossed in front of our headlights and hurried into Nico's friend's building.

We walked the entire length of the short street and poked behind garbage cans, in the hollow space beneath some stoops.

Will rang a doorbell and identified himself over an intercom; a woman came downstairs. I watched the conversation from a half-block away. The woman cupped her mouth with her hand. She followed Will down the front steps to the street and glanced around with him. She shook her head: Aucune idée.

The woman even called out to Nico. "Nicolas. Viens ici. Maintenant. Tu viens. Nico?"

Back in the car, we searched the immediate neighborhood. We must have looked as if we'd run out of gas and were seeing how far we could coast with the occasional push-off with our feet. Will aimed his flashlight low. He navigated, too, although my old map didn't include the gargantuan mausoleum of a building ahead of us, the new national library in the near dis-tance, and we kept aiming for streets that no longer existed.

We worked our way north and west, back toward the river and the center of the city, surveying every cut of a street, focusing on the smallest nooks, the vestibules of closed shops, the corner doors of cafés. A few times we hopped out and would pass the rare person on a sidewalk and, if the man or woman stopped to talk to us, we showed him or her Nico's photo; but it was useless, no one had seen him.

"I somehow think the gang would have driven farther out than this," Will said. "It's just a hunch, but—"

"I agree," I said.

I didn't know on what basis I concurred, but after the first hour of our search effort, I had come to accept our assignment with fewer reservations. We could be looking for the boy for the sake of looking; in the morning, if he turned up on the other side of a city, if a stranger brought him back home, that would be just fine. There was communion in the mission itself.

I surprised myself by being the one who refocused our strategy: "If we cross the river and wander around the Twelfth—"

"There's an address in the Twelfth on Jorie's list," Will said.

"We can start out on the edge of the city again, work our way in."

"Head for the nearest bridge," Will said.

I pulled over to the side of the road and shifted the car into park. My foot slipped off the clutch and once again the car bucked.

"Can you take the reins?" I asked.

I preferred our new arrangement; Will knew how to drive a stick shift well, and frankly, I was the better man with maps. I knew that our assignment was urgent, that the night was not safe, and yet now I found myself relishing the moment. For here we were, lovers in a car at night, driving fast, just the two of us, silent, enclosed. We could have been tearing down a straight-shot, linden-lined road, heading back to New York after a day antiquing upstate. Or traveling a sinewy causeway that tenuously connected a rocky peninsula with the Maine coast. A passenger tacitly expressed trust in the driver, and the driver was always aware of his responsibility to make a safe passage—multiply that pact by an exponent of intimacy: A ritual emerged. No matter the road trip, I never quite wanted us to reach our destination in order to prolong this serene suspension.

What peace I enjoyed, however, did not last; we arrived in a new neighborhood deep in the Twelfth near the Bois de Vincennes, and once we veered off the main avenue, the city looked colder to me, barren, in trouble: We began to pass trees that had been set on fire.

"What is going on?" I asked.

We had entered a quarter inhabited by immigrants, and on every block, one or more trees had either been torched and now smoldered or were still ablaze, the branches electric with fire and folding in on themselves like a time-lapsed flower losing its bloom. What made the sight so eerie in part was that we didn't see anyone trying to dowse the fires, nor for that matter did we see anyone starting them.

"The bread in the river meant something," I said.

I heard approaching sirens.

"But what does this mean?" I asked. "Watch it—"

The high flaming branch of one plane tree dangled and then plummeted to the street. It landed on and ignited a parked car. We improvised a detour, but back on the boulevard, we spotted an entire double row of trees on fire—this was what I must have seen earlier outside the Tuileries, trees on fire—although, at last, a fire truck and a harried crew of pompiers directed hoses at the disintegrating boughs.

Now we also saw more Parisians out and dashing across the street, agitated by the arson and the proximity of some burning trees to dwellings. Now, too, as we followed the arc of a narrow street, we spotted a suspect pack of young men.

"Left, left, left," I shouted.

"Pedro," Will said.

"Left and right, fast," I said.

"Calm down."

"Didn't you see them, the gang? They're coming this way."

One of them banged a mailbox with a bat. Another jumped up to a sign and hung in the air and tried to pulled it down with his weight. They needed something—or someone—to break.

Will drove where I told him to drive, but once we'd lost sight of the gang, he pulled the car over.

"You can't let them spook you," he said.

"That's easy for you to say," I said, "they aren't interested in you. Me, on the other hand—I've already been chased once tonight."

"What do you mean chased?" Will asked.

I told him. Maybe I embellished my account somewhat, adding a couple of bad guys, describing a pursuit that had, in truth, covered little ground. I realized that I was shaking. Will placed his right hand firmly on my bouncing knee as if he were going to shift my leg into reverse.

"Who is she, Will, this woman, that you would do this, have

us drive around on a night like this? Who, Will? I feel like a creep for asking you. But who is she to you?"

Will kept his hand on my knee for a moment before we drove again.

"You've made some connection," I said.

He stared at the road. He nodded.

"You meet a stranger," I said, "and have a lot in common— how often does that happen?"

He nodded again. When he spoke, he was barely audible.

"She's like a lot of the people we used to hang with, Pedro. Once upon a time. I remember that you said you liked us because we were nomads."

A scattered tribe. A people without a nation.

"But look at what we became," Will said. "Is it still romantic?"

Will Law was the only one in our circle of friends who had gone into the Foreign Service, yet that didn't stop the others from continuing a life of constant motion. I'd lost touch with most everyone from that group, as had Will, yet we knew either from alumni bulletins or rumors that came to us years late, we knew that save one or two them, most of the flock had yet to settle.

"It's not romantic to me anymore," I said, "but it's hardly tragic."

"You're wrong," Will said. "*Tragic* is too strong a word, but Pedro, it's no fun feeling homesick when you don't know where home is. When you're twenty, that makes you feel jaded and cool, I agree. But when you're thirty, it's deeply troubling."

Did Will feel that way about himself? I asked him, but he didn't answer me.

We pulled up in front of what appeared to be a minor mansion set back from the street and girded by a smooth wall; all we could really see of the structure was its roof. This was Nico's nursery school.

"Jorie stopped wandering," Will said. "She found something, someone in Luc. A life, a family—she made herself happy. Nico means everything to her."

We sat still for a moment.

"Lately she's been in trouble with the boy's father. They don't love each other anymore, that's clear. She could lose everything."

"She needs her boy back," I said. "I know."

I did not need to have met Jorie Cole to comprehend her fright or despair. It was Will whom I wanted to add up and could not.

"I'm sorry," I said. "You're a good guy who likes to help people, you always have been. It's what you're trained to do, is it not?"

Will blinked. I couldn't read him.

When I stepped out of the car, the map of the Twelfth slipped free from the binding of my pocket plan and landed in a puddle. The page wasn't worth salvaging.

Will aimed the flashlight at the main gate in the wall, a perfect metal seal, and the wall itself was too steep for a boy to scale. We followed its bend around the block and found a couple of excellent hiding places—beneath a recessed bench, behind a bird fountain—but all our hunt yielded was an inexplicable plastic bag full of coins along with an uncorked split of Beaujolais.

We continued around to the back of the crèche, and now I could take in the full expanse of the mansion; it was an ornate house with an unreadable frieze and overripe flowers for capitals; all in all, the building looked less like a nursery school than an opera house. From the back, we pursued quiet residential streets, as yet unscorched; once again we didn't pass anyone.

"Nico," Will called.

"Nico," I echoed.

No one, nothing. We headed down an alley and checked behind trash bins; Will got on his hands and knees and shot the flashlight down an open sewer.

"Nico," we yelled.

Our voices snapped back at us in a warped echo.

In this fashion, working our way concentrically out from the nursery school, we continued, trying to think like a four-year-old. One street collapsed into the next. We'd cover the same ground twice before finding the new avenue. We ended up getting lost, and without a map of the quarter, we had trouble retracing our steps to find the crèche and our car, but we did make it back. We drove again. We entered a new neighborhood. We got out and searched on foot. We were back to speaking Nico's name in the darkness. The wind blew at our faces, kept our voices from carrying very far. With some buildings, we could enter the courtyards without being buzzed in, and if we ran into a resident, we flashed Nico's photo and were met with a

nod—Oui, I've heard about the missing children—then a shrug
—Mais non, I have not see this one.

Before long, it was ten-thirty on an increasingly desolate
night.

The avenue Diderot carried us toward the Seine, the avenue
Ledru-Rollin away. Now we were working our way into and
through the Eleventh arrondissement. We had strayed from our
plan, although neither one of us acknowledged it. Our search
was random. Will rang Jorie to give her a hopeful non-update,
but the cell phone battery was weakening; he kept his conversation brief. He reported that her state of mind had not changed;
she had heard the same news we'd heard, about the two returned
children, which kept her hopeful.

There were more people out around the reliably bustling
place de la Nation, but then no one at all only a few blocks away.
At one intersection, we saw a small person run across the street,
just a few yards in front of us, a child, a boy—and Will slammed
his foot on the brake. I hopped out first, then Will—the car
doors flung open like the wings of a soaring crow. We sprinted
after the child, but by the time we reached the short street he'd
turned down, he was gone, we'd lost him.

I covered the street. Will cut around the corner.

"Nico," he called.

"Nico," I said. "We're here to take you home."

The child had eluded us.

"Damn," Will said.

Back at the car, I asked, "Do you think it was really him?"

Will hesitated but said no.

"I don't think it was either," I said. "You said Nico is small for his age. That boy looked pudgy."

"Not so pudgy he couldn't outrun us."

We searched beneath the generous marquee of a department store. We checked behind a cinema. A loading dock. The sidewalk tables of a brasserie. The green kiosks and newsstands. The corner parks devoted to forgotten republicans. We shuffled along the streets in the shadow of the Bastille, a search for the sake of searching, nothing more.

We turned a corner onto one street and saw a line of bodies moving toward us.

"Umar," a man hollered.

"Umar," two women shouted.

Into the night, Umar, stretching the first syllable, short on the second: Oooh-mar. Oooh-mar. The group consisted of seven adults in all. When they reached us, a woman wearing a scarf over her head and another around her neck wringed her gloved hands and asked us—begged us—if we'd seen a little boy named Umar.

"We're looking for one named Nico," Will said.

"Nicolas Chamoun," I said.

"We have seen no little boys," the woman said. "We look for my nephew Umar."

"We'll be on the lookout, too," I said.

"You have heard about other children?" the woman asked.

"Not really," Will said. "We've just heard the radio reports."

The woman pulled a scarf down from her chin. The rest of her group continued to comb the street, paying particular attention to a bus stand.

"Umar," someone called.

"Some of the children have been found," the woman said.

"Who? Do you know who?" I asked.

The woman's coat blew back and revealed a cane.

"We have heard only rumors," she said. "A little girl."

"Two girls were found earlier," Will said.

"Maybe it was one of them," the woman said. "She turned up hiding behind the Opéra Garnier. She was scared and cold, but that is all."

"Anyone else?" I asked.

"These are rumors," the woman said.

I realized that her cane wasn't a cane but a paddle, a tiny oar.

"A boy in the Nineteenth," she said.

"The Nineteenth," I said. "C'est vrai?"

Will asked if she knew anything else.

"Just that he was not so fortunate. A broken arm. Or leg—I am not certain."

Will dialed the police again and tried to get an update.

"Oooh-mar," the group called.

"Good luck to you," Umar's aunt said and rejoined her group.

Will said: "I understand that the boy who was found was picked up in the Nineteenth. Can you tell me, was it Nicolas Chamoun?"

The group looking for little Umar disappeared around the corner, their chorus fading.

"I see. Thank you anyway," Will said and hung up.

"No?" I asked.

"Nico," he called out, exasperated. "C'mon, Nico. Where are you?"

Back in the car, Will became a little unsteady at the wheel. He leaned forward in his seat. Downshifting from second to first gave him trouble when it hadn't before. He was too large for Didier's car; it was as if he'd borrowed a sweater and was in the process of stretching it.

We no longer looked at the list of landmarks the boy might recognize; we skimmed every street. A short while later, we ran into another search party. We avoided another gang. We noticed more police on the street in the northern quarters of the city. We also passed more burning trees.

We could scout an entire neighborhood without noticing any fires, but then we would come upon a great oak blossoming with flame. Finally we saw a group—we were too far off to tell whether it was a gang—setting a stately chestnut on fire. They poured gasoline around its trunk and dropped a match and were gone. I don't want to exaggerate and depict a scene in which all the trees of Paris were ablaze, but that was what it began to seem like to me. The maples and the yew. We passed a stand of poplars on fire, and I noticed that they drew flames into eerily delicate columns of brightness with long plumes of smoke laddering toward obscured constellations. I'd always thought that the poplar was the sonnet of all trees, elegant in shape, pensive in any breeze, and it made me saddest to see them destroyed. Most of the trees were damp, which saved many from more than a brief charring, but the wind only became more fierce toward midnight, and when a tree did burn, it flashed briefly and then was gone.

I think if we'd found ourselves in a full-blown riot complete with looters and an army moving in, I would have taken some odd comfort in the possibility that for better or worse, the violence had crested and would necessarily abate. Instead we moved through a slow-cook. We didn't ride a slope of action, a paced, metered progression of chapters; we couldn't count on a denouement. This was disconcerting.

We passed a man guarding a newsstand with a rifle. A gaggle of conferring cops wearing white helmets. An older man closing an overcoat tightly around his frail body and carrying an open umbrella, its spokes flipped back in the wind. A woman smoking a cigarette in a parked car, the windows all rolled up, the smoke dense inside as if she were trying to suffocate herself.

At one point, we came across a boy—I guessed he was ten—standing in the middle of a street and crying, and because he and I were similarly complected, I assumed he could have been abducted. Will and I got out of the car; we moved cautiously.

I asked him, "Are you okay? Were you grabbed by a gang?"

He stepped back.

"Can we take you home?" Will asked.

He stepped back again and bumped into a lamppost.

"We won't hurt you. Let us take you home," I said.

"I have to find my father," the boy shouted. "My mother is very sick. My father, he went out. I have to find him now, I have to find him."

Then he ran down the street. He vanished.

It was a night of manifold drama, architectonic, one plot inspiring the next—that much now became clear—and as I scanned the surrounding buildings, I noted a great number of illuminated windows for the hour, bright curtained light, and wondered what the day had done to the average citizen, what the day had done to those who didn't know a missing child or hadn't observed a tree burning or even made it down to the river earlier—what arguments the day spawned, what drinking-to-forget, what doping-up against disenchantment, what fear, what sense of isolation, what melancholy had been violently aroused. There was no way a day like this could not touch you.

Midnight. We drove back to the pont de Sully. Will walked halfway across the bridge. He clenched the stone rail.

I gave him a moment before following.

"They just swooped in," he said. "They grabbed him like he was a fumbled ball and ran with him."

The wind slapped the river against the quay beneath us.

"We can still look for him," I said.

"I'm letting Jorie down," he said.

"We lose nothing by looking for him."

Will took out his cell phone. He started dialing a number but couldn't finish.

"Pedro, could you talk to her?"

"To Jorie?" I asked. "But we haven't met."

"I don't lie well," he said.

"So don't lie."

"Please?"

He finished dialing the number.

"Allô," a woman answered on the first ring.

"Jorie? This is Pedro Douglas. I'm with Will."

And so I met her this way, over the phone. I told her that Will asked me to call because he was in a huddle with some police-men (lying seemed tactful), and I told her that while we were still out looking, we'd heard about the abducted boy who had made it home.

"My baby-sitter fell asleep," Jorie said.

I didn't know what I expected from what little Will had told me about her—a smoky voice, a singsong soprano?

"You're all alone," I said. "I'm sorry."

"Neighbors come down and knock on the door, people I don't talk to at all. Concerned, certainly, but judging me."

"I'm sure they're not—"

"As well they should."

Given the circumstances, her voice sounded surprisingly mellow to me, played through a reed.

"We're out here. And we're not going to stop until we find the boy," I said.

"Can you tell Will something for me?"

I looked at him.

"Tell him I decided to call Luc in Nigeria," Jorie said.

"You called Luc," I said.

Will groaned.

"I didn't speak to him. He's unreachable. But I left word for him to call."

"And he hasn't called back," I said.

"He hasn't, no. I want you to know that I appreciate what you're doing, you and Will. Please: Keep looking."

"We'll call soon," I said. And I added, "With good news."

"I hope," Jorie said. "I hope."

I relayed all the information to Will, who moaned again.

"What's wrong with letting the boy's father know what's happening?" I asked.

"She shouldn't have called him," Will said.

"Because she's having trouble with him? Or what, you think

she shouldn't worry him if he's so far away? He has a right to know even if there's nothing he can do about it."

"It's more complicated than that. Now Luc will find out what's happened and come back to Paris. And if we do find the boy—"

"I'm missing something," I said.

Will headed back to the car.

"Will, what aren't you telling me?"

I added up what I'd been told, and I could intuit some matter of custody, but beyond that, I was at a loss. And so Will told me about Jorie's misery and quandary, her plan, her escape.

"Don't try to reason it out," Will said. "It won't change the fact that a little boy is missing and in danger."

"But you've taken her side, haven't you? You don't know this man Luc, you don't know Jorie. Yet you're cool with this, that she was running off with the boy."

We drove a few blocks into the Latin Quarter.

"I'm not sure what you're thinking," I said.

Will pulled toward a curb behind a police car.

"I'm thinking we should search this area on foot," he said.

"About Jorie."

He scratched his brow. He scanned the rue Jussieu and stared into the concrete quadrangle of academic buildings behind us. A cop was returning to the squad car.

"It doesn't matter what I think," he said. "We find the boy. That's all. Find the boy, and then she does what she does."

I nodded. In my gut, I believed he was correct: First we had to return the boy safely. Then we could afford to enter a conversation about what was moral and what was right.

The cop blinded us briefly with his flashlight.

Will rolled down the window.

"Messieurs," he said.

"We're looking for one of the missing kids," Will explained.

"Ah, oui," the cop said. "Moi aussi."

We got out of the car. The cop was a tall man, taller than Will, with a slightly crooked nose, the tip of which pointed left. He also talked out of the left side of his face.

"We're looking for Nicolas Chamoun," I said.

The cop scanned a clipboard on his dash.

"He is one of the reported missing?" he asked.

"Yes," Will said. "Don't you have his name?"

"We have his name," the cop said.

Dark half-moons beneath his eyes exposed his fatigue.

"Who are you looking for?" Will asked. "Are you following a lead?"

The cop leaned against the hood of the squad car.

"It is terrible. I know a boy, you see. He is a member of one of these gangs. He is fourteen, fifteen at most."

"An informant," Will said.

"He told me where I could find a girl."

"Where?" I asked.

"Not where he said. And so. I am fearing that this girl—she calls herself Yasmine—I am fearing that she was in this place, but now is lost from it."

"What kind of a place did they say they left the girl?" Will asked. "Can you tell us? It might be helpful if we know what kind of place we should look in—"

"It is too cruel," the cop said.

Too cruel to tell us or too cruel where the gang allegedly dropped the girl?

The cop's walkie-talkie interrupted him. He pressed his forefinger against his earpiece. He spoke into the microphone clipped to his epaulet: "J'arrive."

"What kind of place?" Will asked.

"Behind a church," the cop said and got in his car.

"A church?"

"Oui. In a trash bin behind a church," the cop said.

A gust of wind animated the tall trees across the street.

"But as I say, I looked, and she was not there in any trash bin behind a church."

The cop started the engine. He sank back in the driver's seat.

"Good luck," he said and zoomed away.

We stood in silence a moment and together turned in a slow revolve.

"Should we even bother looking in this quarter?" I asked.

"Maybe we should have started here," Will said.

"You said the gang headed east from the pont de Sully."

"But maybe they veered south."

We began to drift around a bend in the street. Soon we were walking up the rue Monge. It was late. The street names began to seem absurd to me. Saint Médard. Ortolan. Dolomieu. French seemed absurd to me, and I giggled.

"What's so funny?" Will asked.

I couldn't explain. La rue de la Clef. La rue de Mirbel. I had spent much of the day in motion, shooting across the city along diverging compass lines, and now I was punchy, crashing, hauling myself up a hill and past gated storefronts with retracted awnings, past the silent cafés, a market. In the distance, I heard the nasal systole of a siren.

Will was walking quickly, whereas I found myself dragging my feet. He would get ahead of me and I'd have to jog a block to catch up. I needed coffee, but all the places normally open at this hour were closed. I took Will's hand, he tugged me along. Once upon a time, he used to be a little skittish about holding hands in public, and I wasn't sure if he'd changed or if the darkness and empty streets emboldened him.

We rounded a corner and reached a plaza in front of a small church. We headed down a hill, down the rue Mouffetard. I heard someone playing a violin, unrolling a lament from a high window.

"That's pretty," I said.

"What's pretty?" Will asked.

"The music."

"What music?"

Was I imagining it?

La rue du Pot-de-Fer. La rue Lacépède.

I let go of Will's hand and lagged behind. I followed his shadow and ended up in the street, across the street. Searching the stoops, doorways, courtyards. Not searching at all and merely walking, walking, covering ground. We were like tourists who needed to get back to the hotel and who had wandered much farther into the old city than intended.

Will scanned the street with his flashlight.

La rue de Navarre. Back to the rue Monge.

I was remembering our first morning three (now four) days ago, and how we ended up in bed so fast, how I lay on top of

Will, still clothed, propping myself up with one arm, touching his brow and cheek with my free hand. But then he rolled out from under me, got up, and ended up at the window.

He said, The apartment isn't the way you described it in your letters.

How so? I asked.

The view, he said. You didn't mention the view of the park.

He looked back at me.

And the high ceilings, he said. They remind me of that apartment we borrowed.

I said nothing and watched Will, who looked outside again and, with his back to me, pulled his shirt over his head.

How was your trip in? I asked.

I wish I'd taken a train, he said. I prefer trains.

He returned to the bed and stretched out next to me, and we remained an arm's length apart. We were very still. I couldn't figure my next move or if the next move was even mine. Finally Will took my hand and placed it on his chest, as if to grant me permission to touch him. He was warm as though he'd just come in from the sun. Soon we were entwined again, and pressed against him, I could read him better, but then—how to explain it? One more time, after he got us going, he dropped back, let me take the lead. I moved, then he moved. I moved him.

In medias love making, I didn't give it much thought, but now, out in the dark, cold morning, sleepy, sad the way a lack of sleep made me sad—now I realized that during our years apart, I had always imagined a reunion of converse kinetics. The solitary beach: He is the one peeling off my wet swimsuit. A steamed-up shower: He stands behind me, I face the wall, he is the one pushing me against the wall. Or in Paris, in a white bed: I am asleep on my stomach and he is awake and he is the one who pulls back the blankets and wakes me by kissing my back and I pretend to sleep on so he will keep going— Was I dreaming or remembering? Remembering: That was Day Two of our reunion, toward dawn. Except I was the one who kissed his back. I woke him and he was the one who (I suspected) pretended to remain asleep.

Back to the present: We ended up next to the steep iron gate of a park. Will was trying to figure out where we might look next. I leaned against the gate and it moved.

"It's open," I said.

Will helped me push the heavy gate aside just enough for us to slip through. I followed him down a dark path, the crushed granite shifting loudly beneath our feet, through a close of fragrant trees.

Last night: We lay in bed postcoitally, on our backs beneath the cotton sheet, talking in flattering moonlight. Will bent his knees, and the sheet pulled away from his chest, down his stomach. Then, languidly, absentmindedly, he stroked his abdomen with his fingertips. Which I read as an invitation for renewed play—he had to feel my eyes on him—but I held back. His forefinger traveled up the main road of his chest. He was giving himself goosebumps. His biceps shifted up and down. I couldn't stand it, and before long I was lowering myself over him. Then he pulled himself up against the headboard, reaching behind him, holding on—he let me do whatever I was inclined to do— and yet this wasn't what I wanted at all.

Fatigue engendered doubt in me. I knew this about myself and tried my best to exhale all uneasy thoughts.

We had followed the park path to a clearing, and I realized where we were. Ahead of us, I could see a crescent of stone built into the hillside, tiers of seating falling away from us down toward a flat oval of dirt. These were excavated Roman ruins, the Arènes de Lutèce, where second-century gladiators faced off. There was evidence that they had used the arena as a theater as well for staging their senecan gore. I recalled one warm afternoon here a decade ago; we lay about beneath a balmy sun; there was a breeze, a bise from far off.

"Do you remember this place?" I asked.

If he did, he didn't say so. Will walked around the highest row. He began to make his way back and forth down along the tiers, all the way down to the pit. He glanced into the chambers beneath what was left of the stadium.

"Nico," he called. "Nicolas."

The rooms were closed off with iron grates, but Will aimed the flashlight inside the vaults. The Arènes offered the best hiding places of all the structures we had checked out; maybe that was why, even after it was evident that our boy was not here, Will made another pass.

Meanwhile, I returned to a higher tier and sat down on the cold stone. The steps had survived almost two thousand years, and considering that fact only tired me more. The sky had lightened with the possibility of a storm, although it would not rain now, and the gray of the stone matched the gray of the sky.

Will climbed up the arena tiers and plopped down one row in

front of me. He pounded the stone with his fist. He stared
blankly at the dirt stage.

The stadium trapped the wind. My hair kept blowing in my face.

Our first evening together, in bed, I had quizzed him about
his romantic life in recent years and—surprise, surprise—he was
vague. I had heard a few rumors while we were out of touch,
and I pursued one in particular, that during his time in Mexico
he'd been seriously involved with a man, a consul from another
country. The rumor went that when the man was re-posted
elsewhere, Will considered giving up his own career to follow.
Naturally this story tormented me. So I asked him, Was the
rumor true? And he told me that, no, there was no truth to the
story at all.

I asked him, So have you hooked up with anyone serious for
any length of time?

And he answered, Not hooked up like you mean hooked
up. No.

He didn't elaborate, and I didn't want him to; I would settle
for my own interpolation. But I will say that I had somehow
expected a different history for him after we split up, that of a
bona fide Lothario, a breaker of hearts; most of the time he had
lived alone, slept alone, unhooked—I couldn't quite square these
facts with my legend for him.

I climbed down two rows so that I could look Will in the eye.

"Hey," I said.

He looked beyond me at first, then he met my gaze. He
pulled up his jacket collar around his ears.

"Tell me what happened in Mexico," I said.

His eyes widened. His shoulders sagged. He studied his boots.

I knew that the untold story probably was not one I wanted to hear, but finally I had to know. I expected him to stand up and lead us out of the park. I expected him to say, There is a child in the night who needs to be rescued. I had stopped checking my watch; it had to be around one in the morning. I expected Will to elude my interrogation one more time.

But he said, "It began with a fairly straightforward assignment."

I sat back down next to him. He stared at the empty stage again, so I looked at it as well. Players, enter from the wings.

The assignment: Look into the past of a certain reform-minded gubernatorial candidate from a southern Mexican state. The United States liked him and wanted to see him succeed. He came out of the establishment, and he said all the right things when it came to matters of trade, but at the same time he was young, a man of new ideas, a popular populist; he appeased the opposition, indeed he contributed to its fracture; he was an institutional revolutionary who blended ideologies of tradition and change. He could be elected governor. Two years later, as the chosen party favorite, he could run for (and capture) the presidency. There were treaty renewals coming up and new treaties in the hopper. State had been following him for a long while. The Administration wanted him in the signing chair.

"So why dig into his past?" I asked.

"There were rumors," Will said.

The assignment more specifically: Look into the gubernatorial candidate's finances. There were unaccountable funds. There were suspicious associates. Men known to traffic in certain leafy illegalities. The State Department did not want to make an investment in this man and then have him turn out to be in with the drug capitáns. That wouldn't play so well in the American heartland.

"And you know, it sounds like we were preying on clichés," Will said.

It did: Latin politicos with money? Must be drugs.

"But State had been burned before. So I was sent in."

Get close. Ask questions. Run the background. Clear him fast.

Part of the reason Will was chosen had to do with the politics on the Mexico team. His seniors were looking for ways to promote him. Partly, too, Will knew about how drug money was laundered. He'd worked Southeast Asia. He had helped the two kids who were wrongly going down for dealing. In order to help them, he had to teach himself who the players were and the rules they played by.

He knew that he would never find anything on paper. In these matters, you never stumbled across an unshredded memo or discovered mistakes on bank records. You only found out what you needed to find out through conversation. So Will had to get himself in a position where he would gain access to all of the people close to the candidate. In which his presence would be innocuous and he would seem to be a good guy, on the right side, and the candidate's friends would trust him and go out drinking with him and prattle.

Officially Will acted as an observer. An administrator of democracy and righteous elections. Unofficially he made himself useful. He helped stage rallies in mountain towns. Someone in the campaign wanted the candidate to wear a suit; someone else thought he should put on a locally woven vest. Will, the candidate asked, what do you think? Will said he liked the vest. He worked on various texts, changing a single line here and there. His contributions were about syntax more than content. If they want an auto plant, they must give us our hospital. You and you alone must determine which cocoa forests you will clear. He gave his spin on poll results. He smiled politely at the commercials they previewed. He played the young veteran. People came to him with questions that he could answer easily. In truth, he actually did very little.

Meanwhile, he spied. He got close, asked questions, ran background.

The wind ebbed in the Arènes de Lutèce, and I noticed the dark town houses across the street from the park, all the buildings silent, at attention, listening.

"It will sound too easy to you," Will said. "But basically, I went out drinking. I was invited places for dinner. Conversations turned one way, I tacked another way."

Did he forget to whom he was narrating? I had seen him work. It was not difficult at all for me to picture Will in Mexico decanting the good tequila and twisting his way toward the question he needed answered: Tell me. You know you can trust me. This candidate, our guy—does he get money from someone I don't know?

"I know how it plays," I said. "You got close. You asked questions."

And as it turned out, the gubernatorial candidate was clean, his finances all neatly upholstered. He maintained no suspect ties and never had. He owed no favors. He was his own man. To some degree, one had to evaluate one's sources; lies were possible. But Will was fairly certain the facts he gleaned were pure.

"Somehow I don't think this is the end of the story," I said.

It was not. Will learned something else about the man. And here he became somewhat ambiguous about what questions he had asked to ascertain what information he received. But I understood, I could infer. Here was what his contacts were telling him: The candidate, our guy, he could be counted on by the party. Counted on—why? He gave speeches in which he often took the side of the Indian cause, in which he talked the talk about the people and their rights, but the party (and the U.S. Department of State) didn't need to worry. Worry about what? Worry about him turning out to be soft on the guerrillas. Soft on the indigenous people's movement. Not to worry. Why? Oh, well, he's proven himself. How? He had a hand in certain actions. He looked the other way. No, he more than looked the other way; he gave specific instructions.

"Will, spell it out," I said.

The candidate had been a mayor before he decided to run for governor. There was a demonstration during his watch. Indians in the town square. The police fired on the demonstrators. Thirty people were killed. Men who may have been guerrillas, who knows. Women died. Several children.

I remembered the news—the international outcry, the universal condemnation.

"Are you suggesting that the man you worked for ordered the massacre?" I asked.

"Indirectly. Yes," Will said. "Which was not at all what people thought. The story was that national generals had ordered the soldiers to fire. But I started hearing it from various sources, you see. I got corroboration. Naturally, if it were known, there would be a backlash and it would open up the candidate to investigation, not to mention make him vulnerable to the opposition. And naturally, I thought, State wouldn't want to support a man like this."

Will paused. His lips were dry, his voice getting hoarse.

"I went back to Mexico City and told my team, The candidate's clean on drugs, but here's something I found out instead."

He paused again.

"And they didn't care. You're not surprised, I know—but I was. Maybe it was naive of me, but I was surprised. All the team cared about was the money and the drugs, and they didn't give a shit about any massacres of civilians as long as it remained quiet, as long as it remained a local rumor at best. They sent me back to the campaign to be of service. By which they meant make sure the guy got elected."

"And you went back?" I asked.

"It was my job," he said. "I went back to the region. I tried to live with what I knew, but I couldn't. I just couldn't."

He let some time go by. The election neared. Finally he decided he had to make a move. He would do his job, keep his job, but at the same time secure public knowledge of the truth. Which was how he came to contact a journalist, one who happened to be writing editorials in favor of the candidate and who therefore would be deemed fair were he suddenly to report on the candidate's role in uncivil events. Will leaked what he knew. The journalist took it all in, came to his own conclusions, and launched a series of investigative reports. The articles ran, validating the darkest fears of the opposition, giving them ample ammunition, new momentum. In fact, the two opposition parties formed a coalition and posed a united threat. The national government in Mexico City had to respond as well, and there was talk of a criminal inquiry. A scandal took on its own life. Will could be satisfied.

Then the Consul-General came down to meet with him. He told Will in no uncertain terms that the U.S. would take no official line, offer no official support, it never did; but unofficially State would stand by the candidate.

"Even with the truth out?" I asked.

Will laughed.

"What truth? It was unfortunate speculation as far as State was concerned. They determined that the candidate could weather it, and they actually thought it was good in the long run that the allegations had surfaced now and not in two years during a national campaign. My boss said to me, Help him through this vetting, Will. He said, Will, spin it. Perform your alchemy. He said, I bet you there's some oro in this yet."

"You didn't quit," I said.

The stories kept appearing, the editorials. The journalist didn't seem to need Will; he ran his own contacts. Will thought if he left, he would be through. Everyone knew there had to be a leak somewhere. Nobody suspected him, but if he left...And then:

"Pedro, you can see it, can't you?"

"See what?"

"How I'd been given a new assignment, an even more significant assignment? How this was an even better way to prove myself. Although I couldn't possibly succeed, right? I had gotten the information out, started something. I had done my part, and now. Now I could pretend at the very least to be doing my job well."

The scandal blossomed; there were protests in the streets, picketing at rallies; the gubernatorial candidate had to respond; so Will himself helped write a speech in the great tradition of the American mea culpa. The candidate would claim no role per se in the massacre but would admit some complicity in not stopping the police from behaving the way they did. The candidate delivered the speech in a televised address. He said that his own life could stand for the lives of the many Mexicans who every single day coped with a rending internal struggle between colonial legacy and native roots. He gave a pitch-perfect reading, he sobbed publicly. It worked. He won.

"I didn't believe it. I'd done my job too well. I was unhappy. I went to State and asked to be re-posted before the end of my rotation. After all, I was owed a favor. I was told it was under consideration. I was also told that I might want to hang around Mexico. I was close to the new governor. Now he needed to run for president. Meanwhile, the journalist, my contact, continued his crusade. Secretly I advised him, suggested new angles. My only pleasure came in how nuts the exposé made the governor. He believed his own speech. The journalist was a liar, he had to be stopped."

Will brought his knees up to his chest and rocked back and forth on the stone tier. I had lost all sense of where we were, what city, what day.

"Then what happened?" I asked.

"The journalist's wife put their kids in the car one day to take them to school and the car blew up. A lot of people said it was the guerrillas because, see, before the journalist had gone after the governor, he used to spend a lot of ink going after the guerrillas in the hills. But it could have been, it probably was the governor who ordered the car bombing. I'm not sure what to believe. I choose to believe the worst."

The journalist's family was dead, and he gave up; he stopped publishing his stories, he quit his cause, which Will learned from afar. The day after the car bomb went off, Will packed his single bag and went to the airport and got on a plane. He left the country without notifying anyone. He disappeared.

He spoke softly: "That was what happened in Mexico."

For some reason, he handed me his flashlight. He headed back up the tiers to the path out of the park. I followed, illuminating the path for him with a delicate cone of white light. We walked silently, and I need to admit that I did judge Will badly. But I chose not to call him on it because what was important to me then—what at that moment, returning to the city from the Roman ruins, I decided to dwell on—was that in the end, Will left.

"You did get out of there," I said.

We'd made our way to the street. We headed for the car.

"I was a coward," Will said. "I couldn't face what had happened. I sent flowers to a funeral home, and yes, I got out of the country as quickly as I could."

"I mean, in the end, you stopped playing the game. You left the Foreign Service."

"That doesn't undo what I did," Will said.

"I'm not sure you can ever undo what you did," I said, I was frank.

"I wonder what my father would say about all this? What would he think of me?"

I didn't know how to answer him.

"In the end you left," I said. "You're out, you're through with all that."

"In the end I left," Will said.

"Yes, you left," I said. "You're through."

"I left."

I wanted to sob. I wanted to see him naked and hold him. He left. I told myself that this was all that mattered, was it not? He left.

The cell phone rang. It was Jorie, she was in trouble.

"Take a deep breath," Will said. "Tell me. Did something happen, did you get some news?"

He whispered the facts to me as Jorie relayed them to her: Luc had called back, they'd spoken. He had received the many messages from the Paris police but called her first, and she'd told him about Nico. He was extremely upset, of course, but angrier than she could have ever anticipated. He was coming back to Paris as soon as he could arrange a flight. Before he hung up, he told Jorie that she was the worst person he had ever known. He told her that if Nico was harmed, it would be her fault.

He said that he wanted his boy back, and he also stated that after his boy was returned, he never wanted to see her again.

Will could barely get a word in. Jorie was crying hard, agreeing that she was to blame. She was a horrible person. If Nico was harmed, if he was hurt . . .

"Jorie, we're coming to see you," Will said. "We'll be there soon. You will wait? Please wait. We'll see you soon."

Will hung up and rubbed his eyes.

"She wants to go out looking for the boy herself," he said. "Pedro, I haven't told you about something that happened earlier."

He described the twilight face-off with the gang boy in the place de Stalingrad.

"We'll go to her," I said. "We'll stay with her now."

Will dialed the operator; he requested the number of a certain hotel.

"Who are you calling?" I said.

"Jorie doesn't deserve to be treated like that," Will said. "She's been a good mother, she should live the life she wants to live with the boy. We're going to find him, and then we will send them on their way."

"What do you mean send them on their way?"

"You go back to Jorie's place. You stay with her, you keep her in her apartment— Allô, oui. S'il vous plaît, je voudrais parler à Monsieur Garrett Jencks. Oui, j'attend. You go to Jorie, and meanwhile I'll— Uncle Garrett? I apologize about the hour."

Will spoke on the phone, but I couldn't tell what was said. I stood right next to him, but I didn't really hear him.

I was remembering how one morning in New York I sifted through my mail and pulled free a thin blue envelope, fragile like a robin's eggshell pressed flat.

I was thinking about how Will unzipped his luggage and withdrew a Gibraltar of dark chocolate.

I was thinking about the way he lay in bed the night before and bent his knees and the blanket pulled away from him, and I examined his body, which I once believed I could map blind-folded and which now seemed to me like entirely unfamiliar terrain.

I was repeating to myself the unadorned facts as I had just

learned them and telling myself, wanting with all my heart to believe that what was paramount, what was key, was that in the end, Will left. He left.

He left, he came to me.

JORIE COLE HAD A round manner of speech, a fullness in enunciation which for some reason I usually equated with height; however, she turned out to be short and fine-lined, small in all the clothing she was wearing, a heavy cardigan over a cable-knit sweater, a scarf wound around her neck. Her lips were gray. Her handshake had been cold, and her first words to me were: I just can't get warm.

"I wish Will would call," she said.

I had dropped him off at the hotel in the place Vendôme and come here per his orders. I was upfront with Jorie, telling her that it was my assignment to keep her quartered until Will contacted us, and she didn't argue with this new plan; she didn't seem to have the strength.

"All night long," she said, "his calls have kept me sane."

"He's a diplomat, he's good at this," I said, by which I didn't mean finding lost boys so much as I meant coming to the aid of strangers.

"He is good," Jorie agreed. "Let's hope he's good. And now, the friend of his family?"

"I think he thinks that this man will be able to pressure the police," I said. That was as much as I understood and as much as I believed Will had figured out when I left him: Garrett Jencks might know someone at the Hôtel de Ville who, as a favor to an old friend, might be able to step up the search for Nico.

"Pressure the police how?" Jorie asked.

This was the third or fourth time we had made our way through this conversation in the last hour, and I couldn't answer her. Frankly I didn't know what Will was up to and didn't want to speculate.

"We'll see," I said. "Will said he'd call us. He'll tell us then."

"His calls have kept me sane," Jorie repeated. "All night long."

Outside the sky had begun to lighten. More than any other part of me, my eyes ached the most. I didn't dare shut them, I'd be asleep with my head on the table in seconds, and the bright lamps in Jorie's apartment didn't help matters. The place was a mess. There was an open cardboard box on the couch, its contents spilled out, a variety of memorabilia as far as I could tell, and the dining table was a disaster. Over the course of the evening, it appeared as if Jorie must have peeled off the teak veneer, exposing a walnut-shell-like surface; a pile of sharp shards littered the dining area. Only an Australia-shaped island remained in the center of the table beneath a mostly empty fruit bowl. In the kitchen, meanwhile, the counters were layered with all manner of foil-covered baking dishes and ceramic bowls: Apparently some neighbors had brought food. I had thought this was a generous collective gesture, but Jorie didn't see it that way at all. People with whom she had hitherto exchanged a minimum of words, she claimed, had leaped at the opportunity to make her feel dismal; they showed up in dark shawls; they slapped their chests. It was wicked—they wanted a funeral. Give them a funeral and they knew how to be friendly.

"I sent the baby-sitter away," Jorie said.

"Why?" I asked.

"She's only fifteen. She's too young for this kind of day." And then, as if this might clarify her, Jorie's, actions, she added, "I tutor her in English."

I smiled and Jorie squinted at me: Why was I grinning? I couldn't help myself. Without sleep, I couldn't check wild mood swings, and what I was experiencing just then was the pure elation of meeting someone new, the world traveler who came complete with a life in which she made a living teaching subject-verb agreement. I liked her right away. I tried to stop smiling—it was rude and inappropriate—but I couldn't.

I noted the various objects strewn about the apartment from which I could construct a more complete portrait. The soccer poster and maps over the cot in the corner, the tall glass jars of couscous on a kitchen shelf, an Arabic primer, pomegranates on the floor like dropped juggling balls. I examined the items emptied onto the couch. There were black-and-white photographs of a dark-haired girl in a white dress and white barrettes, snapshots of an awkward age. There was a wad of old letters, tied with string, and a stack of graph-papered compositions books; I picked one up and saw that it was filled with tiny French cursive. There was a gauzy red scarf basted with a silver thread and a black velvet ring box.

Jorie explained. She opened the ring box for me; it contained two gold bands.

"The small one was Thérèse's ring and the bigger one belongs to Luc. He hides this box up there," she said and pointed to an open closet by the entry; the scarves and hats on a high shelf had been pushed aside.

"Is this Thérèse, then?" I asked about the photograph.

"As a girl," Jorie said. She replaced the letters and photograph and ring box to the larger cardboard box. "This was a scarf Luc gave her. I used to think it might be her favorite or something, but then I got to know Luc and now I figure that he just assumes it was her favorite because he gave it to her. . . . I'm sorry, I'm being mean."

"Go ahead and be mean," I said.

"Once Luc showed me the box. This was early on," Jorie said. "It was one of the only times we talked about her."

"Thérèse," I said.

"You won't find any pictures of her around the apartment. In fact, except for this picture of her at—what?—thirteen, I don't think any pictures of her exist. Luc showed me this box and then instructed me to never touch it."

"But you do," I said.

"From time to time I take it down," Jorie said. She handed me the stack of composition books.

"What are these?" I asked.

"Well, I'm not sure. Luc never told me, but I think they're

children's stories that Thérèse wrote either before or when she was pregnant with Nico."

"Stories to read to her child?"

"The hero of all the stories is a little boy, so I wonder if she knew she was going to have a boy."

"So you do think she wrote them to read to Nico."

"I doubt she could have written them after he was born," Jorie said. "You see, she died not too long after that.... I'm just not sure."

"You've read them all," I said.

"Luc would go to work or go away on business and I'd take down the box, and I more than just read them. I'd read them to Nico."

I flipped through one of the books. I noticed that while all the prose was in French, the dialogue was in Arabic.

"That's sweet that you do that," I said.

Jorie was crying.

"They're all about the same boy, you see, a prince with special powers: He can transform himself into any animal he wants."

"Like?"

"In one story," Jorie said, "a cabal of evil men has taken to the woods—"

"Where?"

"Ancient Lebanon," Jorie said and wrinkled her brow: Don't interrupt. "They've taken to the woods and are conspiring a reign of terror. The prince sees them and follows them and turns himself into a monkey to spy on them from the trees. As a boy again, he warns his father the king, but the king is a peaceful man who does not want to wage war. The boy possesses other powers, too: He climbs a tree at the edge of the forest, and when the army of evil men emerges from hiding, the prince turns them all into fig cookies."

I smiled broadly again, but now it didn't seem inappropriate.

"The prince hands out a cookie to every citizen in the kingdom and all the evil men are eaten up, the end. Happiness ever after."

Tears raced down Jorie's cheeks.

I sat next to her on the couch and held her icy hands in mine.

"I got a recipe for fig cookies from a neighbor," she said. "I would bake a batch and give them to Nico with his bedtime juice and—this was all assuming Luc was away, you see—I'd take down the box and find a story and read one to him. Someday I want to tell him that his mother wrote them. I haven't yet."

I squeezed her hands. Whatever high I'd been feeling began to wane. The light outside began to equal the light inside; it was a sobering effect.

"I've let her down," Jorie said.

"Who?"

"I have so completely and totally let her down. Thérèse."

"I don't see how," I said. "You made the cookies, read the stories—"

"These last hours. Letting her son go. Letting her son stay out there."

Jorie heaved a sob. She was shaking.

"I don't care about Luc. I don't care anymore what he thinks. But Thérèse, Thérèse—I promised her. I would read these stories and promise her I'd take care of her son. Make him my boy. I've let her down."

There was nothing I could do to reassure Jorie, to allay her fears. I wished that Will had provided me with more of a script. He would know what to say. I wanted him to call, but he didn't. And then I realized that perhaps it was better that Jorie release her worst thoughts. Live them out. Rehearse the darkest outcome.

Jorie cried for a half hour straight. Her sobbing gave way to deep breathing.

She said, "I was going to make him cookies tonight. Read him a story tonight—or last night."

I followed her into the kitchen. She removed a bowl from the refrigerator and pushed aside a neighbor's casserole to make room on the counter.

"Then I decided to run away," she said.

I could imagine her with the boy, it wasn't difficult. I could see she was a woman who had surprised herself by happily alighting into motherhood. It suited her, the ready answering of a hip-high kid's constant questions.

"I forgot all about the figs."

Jorie showed me what was in the bowl: oval-shaped plumped fruit soaking in a sticky brown broth.

"We should bake the cookies now," I said. I made the suggestion at the same moment that it occurred to me. It was time for me to help in more concrete ways.

"Bake them now? You want to distract me," she said.

"I want you to picture Nico walking through the door," I said. Jorie sighed.

"He'll be hungry. You can give him his favorite cookies."

Jorie blinked. Then in a snap, she was in motion. Locating a suitable pot. Emptying the soaking fruit into the pot and stewing them briefly, making a bloodred liquid, which she thickened with a measure of honey.

I leaned against a counter. I gave her room. I watched her make dough. Clearly she had done this countless times before. She could roll pastry in her sleep, and in a way, both of us were moving about in a dream state. I felt as though I were studying Jorie through a thin veil. She melted a stick of butter in a pan. She whisked it, added a dollop of vanilla. She got me in the act, instructing me to add sugar to the butter.

"After Will left earlier," she said, "I remembered that a long time ago I saw him play tennis."

This was news to me, that Will had crossed paths with Jorie before.

Jorie poured the sugar-butter into a wide glass bowl. The figs nearly boiled over. She reduced the simmer.

"Did he tell you? I thought we'd been in the same school once. In Cairo or Istanbul. But it was Athens."

"Athens," I said. "Right. But Will was young then. I don't know how old he was when they moved, but he must have been twelve, thirteen."

"This would have been around then. He was skinnier and shorter and he had long, long hair."

"Will with long hair," I said and grinned.

"All the FS kids were always pushing, seeing what they could get away with. How long before someone made them cut their hair. Anyway, I can picture him, a very tan boy in his whites, running in for a volley, making the point. He was a star."

She added flour bit by bit into the butter and sugar. She

kneaded the concoction very gently, keeping the dough airy and light. She sprinkled in a dash of ground ginger. She kneaded some more.

"You were friends," I said. "Did he remember?"

"No, he pretended he did, but I could tell he didn't. We weren't friends. I was new, he was leaving. We weren't friends, but I developed a crush and eventually dated another boy on the tennis team. I'm a year or two older, but I remember having a strong feeling about Will," she said.

The dough was half-kneaded and ready for the cooked figs, which first had to be ground into a paste. Jorie poured the fruit through a strainer and then pressed the skins with the palm of her hand, pushing through all possible pulp. The juice and pulp then went back into a pan for additional simmering, and another dollop of honey was added to thicken the fruit into a loamy paste. The paste needed to cool.

Normally I would have been jealous of anyone who knew Will before I met him. Who knew how he moved as a boy, with what bounce, what stride. Yet that was not the case at all; I wanted more.

"What else can you tell me?" I asked.

Jorie exhaled. "He had older sisters?"

"That's right," I said.

"He was kind of the leader of his crowd, but…"

"But?"

"He never said much. I mean usually a kid who is already playing second singles on the tennis team and whose father could win a Nobel is more talkative. You'd think."

I pictured Will at thirteen. All elbows and knees. Curiously shy.

"He was quiet. That's all, I'm sorry, it's not much."

I said, "No, that's plenty."

"I wish he'd call."

"That's plenty, thanks," I said, as if Jorie had given me a gift.

The fig paste cooled and Jorie spooned it bit by bit into the dough, which she kneaded again. She instructed me to rub a cookie sheet with butter. She showed me how to shape the dough into small crescents and arrange the crescents in perfect rows. We filled two trays and then put them in the oven. This would be the first of many batches.

"What were you like?" I asked.

"Back then?"

Jorie was wan and blush rose easily to her cheeks.

"You don't want to know," she said.

"Tell me. You were what, fourteen, fifteen?"

"I was trouble," Jorie said. She tucked her short hair behind her ears. "The marine colonel's daughter."

"You didn't exactly go to church," I said.

"Oh, I went to church," she said. "I went to church, I did well in chemistry. I also liked the tennis boys. I led two lives— let's leave it at that."

"Okay," I said and chuckled. Had I succeeded in distracting her?

We remained in the narrow galley kitchen, leaning against opposite counters, keeping warm by the oven. I hadn't looked at my watch in a while; suddenly it was almost seven. I hadn't heard a single siren in the last hour. In fact, I thought I could hear traffic, the morning trucks on the périphérique.

It was my idea to check in with Will. He had the cell phone, which I dialed. Will didn't answer; a prerecorded voice indicated

that the phone was either inactive or out of range. I tried the
hotel number and asked for the room of his family friend; the
line was busy.

"Pressuring the police," Jorie said. "Maybe we should go look
ourselves—"

"Not with something in the oven," I said.

"I can't believe we're baking cookies," she said.

It didn't seem odd to me before, but now it did. Cookies for
a boy coming home from school. Were he to walk in the door,
he would need to be wrapped in a blanket and possibly taken to
a hospital and treated for shock.

The cookies took no time to rise and expand. I removed them
from the oven and Jorie shoveled them onto a plate to cool. I
formed another batch of crescents.

"Sometimes, like right now, I wished I believed in a god,"
Jorie said.

I was quiet.

"I'm offending you," she said.

"Not at all. I always assume I'm the only nonbeliever in the
room," I said, "and when people start talking about religion, I
get quiet."

"But here's the thing. I don't believe in a higher force, right,
and yet I'm fairly certain that I'm being punished for my
actions."

"You were leaving town with Luc's kid," I said, I spelled it out.

"Who or what is punishing me, I don't know. But I'm paying
a price."

Jorie tested a cookie.

"Thank you," she said.

I wasn't sure for what.

"For not telling me that I wasn't being punished. For letting me just quietly freak out."

I bit into a warm crescent. It was too sweet for me, but perfect for a little boy, I thought. The cookie tasted more like almond than fig. The apartment now smelled like warm honey.

We watched a pedestrian walk along the canal. Jorie sat down again at the veneer-less table. I collected the daggerlike shards from the floor. We turned on the radio, and there was no new news. I called the cell phone—no response—and the hotel line was still busy. We waited. It was unavoidably morning now and bright, and all we could do was sit and wait, and absentmindedly eat cookies and wait, and bake another batch and wait.

Finally the phone rang. Jorie answered. She shook her head; it wasn't Will.

"Hello, Luc," Jorie said in a flat voice. "Where are you?"

I stared at the table. The veneer was irresistible; I snapped off a peninsula from the remaining island.

"No flights till when?" Jorie asked. "I see. No, nothing. I'm sorry, there's nothing. Well...Yes, Luc. I'm listening, Luc."

Then Jorie became very quiet. She was talking on the wall phone in the kitchen and turned away from me. I thought I should give her more privacy.

"You were upset. I know that," Jorie said.

I stepped into the bedroom. It was a square space, barely big enough for the low mattress and night tables. A salvaged lamp with a turquoise ceramic base. An open closet, a packed bag, that was it.

There was an old phone on the night table, the French kind of phone with the second earpiece attached to its back. I had one like it in my apartment.

There was a lot of static, the connection thin. Luc spoke in a weary bass. It was clear to me that he was distressed, his voice all chopped.

"Yes, but...I should not have said these things to you, Jorie."

"It's okay," she said. "Really, it's not important."

"Nico is all that is important," Luc said.

"Yes, that's true."

"I should not have been so harsh with the words I used," Luc said.

Jorie took a deep breath, which was loud in my earpiece.

"You sit there and you wait," Luc said.

"I'm waiting. I met someone today, an American diplomat. He's been helping me. Helping us."

"Good, good."

A pause.

"You know that box in the closet? The one with Thérèse's things," Jorie said.

"You need to speak of this now?"

"I have to ask you something about those stories," Jorie said.

Luc was silent. Then he said, "You know I prefer that the box stays where it lives."

"The stories about the prince who can change himself into anything. The enemy army he turns into fig cookies. Thérèse wrote them before Nico was born, right? Did she know that you were going to have a boy? And she wrote them in French, not

Arabic, although the dialogue is Arabic—I've always wondered about that."

Luc remained quiet. I thought I heard voices in the background.

"Luc," Jorie said.

"It was my mother who wrote these stories," he said, barely audible. "I am the prince."

"Oh, I see," Jorie said.

"My mother thought French was a literary language. When she was a young woman, she wanted to be French, live in France. She wrote down the stories for me—although I do not know about the dialogue."

"I made him fig cookies," Jorie said.

"You make these cookies? With what recipe, how?"

"I make them all the time," Jorie said.

"I have never seen this," Luc said.

"I know," Jorie said.

"Jorie. I am sorry for the words I used."

Now it was Jorie's turn to remain silent.

"I know," she said eventually.

"The first flight out," Luc said.

"Luc," she said. "I haven't found him yet, but listen to me: I will find him."

"The first flight I can be on," Luc said. "You look, and I will be there soon."

"Luc," Jorie said.

"You look, but—"

"Luc," she said.

"Oui?"

She paused. "À bientôt," she said.

"À bientôt," he said and hung up.

I wondered what it was that she wanted to tell him and didn't. That she loved him. That she didn't love him and was leaving him, and if the boy hadn't been taken, Luc would have never seen him again. That Nico might never turn up—they needed to prepare for a bleak life without him.

I returned the earpiece to the phone and returned to the main room. Jorie still had her hand on the phone.

"I hate myself," she said.

"Now I'm going to tell you to cut it out," I said.

"How much did you hear?" she asked.

I must have turned red.

"At this point, I could hardly care," she said.

"I heard a lot of it," I admitted.

"If I could have just let Nico go to nursery school today. If I hadn't dragged him down to the river—"

"Cut it out," I said.

Jorie removed a roll of currency from her pants pocket.

I stared at the cash. What did she want me to say?

"I was taking his money, too. Sure, some is mine, but mostly it's his," Jorie said.

I looked out at the canal, and now it was sunny enough for me to see that the trees on one side of it had been torched. All that remained were blackened trunks.

"I think that we're going to find Nico," Jorie said.

"You need to think that way," I said.

"We're going to find him. Then we're going to get out of here as fast as we can."

Before Luc returned. I didn't need to say it aloud.

"We can't live in France," she said.

The phone rang.

"Will," Jorie said. "Where are you? At the hotel still?"

I waited for my turn to speak.

"Good," she said. "Soon. I hope."

She didn't look too encouraged by whatever Will had told her, and I understood why: He had little to report.

"What exactly are you doing?" I asked. I didn't mean to sound accusatory.

"We've been making some calls," Will said. "It may lead somewhere, I don't know."

"You can't tell me more?" I asked.

"No," Will said. "You two just wait there, okay?"

Jorie had disappeared into the bedroom and she reappeared wearing a black leather jacket instead of her cardigan.

"Will," I said. I found it irritating that he couldn't supply me with any information. Irritating and suspicious: What did he not want me to know?

"I'll explain everything later," Will said. "I promise, but right now, I've got to get back to these calls."

"Wait," I said—wait to both Will and Jorie.

She was looking for something in the closet—gloves, which she put on.

"Tell me one thing," Will said. "The place where your friend has that cottage."

"Didier?"

"Where is it exactly?" Will asked.

Jorie went out the door without shutting it behind her. I had the presence of mind to turn off the oven, although I didn't remove the burning cookies.

"Will, why?"

"I promise to explain later," he said.

I named the town, the road. A house set back from the road with asymmetrical windows and a low-sloping roof. I had been there once but knew exactly where it was.

"Will, wait," I said.

"I'll call you soon," he said.

I charged down the hall after Jorie. I caught up with her outside a neighbor's door, where she was speaking with a woman in a bathrobe and in the process of borrowing yet another cell phone.

"Merci," Jorie said.

"Oui, oui. J'espère que vous le retrouverez," the neighbor said.

Jorie hurried down the hall.

"Will said to wait," I called after her.

She skipped steps down the stairs to the lobby and headed out to the courtyard and toward the street.

I reached her and grabbed her elbow.

"Will said wait," I said.

"He's had time, he's had no luck," she said. "We can call him later."

"Jorie," I said.

"Go back and get your coat. I'll wait."

Running after her, I had made myself dizzy. I faced her and placed my hands on her shoulders, less to keep her in one place than to steady myself.

"Where are we going?" I asked.

"We have the sun now," Jorie said.

That we did.

"We have to look," she said.

Nico. Nicolas. Come out where we can see you.

WE CIRCLED THROUGH the neighborhood, wordless, drifting along what I imagined would usually be the course of Jorie's errands. Through the open-air market with its battened stalls, past the fish store where a truck unloaded a new catch onto beds of shaved ice, past the bakery, from which the cleansing aroma of rising yeast emanated: Paris was back to normal. But was it? We left Didier's car parked outside Jorie's building and walked south through the Nineteenth, and there was litter strewn everywhere, a carpet of broken glass. We passed a dozen charred and gnarled tree trunks. We walked as far south as the quarried Parc des Buttes Chaumont and even made a tour of its blasted hills and man-made lagoons, and then we swung north toward the concrete housing complexes, north all the way to the train tracks. After Bastille Day, the city looked a tad ransacked; this morning, the battering appeared worse—witness all the freshly spray-painted graffiti, the occasional overturned car, the signs bent in half—and yet, as the morning drew itself out, it also became apparent that Parisians were returning to their usual routines. It was Saturday, and only some needed to go to work, but we saw them emerge a few at a time, then in a steadier stream, people walking dogs and reading the morning broadsheet and descending into the subway. Soon there was traffic coursing the boulevards and swimming toward the place de Stalingrad. Soon we could hear the hum of cars buzzing along the périphérique. Trains leaving the station. The métro arriving, departing.

Didn't the city know that there were children still missing? Couldn't everyone see the broken glass and the charred trees? How could Paris return to its regular pace and beat so easily?

Jorie led the way. My legs ached, my ribs ached, but somehow I followed her, usually a pace behind. It was at least twenty degrees colder this morning than the day before; the wind numbed my ears. Now and then she spoke her boy's name, but it was more a whisper than a shout. We were wandering, circling, pursuing a coil of streets and then spiraling out again, and it seemed to me that we were not so much looking for Nico as we were making ourselves available for him to see us. He was tucked away wherever he had been hiding all along, and then we would meander by and he would ambush us and jump out into the open—what a long game of hide-and-seek it had been. His frown would make clear his frustration: What took you so long?

That had to be the only strategy backing our search now, although this strategy involved neither logic nor method. I was far too burned-out to protest—and if I was tired, I couldn't fathom Jorie's fatigue. How did she keep going?

Another thought: We could wander past Nico's hiding place and his dark eyes would fall upon us and he might let us pass. This would be his punishment, speaking of punishment, for not having rescued him sooner. He was four. A four-year-old would be mad for a very long while.

We searched the Parc de la Villette. We had to walk at an angle against the fierce gale sweeping across the concourse between the concert hall and science museum. The mercuric sphere of the Géode reflected the morning sun and gave me a headache. While we were poking around the science museum, Jorie told me a story:

The museum used to be Luc's favorite place to bring Nico. This was before Luc started traveling so much of the year, a while ago, back when Nico was learning to walk. Luc would steer the stroller here and let the boy (in knee pads) try to gad about on his own. The Cité de la Musique was still under construction, and Jorie remembered how Luc the engineer would carry Nico on his shoulders to the edge of the site and explain to him what was going on: Nico, do you see those steel columns there? Do you see the way they sit on those concrete piers? It is magic. The entire weight of the concert hall will rest on those piers. Yes, and those columns and beams are so strong that there will be much glass. Much glass. You will like it. Nico took it all in, grinning, giggling. It probably didn't matter what Luc said; Nico adored him.

We headed back across the concourse to the boulevard, the wind now pushing at our backs. Jorie told me another story:

One day, also a long time back, Luc came home with a bundle of balsa and a roll of snowy velum. With Nico watching, Luc cut lengths of the balsa and parallelograms of the stiff paper. He narrated his every step, explicating updrafts and wind shear, and he showed the boy where to press the glued paper to the wood, telling him when he could let go. Luc looked after the aerodynamics but ceded complete aesthetic design of the kites to his son. Nico would color the velum with Magic Markers, glue on sparkles, affix a variety of neon streamers as tails. That winter they made a half dozen kites. And then, after the snow melted, Luc and Nico headed back to the Parc de la Villette early on Sunday mornings before there were crowds.

Jorie recalled one March morning when winter was in decline but it was still chilly and the wind was at high tide. Luc held the spool of string and handed Nico the kite. The kite was almost as tall as the child. Nico wobbled a bit but then scampered off across the cement expanse, and Luc let the string roll from his spool and the bright blue-red-green diamond began to lift off. Let go, Luc shouted at the boy. Let go, Jorie yelled, too. Nico didn't hear them at first but turned around to look back, and the act of pivoting inadvertently forced him to release the kite, and it took off, up, up, up.

Nico watched the kite soar. He fell on his butt and sat on the ground. The kite shot off at an angle. Dove down, threateningly low. Luc flicked his wrist. Reeled in some of the spool. Released more string. He knew what he was doing. Nico clapped and bounced and picked himself up and ran back to Jorie; he hugged her thigh. He darted over to Luc, who handed him the reins.

Nico appeared to lift off the ground when one rather sudden gust snuck up under the kite, and it did seem possible that Luc's engineering might have been a little too good, that the boy might be carried off across the plaza. Luc was right behind him, however, kneeling, speaking into the boy's ear, showing him how to maneuver the kite and control the wind. The kite was an untamable bronco, whipping right, left, but Nico had a sweet touch. Luc stepped back. Nico squinted with concentration. He stared up at the kite, anchoring it in the sky with a trusting gaze.

I wasn't sure about the point of her story: Was she trying to tell me that Luc was not a bad father? Or was she merely reminiscing with aching nostalgia for simpler days? A father and his boy and the kites they flew. Where were they now, this father and son? Both at large in the world. Far away. Close but hidden.

We headed down the rue de Flandre toward the place de Stalingrad. The wind made waves in the canal. I realized where we were headed. I could see the Rotonde in the distance. I remembered what Will had told me, about Jorie's showdown with the gang boy, and now I had to speak up.

I said, "Let's stay away from there."

"There's a gang that hangs out here, and there was this one boy who was with the pack that took Nico. He had red hair. I've seen him here," she said.

She stopped when she reached the plaza, however, and I lapsed into my own frozen state, too, when we came face-to-face with the Ledoux monument.

I thought, Why here, why now?

People were cutting across the square, shuffling fast to make an incoming train, and didn't they notice the street lamps that had all been smashed? Or the steady fall of smoke cascading from a torched car outside the entrance to the métro trestle? Ledoux's barrière itself looked as though it had been stormed: There were blankets and wet piles of clothes lying around the steps; the already-soot-and-graffiti-covered columns looked smeared with fresh ash and fresh lettering; many of the second-story windows had been shattered.

Poor Ledoux. C'est la Révolution all over again. The citoyens sacking the customhouses, tearing down his city wall. Un sang impur abat tes maisons.

Jorie moved cautiously across the cobblestone toward the columns and stairs. Commuters pushed past her. I caught up, I took her hand. I didn't stop her from moving up the steps beneath the pediment, but I held on to her. The place smelled noxious, like burned gasoline.

"Nico," Jorie said. "Nicolas?"

We pulled our scarves up over our mouths.

This was the one Ledoux barrière, as I said, which I had never entered. My pulse raced: One of the main bronze doors was pushed back.

"Nico," Jorie said.

I followed her in, and even though it was very dark, my eyes adjusted.

I pictured the architect's engraving for this Rotonde, the clean, fast stroke of his pen delineating his ideal geometric forms, securing his patented balance of proportions, and for a moment I forgot why we had come here; all I could see was the two-dimensional ink rendering as it slowly expanded along a new axis. I held my breath, and the drawing, the volume became real. The vault of the ceiling. The symmetry of arched doorways. The smooth planes of stone. One more time, I found myself well taken care of by the master architect: The rooms were grand, but not so large that I felt lost—he built a monument yet maintained a human scale.

"Nico," Jorie said. Her voice echoed, slapped back at us.

The place was empty. There was no one here, no gang, not a soul—it was clear right away.

Jorie took my hand and led the way into a darker room.

The floor was cold, warped in places. We kept kicking liquor bottles. I noticed an old couch, its springs exposed. We passed a coatrack—the fabric on hangers had been burned. The rot, the stench made it difficult to breathe. Again, my eyes adjusted.

"Nico," Jorie said and went up the stairs.

I let go of her hand.

"I'm here, sweetie."

I stayed behind on the first floor and I took another look around. I strayed back into the first room and leaned against a square column.

Who had trashed this place? What had happened here?

Yes, yes, these were handsome well-made rooms, but now I noticed a heap of broken chairs. It looked like a pyre someone hadn't had time to light. Now I took a step back and nearly tripped over the severed chain of a chandelier.

What kind of place was this? What had it become?

An ax lay on the floor. Canisters of spray paint.

A child's bike with no wheels.

I was very tired, likely delirious, but I blinked and saw a figure, a man standing before me: It was Claude-Nicolas Ledoux, and he wore a velvet waistcoat with gold buttons; his powdered wig was slightly askew, his shirt ruffle torn. Was he speaking to me? What was he saying?

The character of monuments, like their nature, serves—

Thank you, I know the rhetoric.

—the propagation and purification of morals.

But what did that even mean?

Of course, a building expressed the ethos and ethic of its makers, but where was Ledoux headed—what was he truly asserting? You see, I'd always trusted that some deeper meaning had to lurk beneath the surface, ever elusive without just the right context, but I was not so sure that was the case anymore.

"Pedro?" Jorie called from upstairs.

"I'm coming," I answered.

The character of monuments. The purification of morals.

A wave of panic made me shiver—panic, then anger.

I heard Didier's voice in my head: Seulement un homme comme tous les hommes. Full of compromise.

Purification—how? Morals—what morals?

Look around. Look around at your monument now, Monsieur Ledoux. What morals are being purified here? Can you tell me that? Ledoux, please. Explain yourself.

I started up the stairs but paused on a lower step. I had to stop. I suddenly knew two things with devastating certainty: first, that I could no longer separate, indeed save, Ledoux's form from his content—it was a convenient reading that could not stand; and following that, a second revelation, that my time with the architect was finished. I could not devote any more of my life to him. His stone surfaces would always take my breath away, but in the final analysis, I did not like him very much.

I wanted to sleep for a very long time.

"Pedro. Come here."

There was more light in the round second-floor room, but
the clerestories had been covered with brown paper and it was
still difficult to see. There were mattresses on the floor. Another
rack of clothes, this one not burned; they looked like new overcoats, still wrapped in plastic. A large pile of empty bottles. The
French flag taped to the wall. And in the center of the room, a
plaster statue, a three-quarter-sized portrait of a young woman
with a pageboy coif, dressed in armor, holding a shield and
sword, gazing upward toward her divine protector. I assumed
that it was the maid of Orléans, Joan the Saint, but I couldn't be
certain.

"Over here," Jorie said.

She was standing next to a pillar, and when I was close
enough, she pulled me toward her, behind the pillar. She
pointed. I looked where she wanted me to look and I gasped.

A pair of eyes blinked at us from behind another pillar. They
were small eyes, low to the ground. They could have belonged
to a cat. It was a child.

My heart beat fast. Could it be?

"We don't want to scare him," Jorie said.

I clutched Jorie's arm.

"Nico?" I whispered.

Jorie breathed deeply.

Of course not. If it were Nico, Jorie would have already
scooped him up. Even in the dark, a mother knew her child.
Especially in the dark.

We stepped out into the open.

The child stepped out from behind his pillar, too, but then
back into shadow.

Jorie got down on her knees. I did the same.

"Qui est là?" she asked. "It's okay, you're safe with us."

The child had pressed himself now against the wall, blinking at us, paralyzed.

Jorie crawled forward. I remained where I was, frozen, too.

"We won't hurt you," Jorie said. "Let us see you."

The child didn't move.

"We're looking for a little boy named Nico," Jorie said. "Instead we found you. We can help you. Let us see you."

The child came forward a step away from the wall, but that was all.

"Let me see you, sweetie."

Jorie reached out her hand.

I sat on the floor and watched.

Then Jorie must have been close enough to know that she should try another language.

She said, "Mumkin tanee. Mumkin tanee." Then she laughed.

"What?" I whispered.

"My Arabic is terrible," she said. "I think I just asked for another helping of food."

But the child had responded by stepping into a shaft of light, a streak of morning coming through a broken window. I could see now that it was a girl. She wore jeans and a fleece-collared jacket. She must have been about Nico's age, but it was hard to tell.

"Try something else," I said.

"Tísbah àla khayr," Jorie said.

The girl blinked.

"Àna musàfir li-wàhdee."

The girl took another step. I could see her well. She wrinkled her brow.

"I thought of something," Jorie said. "A song."

"Sing it," I whispered.

"Màtkhefsh al-layl," Jorie said.

Tears streaked down the girl's cheeks.

"Màtkhefsh al-layl," Jorie repeated, drifting into melody, into a quiet chant: "Màtkhefsh al-layl."

She chanced a move. She reached forward and pulled the girl toward her, into her lap.

The girl shivered. Jorie stroked her matted hair. She held her very close and rocked her back and forth.

"You're safe," she said. "I'm taking you away from here. Right now."

I crawled over and sat on the floor next to them.

"What was that you said?" I asked.

"Màtkhefsh al-layl," Jorie said.

The girl was crying.

"Don't be afraid of the dark."

Jorie carried the girl down the stairs and out to the square. The sun made the girl yawn. Her face was dirty. Jorie sat down on the steps of the Rotonde while I looked for a cop. It took me a little while, but finally I found two officers in a squad car parked over by the canal. They were still wearing riot gear, but once they sized up the situation, they removed their helmets.

"A missing kid," I suggested.

"You are such a pretty girl," Jorie said to the child. "You are. Your parents will be so relieved to see you. Could you tell us your name? Ismak ay?"

The girl wouldn't answer. She wouldn't speak.

"Let's hope it is one of the ones who is already reported missing," one cop said.

The other returned to the squad car to retrieve a list.

"Is there any news we should know about?" I asked. I explained who we were and specifically requested information about Nico.

The second cop returned with a computer printout.

"No news as of yet about Nicolas Chamoun," the cop said.

Jorie didn't appear to hear us at all. She kept speaking to the girl and stroking her hair, holding her close to her breast.

"Màtkhefsh," she said.

"I am happy to say that three children have been returned," the cop said. "There is an unconfirmed report about a fourth."

"That's good," I said. "That's very good to hear."

"But not good enough. Most remain missing," the cop added. "So if we could now figure out what this girl calls herself, that would be helpful."

"Let's see your list," I said. "Maybe we can figure it out by process of elimination."

"No, it is better not to guess," the cop with the printout said. "That might be risky. Notifying the wrong parent."

A rush of pedestrians suddenly made a lot of noise and the girl winced.

A few Parisians noticed Jorie and the girl on the steps of the Rotonde and formed a circle around us. A cop asked them if they knew who the girl was, but no one recognized her.

"Ismak ay? Màtkhefsh," Jorie said and shifted the girl in her lap so that she could look in her eyes. "Ismak ay?"

The girl opened her mouth.

"Ismak ay?" Jorie asked again.

Then, in a meek voice, the girl responded, "Ismee Sarah."

The first cop glanced at a clipboard and began to grin.

The second cop spoke into his walkie-talkie.

Sarah. The girl was called Sarah, and with some reluctance, Jorie handed her to one of the cops. They knew who she was, to whom she belonged. They would call ahead and let the parents know. They would bring her home.

"You would like to come with us?" a cop asked. "The parents, I am sure, will want to thank you."

"We need to keep looking for Nico," Jorie said.

She kissed the girl good-bye before the girl was strapped into the backseat of the squad car. The car drove off, its lights flashing.

Widening fissures in the cloud cover allowed more sunlight to wash the place de Stalingrad. I suggested we go back to her place, but Jorie said no.

"We need to check in with Will," I said.

Jorie agreed, but she walked back to the steps of the Rotonde and sat down. She said, "I'm so tired, Pedro."

"I know," I said.

"How will I live without my boy?" she asked.

"Let's take you home."

"I can't go back there," she said.

She feared the worst now, and she had every reason. You find one child a day, and you consider yourself very lucky. We were not going to find another child that morning, simple as that; all odds were against us.

"You sit there," I said, "and I'll call."

Jorie folded her knees against her chest and rocked on the step. There were honking cars and women with briefcases and shopping bags. Men with dogs and a few teenagers with backpacks. Newspapers for sale from a green kiosk. A shopkeeper across the street cranking open an awning. A woman with a loaf of bread. Paris was in motion, but Jorie Cole made herself small. Time did not exist. Time had stopped.

I didn't want her to listen to my conversation with Will; no news would be bad news, and I didn't want her to hear it. I kept my eye on her as I stepped across the square. I watched her while I dialed the number of the hotel and while I was transferred by the operator. A man answered, I asked for Will.

"May I ask who is calling?"

"Is this Mr. Jencks?" I asked.

"I'm his assistant," the man said.

Street noise enveloped me—I couldn't hear well. The assistant was telling me something, but I couldn't make out what he was saying.

"Speak louder," I said.

"You must be Pedro Douglas," the assistant said.

Jorie stood and headed toward me. The sun lightened her hair. She wobbled as she walked, as if she were dizzy. Or I was the one who was dizzy.

"Will tried to phone you earlier," the assistant said. "He had to leave."

"Where did he go?"

"He left a note for you. Let me read it to you so I get it right. Are you there?"

The earth lost some spin. My legs became heavy. I leaned against an already-leaning signpost.

"I'm still here," I said.

"'Tell Jorie that I will have Nico soon,'" the assistant said.

"You will have Nico?" I asked.

"Not me, Will. This is Will's note," the assistant said.

Jorie came closer. She was reaching her hand toward me the way she had reached out for the girl in the Rotonde.

"'Tell Jorie that I will have Nico soon,'" the assistant read again. "'I have taken care of everything, I have made all the arrangements.'"

"He found Nico?" I asked.

Jorie stood next to me. She leaned into the phone so she could hear.

"He says he will have him soon," the assistant said.

"How?" I asked. "How will he have him soon?"

"There's more." The assistant read the rest of Will's note, but I heard Will himself speak, Will telling me what to do next:

> You and Jorie drive to your friend's house in the country. Leave now. I will meet you there. This is how we must work this—I can explain later. But Pedro, tell Jorie that I will have Nico with me. I will have Nico back to her by noon.

"'Love, Will,'" the assistant read, which sounded to me less like an epistolary valediction than a final instruction: Love Will.

$\dfrac{4}{\rule{2em}{0.4pt}}$

AT WHAT POINT did he understand exactly what would be required to find the boy? When I dropped him off at the hotel or while we were combing the city in a borrowed car—or even earlier in the evening? When did he know what would need to be transacted? When did he anticipate the role he would play? I will never be sure.

What I have decided is that rising in the hotel elevator, Will caught his reflection in the polished bronze panel of buttons to the right of the doors and startled himself, although not because the metal cast gave him a radioactive glow or because he looked gaunt to himself and could measure the deep gouge of his fatigue. He was surprised because he noticed that he was grinning—why? He had come looking for help at a moment when he did not know where else to turn. The hour was urgent, tragedy increasingly possible. Yet here he was, alone at intermission, unexpectedly looking forward to the next act, authoring it in his mind before seeing it staged. He walked down the dimly lit hall with the sure, even stride of a tall man. Here he was, retrieving a long-forgotten blazer from the rear rack of his closet, trying it on, looking smart—it still fit and fit well. I suspect that when I dropped him off, his agenda may have been obvious to him, but the particulars of his plan remained murky. Then, only minutes later, by the time he was knocking on the door to the suite, he became confident. He knew what he had to do.

"Aloha and bonsoir," Garret Jencks boomed. "Or do I mean bonjour?"

He was wearing a paisley robe over a pale blue shirt, corduroys, and black suede slippers. His hair was brushed back, he did not look the least bit flagged, and the only indication that it was past his bedtime was a smattering of gray stubble.

"Uncle Garrett," Will said. "I'm sorry to wake you."

"No need to apologize. Like I said, I wasn't really asleep. Quite a raucous dinner in Berlin, you see, where by the by, the food has gotten quite fine. Then we had to make our plane—I was just coming down, as it were."

"Coffee?" his assistant asked.

"Much," Will said.

Jencks's assistant, on the other hand, wearing the same black suit he'd had on earlier, now with a rumpled T-shirt, looked entirely tousled. He clutched the silver coffeepot with both hands. His pour was unsteady. Once he was done serving, he sank into an armchair in the corner and immediately appeared to doze off.

Jencks balanced his cup and saucer in his palm.

The java went right to Will's heart. He sat at the edge of the couch.

"I'm unhappy about the architecture there," Jencks said.

"In Berlin," Will said.

"So much building, you know, but it's all very different, one structure from the next. What Berlin truly needs now is a master planner. Someone who can come up with a look. I have a friend. I may see if it's not too late."

"I would understand if that wasn't too popular," Will said. "A master plan for Berlin. It carries an echo."

Jencks scratched his chin.

"I suppose," he said. "Anyway, fill me in. Brief me. Your friend, the woman in distress. You say her child was kidnapped?"

And so once again, he narrated the events of the day. He described the night so far. He mentioned me now by name. He did not, however, disclose the truth about where Jorie had been heading with Nico, nor did he lay out the troubling new development, a dilemma he had yet to sort out: Even if Nico turned up, Jorie faced losing him. Luc had issued his threat, he would cut Jorie out; one way or another, it seemed, her life with the boy was in jeopardy. Nevertheless, first things first:

"I need to find this boy," Will said.

Jencks fingered the lapel of his silk robe. He nodded, let the information hang in the air, settle. He took several sips of coffee.

"Is he worth it?" he asked.

Will knew the question would come.

"Worth negotiation, you mean?"

Jencks hummed.

"Because he's just a kid, and not even an American kid at that," Will said. "In fact, he's of Lebanese descent—"

"That's not what I mean and you know it," Jencks said.

"We are talking about human life here. The life of a child."

"Et cetera, et cetera," Jencks said.

"If I had told you that I was involved with Jorie, you wouldn't hesitate, would you?"

"Oh, no. You're underestimating me," Jencks quipped. "Then I would ask you this, young Will: Is she worth the risk?"

It was Will's turn to sip coffee and collect his thoughts.

"You always run a risk when you help someone, you know this," Jencks said. "You get a dissident out of jail, but you have to consider what he will do with his freedom."

Will sighed loudly. "The boy is a treasure, Garrett, not that it matters. He's four years old, and a gang of fascist teenagers took him because he threatens them. At four, he is the enemy."

Jencks crossed his legs.

"I do like a good puzzle," he said.

Will waited.

"I'm not sure how this game is going to be played just yet. We may have to go a few hands before we actually know what's wild."

"What can we do?" Will asked.

"We make some calls. See where it gets us."

"I actually thought I could find the kid by just looking."

"It's not absurd," Jencks said. "I heard the news. That is in fact how a couple of them have turned up."

"Maybe I should still be out there," Will said.

"If you thought that," Garrett Jencks said, "you wouldn't have come here."

True, Will thought.

Jencks looked at his snoring assistant: "Hello, coffee-boy?"

The assistant cleared his throat. He grabbed the silver pot, refilled cups.

"I'll need some numbers," Jencks said.

"Yes, sir," the assistant said.

"You're going to wake up some very important people. But you enjoy that, don't you?"

"Yes, sir."

The assistant located an attaché case and removed an electronic address book. He wiped his eyes and awaited further instruction.

Jencks squinted at Will.

"Uncle Garrett?" Will asked.

"What's in it for you?" Jencks asked.

Will didn't know how to respond to the question or why it needed to be answered.

"Something should be in it for you," Jencks said. "You didn't want to come to me. Don't worry, I am not offended. Believe you me, I understand who I am to you."

"No—"

"Look. At this moment, you are my son. I am the father, and so be it. But this is business. This is our business, Will. We trade and we get something in return, a commission if nothing else."

Will was lost. "I've said what I want. The boy back, that's all."

Jencks squinted again.

"You don't get it?" he asked. "What you want?"

Will shook his head no.

Jencks shrugged. "I suspect you will. As for me, what do I get?"

Why should he get anything?

"I am happy to agent what I can agent," Jencks said. "But…"

"What do you want?" Will asked.

"I'll get back to you," he said.

He gave his assistant a name to call. He licked his lips. He hummed again.

The assistant pulled a chair over to a rolltop desk and went to work. When he had someone on the line, he spoke in pitch-perfect French: "I apologize, Monsieur, for interrupting your sleep. However, I have Monsieur Garrett Jencks for you with a matter of some urgency."

Pause.

"My client in the French government," Jencks said.

He picked up a phone on the end table and pushed a button with his pinkie. Before he spoke, he winked at Will.

Will's heart fluttered: Did Jencks realize what was at stake?

Jencks opted for English. He made a brief amount of small talk before explaining that someone close had come to him with a crisis, which he laid out gradually like a math problem.

"The police have proved useless, forgive me, as they tend to be in these matters," Jencks said. "How I miss the old Interpol. Anyway, I need your help."

Will watched Jencks listen for a long time. Jencks's nostrils flared.

"I agree. What happened today in Paris does not make anyone look good. You have reason to be alarmed. Look, back to the reason I'm calling. I know that our business together is nearly complete. You won't find your name anywhere you don't want to see it, and I know that you are grateful. This is extra, I acknowledge that, and let me be clear: I do not want you to feel as though I am fishing for any gratuities. I will return the favor."

A swift conversation ensued. Jencks asked his client to make a phone call. The client agreed and said he would phone Jencks back shortly.

Fifteen minutes later, the phone rang. The assistant answered. Jencks took the call without delay.

"Ah, très bien," Jencks said. "That is just the response I was hoping for. By the way—have you been checking out the restaurants lately in Berlin? The food is awfully good now. I know a place, it's called A Hole in the Wall. The next time we meet, my treat. They're doing French cuisine better than the French. Only kidding. Go back to sleep."

Jencks hung up and flexed his fingers.

"Access," Will said.

"We're in," Jencks said.

The assistant had listened in on the second call and knew what telephone number to dial. Jencks's client in the French government had contacted a friend of his in the French Front. In theory, the former should have been the sworn enemy of the latter, yet that was not the case.

"They probably went to the ÉNA together," Will said.

"Oh, I'm sure," Jencks said. "This is too easy."

The assistant: "I apologize, Monsieur, for interrupting your sleep."

"How so?" Will asked.

"This fellow we're calling now—I've had some dealings with him. Once upon a time."

"I see," Will said.

Jencks took the call. He offered a somewhat less succinct plot summary. He also spoke about the day, the gang abductions, the political implications.

"I can't say I understand," Jencks said. "You have your new laws. Shouldn't you rein in your young friends in the street? Wait, hold on. I'll have my assistant translate."

The assistant picked up the phone again. He converted what Jencks said into quiet French. Will knew that Jencks understood the language just fine and could speak it adequately; clearly he wanted some distance, some words lost. He didn't want to be too friendly just yet.

"So much discord these days," Jencks said. "I agree, it's troubling."

"La dissension est partout," the assistant said. "Je suis d'accord, c'est troublant."

Will got up and paced. He understood Jencks's strategy now and it made sense to him. He was playing his contacts off of one another, perhaps without being sure of what he'd gain in the end. But it was a baseline game, merely an opening, by a baseline player who would be happy, when necessary, to come to the net.

"I may be able to present you with an attractive opportunity," Jencks said. "Your friend in the government tells me that you're unhappy with the way your party looks—I've heard that elsewhere this week—and frankly, I don't blame you. Today is a fiasco as far as you are concerned. Today is the disaster, the undoing of all your hard work. I can imagine that you've been sitting up with the people you'd like one day to call your cabinet and that you were all trying to figure out your next move, how to save the day, how to turn the day against the party leadership."

The assistant had difficulty keeping up with the translation.

Jencks indicated to Will that he wanted more coffee and Will poured out the remainder of the pot.

"Yes, I see," Jencks said. "Right. I hear you, I hear you."

The conversation chug-chugged along slowly. Jencks, Will gathered, now played the confessor. He listened well, an acquired skill. Several times he glanced up at Will and rolled his eyes.

"I know how it is," Jencks said.

Will regretted how little news he had read in the last year. Isolation from the events of the world seemed reckless. All Jencks needed was minimal knowledge of regional politics to appear as if he grasped much more, and that proved useful.

"I can see where you want to go," Jencks said. "You have ideas, policies. You're a practical man, do I read you right? The last time you and I spoke, you said much the same thing. The current leadership will lead the party to its demise."

Another regret Will had was that he hadn't tried to contact Jencks earlier in the day, called him in Berlin or left word at the Paris hotel sooner. What had kept him from asking the favor? In some part, pride—Will wanted to be his own man. Which may have been foolish and selfish, if that meant that a boy could have been retrieved from the cold any faster.

"Let me tell you what I want," Jencks said. "It's simple. Très simple, écoutez. A little boy. He was taken—where?"

"The pont de Sully," Will said.

"Au pont de Sully," the assistant said.

"He needs to turn up now," Jencks said. He examined his manicure. "You do that. You speak to the people you trust, your colleagues in the party. See if we can work together. I can wait."

And he hung up.

The assistant called room service and requested more coffee.

"See if the kitchen can make us something to eat," Jencks said. "You know what I like when I'm digging in for a long negotiation?"

Will didn't guess.

"Falafel," Jencks said.

"Did you pick that up in Israel?"

"That would seem likely," he said. He asked his assistant to make the special request to the kitchen. "And hummus and plenty of pita. I remember one tough game I got into, an all-nighter. The delegation was supposed to go back to Washington the next day. I was working on the timing of the troop withdrawals. We came to a real impasse. Had to do with the fact that the point men on either side couldn't stand each other, and this clause would be the deal-breaker. The Secretary would have to go home with nothing, and that would look rotten. So we're talking, it's getting later and later, and I ordered some falafel from the kitchen of whatever hotel we were in. Soon enough, room service interrupts us with this big platter like you've never seen, a mountain of the stuff. And we all stop talking and we eat. We're loading the pita with the falafel and the hummus and red onion and tomatoes—"

Will's stomach growled.

"I heard that," Jencks said.

"Sir?" the assistant said.

"What happened?" Will asked.

"The warring point men started giving each other tips—you know, try it with olives, try it with cucumber. We had the clause drafted by five, stayed up for the press conference. You know the history."

"Sir, the kitchen doesn't have the ingredients for falafel," the assistant said.

"Well, darn it all," Jencks said.

"They'll send up an assortment of cheeses and pâtés, if you like," the assistant said.

"The French with their assortments," Jencks said.

He kicked off his slippers and massaged each foot.

Time moved slowly, an hour slipped by. No one called back. Will suggested that they try another contact, if Jencks had one, but the older man prescribed patience.

"We have two things going. This man in the French Front has been looking for a way for some time to impress my client in the government. Later in life, they imagine themselves running their respective parties. They will want to be able to get each other on the phone. It's a rising-star thing. And then there's the split within the French Front itself. The old men think they can win the war their way. The young guns get all goofy with their new theories—they speak of the new pragmatism. When you see a rift like that, you have to mine it. Sparkly minerals are there for the scraping."

A waiter arrived with a silver tray. They cleared off the piles of magazines and faxes on the glass coffee table and soon all three of them, Will and Jencks and Jencks's assistant, silently spread Camembert and foie gras on soft bread. Another hour went by.

"Let me ask you a question," the assistant said to Will. "Did you feel that your time at the UN helped you get your first posting?"

"I'm going to lose my compatriot here to the FS, I think," Jencks said.

"I mean, I've heard that you can get, like, really lost there if the Delegate doesn't notice you right away," the assistant said.

"I've been telling him your story," Jencks said. "Stupid me. Now he wants to be you."

The assistant turned red.

"My story," Will said. How much of my story? he wondered.

Fortunately the phone rang. It was the French Front contact.

Jencks seemed pleased. He continued to eat cheese while he spoke on the phone.

"I agree completely," he said. "And I don't need to tell you that we will be eager to demonstrate what we can do for you. You will let us know how we can make all of this easier for you."

Will had been sitting on the couch next to Jencks and Jencks was next to the phone; Jencks waved Will over to an adjacent wing chair.

"To move this forward now, I am going to hand you over to my associate," Jencks said. "His name is Will Law. Play nice."

Jencks handed Will the phone.

Will was unprepared, he stuttered.

"Bonjour," he managed.

"This, I believe, is what you want, young Will," Jencks said.

Will didn't have time to get his footing. He didn't have a

plan, he didn't know what was possible. He wanted to respond to Jencks—whose presumption agitated Will—and he had to get rid of the assistant doing the simultaneous translation.

The man on the other end spoke with a pleasant baritone, officious yet cordial.

"You realize, of course, that we are as unhappy as you must be about the events of the day," he said.

"I realize that," Will said.

"But you must understand as well that we do not operate these youth clubs. Contrary to popular belief. No orders were given."

"I can accept your word," Will said.

"The party is otherwise engaged."

Engagé. Will wasn't sure if the word carried quite the same color he thought it did.

"Of course," Will said.

Jencks nodded in encouragement.

"But a little boy is missing, it comes down to that," Will said. "And if you have any influence."

"Perhaps you need to define *influence*. You see, I could be asleep. At this hour, I find myself usually asleep."

Jencks stretched. He disappeared into the bedroom of the suite.

The assistant, however, kept his eyes fixed on Will. Negotiation often became a spectacle. You performed for your own team as much as you did for your opponents.

Be cool, Will thought. Be cool, be clear about what you want, what you can trade.

"Do you think you know who might have taken this particular boy?" Will asked.

A moment of silence.

The French Front contact said, "Yes. It is possible. The information may exist."

"Some of the, um, youth clubs actually may have held on to the kids rather than drop them off the way they did in the past," Will said. "Don't you think?"

"We are otherwise engaged."

"You have your programs," Will said.

"We worry greatly about unemployment. If the French do not look after the French."

You have your rhetoric, Will thought.

"There are so many young people who do not see a future for themselves," the French Front contact said. "Thus, they form their various unions. They express themselves."

"You can encourage them to release the children at once," Will said.

"That is what you want."

"Yes," Will said. "It would be humane."

He eyed what was uneaten of the pâté; the discarded aspic looked like jellyfish remains. The crescents of cheese rinds looked like broken tusks.

"It is not so simple," the French Front man said.

"No one thinks it will be," Will said.

"Earlier your colleague Monsieur Jencks suggested that this was a terrible day for the French Front, whom he rightly asserts believes it can achieve a greater following. However, he is not entirely correct. Twelve boys and girls. Yes, that might look bad. A few—three, for instance—that is not terrible."

Will wanted to tell the French Front politician to take a flying leap from the Tour Eiffel. But he took a deep breath. He knew he was being tested, pushed. He had no room for error. He composed his words and translated them before speaking.

"What I think you are saying—I cannot say I like the sound of it very much," he said.

Jencks had returned from the bedroom reeking of a caustic cologne. He rubbed his hands with a white unguent. He took his seat on the sofa and reclined and listened and made no motion that he wanted to intervene. Then again, why would he—what did he have to lose?

Will thought about handing back the phone. Maybe he had made too emotional an investment. But he continued.

"What I think you are saying is that some terror is useful," Will said.

And if you appear too soft, you will never rally the more reactionary members of your own party, whom you will eventually need.

"You are saying this, not I," the French Front man said.

"In the end, you wouldn't mind a statistic."

The line was silent.

"You may or may not be able to speak directly to the youth clubs that have taken the children who are still missing," Will said. "And you may or may not be interested seeing all the children return home."

Nothing. The longest pause yet.

Finally the man on the other end spoke: "The way this would work, to get the boy back—we need more time to make arrangements. It is not as easy as you make it seem."

Will glanced at his watch. It was three-thirty.

"Think how long the boy has been missing," he said.

"We speak now to our friends," the French Front man said. "Then you and I can talk again. Determine where we are."

"And we'll make sure we discuss what we can do for you," Will said.

"I respect your candor in these matters."

After he hung up, Will had to pace the perimeter of the room.

"Well done," Jencks said.

"May I say that I'm impressed," the assistant said.

By what? Will wondered. He had yet to accomplish anything concrete.

"He's a fucker, isn't he?" Jencks said.

"You looked like you got along so well. You listened. You didn't challenge him," Will said.

"This man, our contact—in the end, he has no reason to help us," Jencks said. "What can we really offer him? For all we know, before we even got in this game, he and his colleagues tried and failed to pressure those gangs to release the kids. We will never know. Look: He knows who we are, what we represent. He wants to play the network. He dances with you because you're pretty. Stay pretty, he'll keep dancing."

"I feel like I need a shower," Will said.

"Take one," Jencks said.

"A very hot shower," Will said.

"Please. There are fresh towels."

Will tried to be quick, but as soon as he shed his clothes and found himself beneath a warm spray, he had to sit down on the floor of the tub. He thought about the day he left Mexico—it rained. He had to take a series of small planes out of small airports, and he remembered standing on the tarmac, refusing the umbrella that someone offered him, letting the warm downpour soak his clothes. It would be too easy to say that he hoped the rain could cleanse him of his sins or that letting himself get so wet somehow reconnected him to the natural world from which he had strayed. What the rain afforded him, however briefly, was the chance to lose himself, to let go of his darker thoughts. He imagined the puddle at his feet—the water collecting around his legs in the tub—swelling into a river, and the river then drawing him wherever it would. To be a diplomat was to live a public life, and living a public life fostered fantasies of an opposite exis-tence, the life unobserved. Stand in the rain, pretend: No one can see you. No one can run you. You are your own man.

But Will was dreaming and he knew it. The real world made its demands. The real world had its evils. And he was to ready to face them. He toweled off, he slicked back his hair. He was restored.

"Look at our hero," Jencks said. "He's freshened up."

"I'm not the hero yet," Will said.

"You will be," Jencks said.

"Glad you think so. I wish that creep would call me back."

"He will. He has to, although he won't admit it."

"Why does he have to?" Will asked.

Jencks started to answer but then didn't respond.

"I took a shower. I still feel grimy," Will said.

"Please," Garrett Jencks said. "Please don't get lofty on me now. I listened to you. You played. You played well so far."

"I played, and I feel grimy."

The assistant frowned, he wasn't following.

"Your problem is you don't know who you're fighting," Jencks said.

"I think I do," Will said.

"No, your whole generation," Jencks insisted. "You don't know your enemy, you don't have a clue."

"While your generation did."

"Yes," Jencks said.

"Is it that simple?"

"Actually, yes, it is," Jencks said. "We had a code. Any idiot could recite it."

"I've heard this all before," Will said. "My generation is supposed to be post-partisan, post-ideological. Hence our quandaries."

"I took a course in postmodern ethics," the assistant said with a stupid smile. "I didn't understand a word."

Will and Jencks both ignored him.

"I think that's dangerous," Will said. "To be talking post-this, post-that. It implies maturity."

"Maturity is knowing the face of your enemy," Jencks said.

The phone.

"Let's hope it's my enemy. Not that I can see his face," Will said.

"Have you thought about your next move?" Jencks asked. "You need to make this guy think you're giving him something."

Will didn't answer. He took the call, and it was the French Front politician, who sounded cheery.

"We may now have the information that you seek," he said.

Will was cautious. "Good," he said.

"Of course, there are certain risks for us."

"Naturally," Will said.

"We would like very much to help, you see, but at the same time, we need to acknowledge our gambit."

"I understand," Will said.

He took a keep breath. His move. Something had occurred to him while he lay in the tub beneath the shower spray. The pieces of the puzzle laid out before him. There was Nico. There was Jorie and what she wanted, what he had come to believe, especially after this ordeal, she deserved.

"Allow me to clarify a point," Will said. "The boy can be returned to us, but he does not necessarily have to reappear."

"How's that?" Garrett Jencks asked.

"I'm missing something," the assistant said.

"I do not follow this," the French Front contact said.

Will explained again: "What if the boy returns, but he isn't reported found? What if he remains missing?"

The French Front man sniffed.

"Some useful terror, as you put it," Will said.

"It is you, Monsieur, who state it such."

"I state it such," Will said.

"You are telling me what? That this boy will simply vanish?"

"That is what I am saying," Will said. "The boy won't go home. He and his mother will leave the country."

"Wait," the assistant said to Jencks. "Why?"

"This is getting interesting," Jencks said.

"I see, I see. This may prove fruitful," the French Front contact said.

"Assuming the boy is fine," Will said. "You help us. We will make sure that our friends know how you helped us."

At the same time, he thought, you appease your ranks. I know how it works, my friend. You play both sides.

"We will call again very soon with additional details," the French Front contact said in a smooth voice. "Of course, we are not directly involved. We serve as mere intermediaries."

"Of course," Will said. "And perhaps if the boy we've been talking about, Nico, if he never surfaces, then maybe the other children can be released now, too."

"Ah, oui. Perhaps."

"It is possible you might desire that outcome," Will said.

"It is, yes, possible. We shall see," the French Front man said.

The conversation concluded with the usual pleasantries often exchanged by people who feel they know each other better through an act of bartering. We should have a drink when this is all over. We may not be so far apart. Yes, I have a child myself. He is ten. No good in algebra, but then neither was I. So long for now.

Will hung up and the hotel room seemed very still.

"Tell me we can get a woman and a child out of the country," Will said.

Jencks smiled. "Sounds like a caper."

"Please."

"So serious," Jencks said. "You who kill multiple birds with the single phone call. Well, a few calls."

"Uncle Garrett. Jorie Cole is a good person, a good mother—"

"Stop," Jencks said.

"The boy adores her, and she's had a rough time—"

"Will, stop. The less I know, the better I sleep. On the nights I do get to sleep."

"You don't want me to explain," Will said.

"This is your game, not mine," Jencks said. "And by the way, it's seven in the fucking morning, excuse me, in case you haven't noticed. I know what needs to be done."

Will hadn't realized the hour. He also didn't notice until now that the cell phone battery had run out. He used the hotel phone and dialed Jorie's apartment.

"Will," she said. "Where are you? At the hotel still."

"Yes," he said.

He didn't ask if we had heard anything about Nico because at that point, he knew more than we did about the boy. He thought about telling Jorie that he was close, very close to handing him back to her, but there was still an endgame to be played out, and he didn't want to give her false hope.

So all he told her was, "We're making calls. Contacts in the French government. We're calling everyone we can think of," he said.

"Good," Jorie said softly.

"Soon I'm going to call you with very good news. You can count on it."

"Soon," Jorie said, "I hope," and that was when she handed me the phone.

Will repeated what he'd said to Jorie, except when he spoke to me, a sour-fruit taste made him pucker. He hadn't actually said anything untrue, but withholding information from me might as well have been a lie. He had his secrets. He would always have his secrets, maybe not covert facts so much as a furtive way of moving through the world.

"You can't tell me more?" I asked.

"No," Will said. "You two just wait there, okay?"

He promised to explain later. He asked about Didier's cottage. He was thinking that he needed a safe house. Once he had the boy, he would meet us there. From a safe house, he would figure out a way to get Jorie and Nico out of France.

"Will, wait," I said.

"I'll call you soon," he said, and that was that.

Jencks yawned. He said, "You are your father's son."

Will wanted to believe that the comparison was flattering.

The assistant spread some cheese on a cracker for Will.

"So now what's in it for me?" Jencks asked.

Will blinked.

"You have to get this woman and boy out of the country? That's what you promised, right?"

"But we can call your contact in the government—"

"We? I think you mean me," Jencks said.

"I still need you," Will said.

Jencks's wide smile revealed his fillings.

"Did you enjoy yourself this morning?" he asked.

"*Enjoy* is the wrong word," Will said.

"It's what you wanted. I gave you what you wanted."

"I always feel like I'm missing something," the assistant said. He retreated to his chair at the rolltop desk.

"And what do I want?" Jencks asked.

That Will return to the Foreign Service. That he take the job in Jakarta.

"I can't say yes yet," Will said. "I need to think some more."

"Speak to your friend," Jencks said.

He was a tall man. The early-morning negotiations had made him look hale. He stretched both arms high.

"Anyway," he said, "I shouldn't make these calls now. It's not wise. I'll wait a few hours. Let my friends in high places have their big bowls of coffee. Then I'll get to work. You did enjoy all this, did you not?"

A boy was missing and Will knew how to find him, simple as that; any sacrifice on his part that he might have made or would now make seemed right. He convinced himself that this was true. Yes. He had done what he had to do.

He stood by the window that overlooked the place Vendôme. The morning light came up behind the column in the center of the square. Its shadow pointed toward the hotel like a finger.

"What a fine morning," Garrett Jencks said. "Everybody is getting something for his troubles."

AND THEN NOTHING went as planned. The arrangements were simple enough, who would appear where and at what hour. Jencks provided Will with a car with tinted windows, but then Will called us at Jorie's apartment to tell us the plan. He wanted to wait for us to surface, but he ran out of time. He dictated his note to Jencks's assistant. He picked up the car from the hotel valet. He headed out into the city, and the morning traffic, however minimal, surprised him as it had us: How could Paris return to normal so quickly? It did not seem just.

Will made his way into the Fifth. He spotted the white van parked at the corner of the rue Cuvier and the rue Linné. The dome of the mosque down the block reflected the rising sun. He pulled up behind the van. He saw a sole gang kid—which in and of itself was curious, a single boy in frayed jeans and the heavy steel fop chains and stubby boots—before he spotted a second gang member, who didn't quite look right. The kid was running up and down the block, back and forth beside the tall fence around the Jardin des Plantes, peering through the iron bars. He wasn't wearing a jacket, just a T-shirt, so his bare arms revealed the French flag tattooed on one forearm, but he didn't have the usual buzz cut; indeed his hair was long and very red. The boy Jorie claimed she saw.

"Qu'est-ce qui se passe?" Will asked the first gang boy. "Où est le petit garçon?"

The boy made all manner of gestures, which involved sneering and shrugging. It was the red-haired boy, a gangly kid, all teeth, who spoke.

"Il y a un problème," the boy said. His voice cracked.

Will waited for an explanation.

The red-haired boy described what had happened. The first boy was driving, the red-haired boy was in back with Nico. They had arrived on the scene. The red-haired boy slid open the side door to hop out, and when he did, Nico made a run for it. He slipped away fast, and the gang boys chased him, but Nico was too quick. The gate of the Jardin des Plantes was open. Nico scampered off into the park.

Will swore at them.

"You stay here," he ordered the first gang boy, and he took the red-haired boy with him, grabbing his elbow, and headed toward the gates of the botanical gardens.

This was a disaster in the making. Within the park, there were an infinite number of places to hide. Will didn't know where to begin.

"Nico," he called out. "Nicolas."

He headed down the main path beyond the gate. The red-haired boy followed. They fanned out.

"Nico," Will called. He tried to sound friendly, as if this were nothing more than a game of hide-and-seek. Come out, come out— "Nicolas?"

They circled the Natural History museum, investigating every exterior nook, and from there headed down to the hothouses, the steep edifices of iron and glass which in the morning light looked like enormous interconnected spiderwebs; the palms and various tropical flora within were giant insects caught in the spun stick.

They wove their way through the vast parterres, the orderly encyclopedia of plantings, squared off and divided by crushed-granite paths. Even with some moisture, the ground remained hard. Many plants had not yet been cut back for the winter ahead, but they had long ago stopped blooming. It was a barren sight, easily surveyed, and Will did not seriously expect to find Nico out in the open.

"Nico? Nicolas?"

They began to explore the perimeter of the gardens, the forest of exemplary trees. Will decided that he and the red-haired boy had to split up. The red-haired boy had a mournful look, his eyes welling up with tears. He was shivering.

"I was the one who stayed with the boy, you see," he said.

"Where did you hold him?" Will asked.

"We were in our pub. The basement of the pub we hang out in," the red-haired boy said. His teeth chattered. A tear ran down his cheek.

Will wanted to tell the kid that his tears were worthless as far as he was concerned. He didn't. And now it occurred to him that he'd been dumb to drag the gang boy into the park; if Nico spotted his captor, he'd hardly emerge; he would dig deeper into his hiding place.

"Why don't you wait back by the main gate," Will suggested and continued on without him.

He passed the famous cedar of Lebanon, a magisterial sixty-foot green plume, and it seemed possible for a moment that the boy might take refuge around here, identifying with ancestral botanica, but that was silly; Will knew better than to apply adult logic.

He called the boy's name, stretching it, a plea wearing thin.

To come this close, to get this far. It all came down to this moment. Without the boy, he would have achieved nothing.

He headed back through the neat parterres. He thought about Jorie's assertion that if Nico knew where he was, he might take shelter somewhere familiar. So what would seem familiar to the boy? He hadn't hesitated, he'd run right into the park—why?

Will walked up and down the parterres on the off chance that the boy could lie low enough to hide next to a bed of withering lavender and go unseen.

He doubled back to the cedar. He circled back to the museum, the greenhouses. The better part of an hour got away from him. Then it hit him.

He remembered the ménagerie. He jogged down the path, all the way across the park. The zoo was fenced off from the rest of the Jardin; however, there were many opportunities for someone under four feet to slip in. Will had to climb a wrought-iron gate. He pulled himself to the top, negotiated some nasty spikes, then dropped to the ground on the other side; a stab of pain shot up his ankle.

The zoo was a collection of small buildings, all of them locked, some of them under renovation. The vivarium with its snakes and crocodiles smelled like a swamp. A mammoth aviary for exotic birds had been emptied out for the cold season. In fact, none of the outdoor cages looked occupied; the animals had either been removed for the winter or possibly removed from the zoo entirely since the ménagerie had clearly fallen into disrepair. The signs outside one round building described a permanent exhibit on evolution inside, but the entrance was padlocked and there were missing bricks all around the exterior.

Let me find you, Nico. I need to find you.

Will hobbled around the zoo several times, speaking the boy's name, then saying nothing at all.

He had thought for a moment that maybe, just maybe he could think like a four-year-old. The zoo had seemed so promising. He kept passing the monkey cage, a miniature town house of steel bars and wire mesh decorated within with hollowed oaks, rope ladders, a fort constructed on lower branches. The animals were gone, but then something caught his eye. Will limped closer.

Had one chimp been left behind?

Will stepped up to the bars of the monkey cage in the zoo of the Jardin des Plantes.

The chimp came toward him. Not a chimp. A boy.

He was wearing a cape—no, a large leather jacket, which fell off his shoulders, revealing the boy's own coat. His pupils were wide and brown.

What's the best thing you ever did for someone? I rescued a missing boy.

He didn't come any closer.

"Nicolas Chamoun, it's you," Will said and crouched down, and he had to smile.

The boy in the monkey cage wouldn't move.

"You remember me," Will said. "I met you with Jorie. We went to the bistro."

The boy blinked. He stepped forward slowly.

"Jorie will be so glad to see you," Will said. "You are all that matters to her. Jorie, she's like your mother."

Closer. Closer.

"That's how you think of her—am I right? As your mother."

Closer, yet the boy maintained some distance.

"Jorie is your mom," Will said.

Then he removed a chestnut from his pocket. He held it up to a hole in the wire mesh.

The boy took another step closer, at last into the sunlight.

"I believe this is yours," Will said.

At which point the boy, Nico, Nicolas Chamoun, reached out for the nut.

THE DAY BECAME A DREAM: The towns and villages of France fell away from us as we sped along the autoroute—the clusters of tiled roofs in the distance looked like scattered leaves. Jorie drove the entire distance, leaning forward against the wheel as if by pressing her whole weight behind the engine, she could push the car beyond its maximum speed. She passed every truck on the road, she took on any car in our path. Her frayed patience left her angry. She barked at me when I made us stop so I could call Didier and be sure he didn't need his car back (he didn't seem to care; he was hung over and staying in bed); she yelled at me when I didn't supply her with directions well in advance of when they were necessary; and she exhibited hostility toward Will.

"I don't see why we have to drive all this way," she said. "I don't understand why he couldn't just bring the boy home."

The only defense I could make was to say, "He promised to explain later."

"Explain what exactly?" Jorie shot back.

She gripped the steering wheel, her forehead almost touching the windshield.

We exited the autoroute, we rushed a narrow road. We must have driven for an hour and a half, yet I had no sense of how long we'd traveled or how far. We floated through a town. There was an inn, some shops. Then another empty road, only occasionally punctuated by a house or a stretch of a stone wall, and then another village, an abbreviation of the previous one. I thought we might be passing through a town built up around a château, except the castle was long gone, and why anyone would choose to live here between a rivered valley and the hard coastal bluffs was a mystery. Eventually we turned onto a flat, unpaved road and entered a meadow of tall grass with the faith that somewhere amid the field, before we reached the forest on the horizon, we would come upon a house.

And we did. It was a white stucco cottage with an erratic array of shuttered square windows and two obese dormers breaking through a thatched roof. There were no other houses in sight. There was a forest, as I said, beyond the field, and while we would have needed to drive much farther to reach the Atlantic, the cold air smelled heavy with salt.

We had arrived before Will.

"He did say noon," I pointed out. We would have to wait.

Jorie pulled her coat tightly around her and took a walk around the house. I went inside, opened some shutters. There was a large room downstairs, along with a kitchen, and two bedrooms upstairs. I checked the flue and assembled the wood for a fire, but I didn't light it. I went back outside and found Jorie sitting on the stone stoop. I tried to coax her in from the cold. She wouldn't budge and now she wouldn't speak. It did seem cruel to me that Will had ordered us out here for no apparent reason. Jorie's lips were gray, her face blank like a frozen pond. I found a musty wool blanket in a bedroom and took it out to her. She stared at the road.

Noon came, noon went.

Gradually I became queasy. I was severely fatigued, of course, and the last thing I'd eaten were the too-sweet fig cookies; add to that the anxiety of the hour—I couldn't watch Jorie any longer. I tried to believe that Will was on his way, that his reasons for sending us all the way out here were sound, but at the same time, I could imagine a contrary scenario. Will would show up with grim news. The boy was gone—maybe found but found dead.

I told Jorie that I was going to look for more firewood and went around to the back of the house, where I promptly threw up. I sat on the ground awhile, then I walked away from the house along a beaten path through the tall grass.

I remembered how I awoke alone one morning at Will's family place in Maine and was unable to find him anywhere in the house. I called out to him, he didn't answer. I went outside and didn't see him. I may have panicked. I didn't believe that I had been abandoned so much as I worried that he'd slipped off on some errand and maybe there had been an accident. I had the presence of mind to follow the white wooden stairs that went down to the beach and checked the boathouse, which was where I found Will, merrily scraping barnacles from an overturned dory. And that scene, I remember, troubled me: boats, boat upkeep, boat lore—all of it was alien to me, and the fact that Will had a nautical past about which I knew nothing made me wonder if I could ever completely know him. Just when I thought I could chart him, I would forever discover yet one more hidden glade.

I must have walked a fair distance from the cottage without realizing it because when I turned around, all I could see was the roof of the house hanging above the browned grass. I headed back, and when I was close enough to see the kitchen door, I spotted Will.

I ran. I slipped and my knee was suddenly cold with mud. When I fell again, it was into his hug. His breath warmed my neck.

Jorie was around front, kneeling on the dirt drive, swallowing Nico into her embrace, swaddling him with the wool blanket so that all I could see of him was his round face, his eyes shut. He was smaller than I expected him to be, much more compact, and when he opened his eyes and blinked at me, I didn't think that he so much resembled a child as he did an old man, diminishing a fraction each day, shrinking, retiring; soon he would exist no more. Jorie was kissing the top of his head, brushing back his black hair with her lips. Kissing him, and pressing her cheek against his ear, kissing him again. I couldn't hear what she was saying. Nico looked dazed; he didn't cry, he didn't speak.

Inside, Will lit the logs in the hearth, and the crackle of dry wood burning fast became the only noise in the house. Otherwise we were quiet. We sat by the fire. Jorie wouldn't let go of the boy, who allowed himself to be held and eventually appeared to fall asleep.

A long while went by before I broke the silence: "How on earth did you find him?"

Jorie looked at Will, and Will let out a deep sigh.

"It's a long story," he said.

It was apparent, however, that the pure joy of the boy's return would remain qualified without some explanation. We needed resolution. We knew that Will had gone to the hotel to see his family friend; I asked if the retired diplomat had intervened in some way.

"As a matter of fact, he did," Will said.

"He pressured the police?" I asked.

"He called a client in the government. Contacts were made from there."

I decided not to pursue what he meant by contacts; I didn't like the sound of the word.

Jorie stared at the fire again. She rubbed her nose against Nico's head. Sleeping, he seemed to me more like a four-year-old, protected in the somnolent depth where only a child can burrow.

"I can explain more later," Will said.

"But why here? Why did we have to meet all the way out here?" I asked.

Again Jorie looked at Will.

Will crouched in front of the fire and poked a log. When he turned back toward us, he faced Jorie.

"I know it's perverse. Given all that's gone on, I know it may seem devious to think this way. But don't you see?"

She shook her head no.

A queer grin formed on Will's face.

I didn't recognize his smile.

"The boy has been reported missing," Will said. "Don't you see? It's what you wanted."

Jorie cleared her voice. She spoke softly so as not to wake Nico. She said, "We leave the country."

"Yes," Will said. "And no one will look for either of you, no one will have any reason—you have your cover. The boy was lost. You were distraught, you left."

I understood now. I said, "So right now, you could say we're in hiding."

"Later today," Will said, "I'll get word about how we'll get you two out of the country. That's the next step. I figured this place would be in the middle of nowhere, and it is. I'm sorry it was so far. I didn't know where else we could go. Soon I'll get word, and then we'll move fast. This is what you wanted, Jorie. You and Nico—you're free."

Jorie studied the boy in her arms. He slept with his mouth open. She wiped his nose.

"Can we go upstairs and lie down?" she asked me.

She carried Nico up to the second floor and lay down with him on a lumpy bed. I made sure they were comfortable and shut the door. Will met up with me in the other bedroom. We lay down. He was asleep in a matter of seconds, and so I let myself go, too, at last, into a deep cove of slumber.

When I woke up, it was dark out. Will was no longer beside me. I noticed that there was a lamp on in the other bedroom, but only the boy remained beneath a blanket, which rose and fell in a tranquil tide.

Jorie and Will sat at a butcher-block table in the kitchen. I didn't know how long they had been talking. They had apparently found some canned soup in the cupboard and heated it up, although neither one of them appeared to have eaten much of what was in their bowls. It occurred to me that I had taken for granted before what would be involved in ferrying a woman and child out of the country unnoticed, undocumented. Some degree of bureaucratic complicity would be necessary. I ladled myself some soup and sat down across from Will. Jorie's face was locked in a frown.

"How long did we sleep?" I asked.

No one answered me. Will spooned some of the soup. Jorie exhaled.

"What he didn't mention," she said, "was that the way he got Nico back was by promising, by pledging that we would disappear."

"Which in the end was what you wanted," Will said.

"The story might run in the papers or on television," Jorie said. "At least one boy never made it home, and it will be a lie."

"Maybe the lie will inspire some people to do good," Will said.

I wanted to go back to bed.

"You made a deal," Jorie said.

"Yes, I did," Will said.

I could read his frustration: He was thinking, I got you your boy back, isn't that what matters most? Why aren't you thanking me?

"You did what you had to do," Jorie said.

"I suppose I did," Will said.

Jorie stood and said, "I need to see how he's doing. He hasn't said anything yet."

"He's probably going to take a while to come out of shock," I said.

Jorie placed a hand on my arm before leaving the room and heading back upstairs. Moments later, the ceiling creaked.

I glanced at the black rotary phone mounted on the wall.

"Have you worked out the rest of the details?" I asked.

"Not yet," Will said. "Since it's Saturday, Jencks is having trouble reaching people. It's going to take a little longer than I thought it would. We'll probably have everything in place by tomorrow morning."

He needed a shave. He rubbed his chin. He watched me eat the soup, but let what was in his bowl get cold.

"I think it's amazing you found him," I said. "I stopped thinking we would."

He stared at the table awhile, but then a lazy smile broke.

"Can you tell me how?" I asked. "Who did you have to call?"

Once again, Will said, "It's a long story."

And I suspected the contrary; his explanation would be brief, but he didn't want to render his version of events, not yet. I could only infer that he was worried I would judge him the way Jorie evidently was judging him. However, I wanted him to believe I was on his side. I needed to believe that he had played the hero. I took his hand, I led him back upstairs to our room. I shut the door quietly and for some reason turned the brass bolt. I sat on the edge of the bed and undressed him partway. I pulled him onto the mattress, and he lifted my shirt and sweater over my head. It was cold, we slipped beneath the duvet. We left the lamp on. We found our tempo. We rafted our familiar current, but only for a time.

Here was where the years had carried us: There was a loneliness in the way we made love, finally impossible to ignore. Our history could be chaptered according to a succession of rooms with low slanted ceilings and cracked-plaster walls and shuttered dormers like this one—small rooms made smaller by everything between us that remained unsaid.

Later Will switched off the lamp, but we didn't sleep right

away. I guessed what he was going to tell me before he said it. His hesitation was tactile, the heat of his words before he spoke them.

"I've been offered a chance to go back into the FS," he said. "If I want to."

I may have said something, I don't recall.

"It would be Jakarta again."

I got up and opened the window a crack.

"You could come this time," he said. "We could make it work."

And so once again, it seemed the choice was mine: go or don't go. I didn't want my life to run in a circle, no one does.

"I haven't said yes," he said.

Not yet you haven't, I thought. I didn't know what to say. The day was a dream, the night a trance. Maybe by morning I would wake up and not feel so strange. Could sleep repair us?

I got back in bed and placed my hand flat against his chest.

"We can talk about it all," he said. "I want to talk about it."

He turned onto his side. I kept my hand on his chest. This was how we slept.

Early the next morning, a ladder of light fell across the bed, the sun through the shutters. Will had pulled a pillow over his head. The duvet covered half of him, and half of him was exposed. He appeared to sleep easily and, as always, with enviable disregard of time and place. I watched him for a while and then I dressed.

Downstairs I found Jorie with Nico in the kitchen. She had already taken the car to the village and bought food. She had spread a thick red jam across a baguette. She had made eggs, and the kitchen smelled like a buttered skillet. Nico sat at the table and slowly ate the jammed bread; he ignored his eggs. Jorie was washing the dishes, drying them, putting everything away.

She sat down at the table next to Nico and whispered something to him. He looked listless to me, still disoriented. He had not yet spoken. He glanced at me and furrowed his brow; the very fact that I was a stranger and that he had woken up in a strange house seemed like unnecessary injury after what he'd been through. I didn't like seeing a child so obviously distressed, it troubled me.

Jorie, on the other hand, appeared calm. I didn't know whether she'd slept; I suspected she hadn't drifted off for very long, if at all. Even so, her skin looked smooth and pink, as if this morning she breathed more oxygen. Or she had reached some decision, the inner arbitration of which had been difficult, and in the end she accepted her chosen destiny. With retrospect, of course, I know that this was the case because Jorie informed me that, with my permission to take Didier's car, she and Nico would return to Paris immediately.

"Home," I said.

Jorie nodded.

"What about Will's arrangements?" I asked.

Jorie didn't respond.

"You're not going to leave the country?"

"We will eventually, I hope," Jorie said.

"Will is still asleep," I said.

"I know," she said.

"You want to leave before he wakes."

"Yes," she said. "We'll leave in a few minutes. I can return the car to your friend's place, and we'll take the métro from there. You just need to tell me where he lives."

I rubbed my eyes.

"I don't understand," I said.

The boy watched us speak. He blinked at me, concerned.

"You do," Jorie said. "You do understand."

I took a piece of bread and swiped some jam across it, although I wasn't hungry.

Jorie stroked Nico's hair. He looked clean, his hair was wet; they must have been up awhile, if she had bathed him, too.

"I will always be grateful to Will," she said. "Please believe me when I say that. He did find Nico, I know, I know. I hope he will know how grateful I am. But he went too far, and I can't participate in the rest."

"He did what he thought he had to do," I said.

"But at what expense? Of course, I wanted Nico safe, of course, of course. And I admit that if Will had said to me first, Look, here's what it will cost, I would have said, Pay that, pay whatever you have to pay."

Nico took a bite of bread, leaving a fleck of jam on his cheek. Jorie wiped it away with a napkin.

"I'm just lucky that I happened to meet someone who had access to someone who had access to someone, and so on. But, Pedro, it never ends. They trade favors, they cut deals with each other—this is their business. The French Front politicians and the government politicians and this ex-diplomat friend of Will's family and—"

And Will himself. She was going to say, And Will.

"Look, I haven't known Will—or you—for very long, have I? Just a day. I don't mean to make so many assumptions, but..."

Jorie bit her lip, she hesitated. She lowered her voice:

"When I was a girl, my father used to talk about all the horrible men in the world who were the enemies of our country. The fundamentalist clerics, the despots with their personal armies. They were not so far away, which was why we were living wherever we were living—so my Dad could keep them where they were. Okay, late one night—I'd say I was about ten—I couldn't sleep and got up to get a drink of water. I went down to the kitchen and found my father there playing cards with some of his Marine buddies and the diplomats he worked with—no big deal, right? But also at the table, I saw that there were men wearing different uniforms, the wrong color uniforms, the uniforms that I knew belonged to the enemy. The wrong berets, the wrong flag patches on their shoulders—and they were laying out their gin-rummy hands and drinking scotch and laughing and laughing. I'll never forget this. I was young, I didn't get it—although this kept happening everywhere we lived, and after a while I did understand. Anyway, that first night, I started crying and my father put me back in bed. And I asked him, I said, Those men down there—don't we hate them? To which my father said something like, Don't worry, honey, Daddy will make sure you're safe. Don't you worry."

Nico took a few more bites of the bread. He stared at me. He barely blinked. I felt conspicuous. Read by him, read by Jorie— fully exposed in all my confusion and doubt. I heard her, I most definitely understood what she was saying. I could add to it what Will had told me about his time in Mexico and what he told me before we went to sleep, about the offer to go back to the Foreign Service. Even after all he'd been through, he would return to that life. In some sense, I could see, he already had returned.

I buried my head in my hands.

"How was it that Will Law could secure the release of my boy?" Jorie asked. "How does he possess the power to make that happen? You don't want to hear it, but you know it deep down. Someone who you and I probably don't like so much wanted to do business with him. Ask yourself why. Ask yourself, How does someone like Will—"

"You've made your point," I said without lifting my head.

I felt Jorie's hand on my shoulder

"And I've made you mad," she said. "I'm sorry."

I looked of her and said, "You don't need to apologize."

"I need to do what is right, simple as that," she said. "I can't turn Nico into a news story, I can't lie about him. I couldn't live with myself. We're going back to Paris now, and we're going to let the police and whoever else cares know that Nico is safe."

"And Luc?" I asked.

Nico looked at Jorie. She sat up straight.

"I was wrong," she said, "utterly and dangerously wrong. I can't run away."

She found their coats in the main room and she began to zip Nico up in his. She asked me again where she could leave Didier's car, what to do with the keys.

"Can you wait a minute?" I asked.

I went upstairs to the bedroom. Will lay on his stomach, one knee pulled toward his gut, the other stretched long. The pillow had fallen away from him. He slept. I kissed his back between his shoulder blades. He didn't stir. I kissed him again. He reached for the headboard. I kissed him one more time, on the golden rough of his face, and he flinched but didn't wake.

You know where to find me.

Then I went downstairs. Then I took the car keys from Jorie and told her that I would drive.

$$\underline{5}$$

ONE YEAR LATER, I traveled to Lebanon. Nothing Jorie had written in her letters had prepared me for the sun, from which there was no relief, not even in high autumn. An implacable light pressed steadily against the coast and made the ground crack beneath my step. On the bus from Beirut to Byblos, I felt myself developing a burn. Jorie had to stop twice to add water to the radiator of her aging car, a wide sedan with blankets spread across its torn upholstery. I didn't know how Nico, sitting in the backseat, could stand the heat, but I imagined that he had acclimated. Eventually we attained some altitude, and only then did the sun fade in volume. The mountain trees provided some screen, although a fair amount of light still bore through the cypress, then the cedars.

"How are you?" Jorie asked me.

We had not driven too far up into the mountains before coming to a road-check. A Syrian soldier with a semiautomatic strapped to his back examined Jorie's papers and my passport and glanced at Nico before having a look in the trunk. We waited patiently.

"I feel like I fell asleep on the beach and now I'm going to pay," I said.

"You'll do better when we get to the house," she said.

I turned toward Nico.

"And how are you doing back there?" I asked.

He blinked at me and then looked away; he watched the soldier. I had not expected him to answer me.

"I kind of meant how are you doing in general," Jorie said. "These days."

Her skin was tan and her hair blond and dry, pulled back into a ponytail.

"These days," I said.

I would have liked to have given her a pat response. Each day isn't so dark, each day I feel stronger. But the Levantine sunlight made me honest.

"I feel as lost as I did the day Will's sister called to tell me he was dead," I said.

The soldier returned the documents to Jorie and mumbled something in Arabic. He pushed aside the gate blocking the road, and we headed up a tree-lined incline.

"I'm glad you came," Jorie said.

We talked more now, although not about our lives but about Lebanon and its qualified peace. The road we were on had been closed during the decades of war, and so for a long time Luc's family had no safe access to the property they owned in the mountains. They all lived in Beirut and Byblos, and even after the road was reopened, they did not make the trip too often. We drove an hour, and then we reached a clearing in the forest and made our way through a modest grove. The silvered leaves of unpruned olive trees flickered in the morning sun. Closer to the house, there were fruit trees, apple and plum. An older man was busy twisting the fruit from the lower branches of one tree, collecting it in a deep basket. He waved hello. Jorie explained that he lived in the white cottage we passed before arriving at the main house; he was the man whom the family had employed during the war to protect the stead against squatters, and he had stayed on, which now enabled Jorie to live here with Nico. It would have been impossible otherwise, a woman alone in the mountains with a child.

The main house turned out to be only slightly larger than the caretaker's cottage. It was a low-lying cement structure with a gentle gable and surrounded by a broad covered porch. The ground sloped away from the house in back, the hillside dense with jasmine. A swing swayed in the breeze. A vegetable garden looked well-tended but beyond profit at this point in the season. As promised, the rooms inside were cool; all the windows and doors were open. I looked forward to a nap.

Jorie set out some plates of food on a table on the back porch—a blue cheese, bread, a bowl of miniature pears—although I wasn't hungry. Neither was Nico. He brought out a pad of blank paper to the table and started coloring with crayons. He drew a house not unlike this one, and I noticed that he

selected the same colors that could be found in the horizontal
stripes of the shirt he was wearing—blood-reds and earth-
browns—and the green of the arbor around us.

"Are those your favorite colors?" I asked him.

Again he blinked at me but said nothing.

Jorie beamed at him.

"Nico, that's a smart-looking house," she said.

His lips were tight. He looked out at the slope and the forest
of firs in the distance. He began to draw a tall tree next to the
house. A house, a tree, the sun—but no stick-figured boy in his
landscape; he did not draw himself in. He sat with us for a while
but then went inside, and when I looked at Jorie after he was
gone, I could see through her summer tan and know that she did
not sleep all that well at night. She worried constantly about the
boy. At rest, her mouth formed a frown.

In her letters, she had reported that Nico had not uttered a
sound since his ordeal in Paris. One year later, he had as yet not
spoken a word. French doctors had determined that his hearing
was fine; other tests determined that there was no overt medical
reason for his speechlessness. Psychiatric evaluations became difficult without dialogue, and in the end, recommendations for
treatment remained elusive. In her heart, however, Jorie believed
that Nico would heal with time if he could feel safe, and she
believed he would feel safe in Lebanon. Indeed, he had made
progress, she told me now, during the months that they had
lived here.

"I know it probably doesn't seem like it," she said, "but he's
much more social, much less afraid. He sleeps through the night,
he's not on any medication. I can even leave him for an hour

with a sitter and go down to the village and come back and he
will be okay. A few months ago, if someone like you came to the
house, he would have run to his room and shut the door."

"He sat here with us and made a drawing," I said.

Jorie nodded and tried to smile.

"I take what I can get," she said. "Although I don't want to
pretend. I see him, I watch him, I follow his eyes to know what
he's looking at. His recovery is slow. Life is hard for him."

"And how are you?" I asked. "In general."

Jorie shrugged. "I do see his progress. That makes me happy."

"Are you lonely up here all by yourself?"

Jorie's answer was immediate: "Not at all. I couldn't live like
this forever, mind you. But right now, even with all that's going
on with Nico, I'm content."

I had no reason to doubt her.

"You look good," I said.

"I live in the sun," she said.

"I can see that."

I wondered about Luc and her arrangement with him. I knew
that when she returned to Paris with Nico, he had not yet
arrived, but when he did make it home, she told him everything.
She was completely honest about how if the day had gone dif-
ferently, she might have run away with his child. She was frank
about her fondness for Luc but spoke openly about how the love
they had known had vanished. She didn't know what to do. She
couldn't live with him. She couldn't live without Nico, and now
all that mattered was the boy's happiness.

Then Luc surprised her. His arduous journey home, not
knowing what or whom he would find when he returned, had

made him clear. He, too, was willing to admit their love may have passed, and he, too, was most concerned about the boy. If that boy had been lost for good, he would have been sick the rest of his life. Yes, now they had to secure the boy's welfare. Yes, now his son needed to believe he was safe. But moving to Lebanon was out of the question for him; it was simply not a sacrifice he could make. So Jorie said, Let us live there, Nico and me. Let us live there, even if you cannot. Luc had to think about it, but when the French doctors failed to provide direction, he acceded to Jorie's wishes. He visited once a month, although lately less. He sent money.

"Do you worry about Luc suddenly changing his mind about all this?" I asked.

Jorie raised her chin toward the sun and closed her eyes.

At first I regretted the question, but then Jorie looked at me and said, "It's very sad. The truth is Luc has moved on—he had moved on even before Nico was taken. Why do you think he was traveling so often? His son is a part of his old life. As for me, I suppose I unwittingly played a part in Luc's passage into his new life. The truth is that Luc is gone, and it's sad for us sometimes, but there it is. This is how we live now, without him. This is our life now."

A breeze ruffled the jasmine on the hill beneath us, sweetening the air.

"Do you miss Paris?" I asked.

"I will never go back," she declared, bitter. "I avoid all news of the place."

I wished that I could match her sentiment. But the fact was that I would never escape my nostalgia for the city. Unlike Jorie,

I did read the news from afar: The French Front was still on the rise, but centrists continued to govern. Parisians opposed to the right wing sometimes managed a rally. And the gangs still swiped dark-skinned children in broad daylight. I gathered that most people did not speak about the day that people tossed bread in the river and a dozen children were abducted, perhaps because it was known that in the end all of them were returned one way or another. More recently there was a hunger strike by immigrants who sought asylum in a church. They were all scheduled to be deported but given clemency after one of them died. And the previous month, there was a story about a man, an immigrant, who climbed to the top of Notre-Dame and, once he had secured live media attention, shouted, La France m'assassine—France kills me—before falling to his death. The man became a martyr, his likeness postered everywhere, but I had reason to suspect that in time he, too, would be forgotten.

"Have you gone back to work on your dissertation?" Jorie asked.

I had not. I had seen the Ledoux show come to pass, and it was a critical success, for which I could receive some credit, but my passion for the man and his architecture had expired. I had flailed around in search of a new topic but was blue all the time, and it was Didier who suggested I take time off.

The morning I went back to Paris, I had gone to his place to return his car and found him in bed, fevered. I took care of him for two days, during which time, I should mention, Will came back to the city as well, went to my apartment, retrieved his belongings, and slipped away without seeing or speaking to me. Once Didier was better, I found myself not wanting to give up his company. Maybe I am not so stupid to wait for you after all, Didier said. He stayed with me in New York when the Ledoux show went up; this was when our romance began. He landed a job in a Chelsea gallery, and we began to make a life together, which proved gratifying. Then there was the news that Will was gone, and I found myself weighted with grief. The funeral was a cold affair; my mourning only deepened. Didier, as I said, suggested I take it easy for a while, and it was also Didier who suggested that the only way I could achieve any resolution would be if I made real all that had happened, if I faced it somehow; it was Didier who urged me, indeed insisted, that I travel to Lebanon and stay with Jorie and Nico.

"Every time I'd get a letter from you," I said, "I felt some relief."

"I'm your connection to Will," Jorie said.

"Is that strange? You'd write to me, and I'd believe that in the end I did the right thing when I drove you back to Paris."

"I thought you'd never want to hear from me," she said. "I wrote you the first letter just to thank you, but I never expected you to write back."

"And here I am," I said.

"I'm glad you came," she said for the second and not the last time that day.

I yawned. Jorie showed me a bedroom where I could lie down.

"Nap as long as you need to," she said.

There was a treelike crack on the wall next to the bed. I traced the branched fracture in the plaster with my fingertip. The walls were pale blue like the airmail letters Will used to send me.

A month or so went by after I left him in the country house, and then he began to write to me from Jakarta, except unlike the letters he wrote before our reunion, he never as much as alluded to the past, deep or recent; instead he only offered me some surface details about his present life. He described the view from his room. His subject became the rainy season.

These letters came to me monthly. I composed responses that I never actually wrote down, that I never sent. I was too angry. What would I write now, here, from this mountain cottage?

Dear Will: Jorie has let her hair grow. She looks like she spent all summer tending her tomato plants. The boy you rescued won't speak.

Dear Will: How could you choose me but then choose a life in which I had no place? A life that I thought you had abandoned. A life I will never comprehend.

Seven months after we'd parted ways, a woman phoned me and said her name, her married name, and I couldn't place her. She said, I'm Will's sister—I hadn't dealt with her in years. I started shaking. She said that she was sorry to be speaking to me again under these circumstances. She had found my name in his address book. Apparently he had started a letter to me and left it on the desk in his apartment but proceeded no farther than Dear Pedro; from this, Will's sister inferred that he and I were in touch, that she should contact me.

She relayed the cold facts: Maybe I had read about the rash of car-jackings, the unrest. That was what the police concluded, that it was an attempted car-jacking, although Will's car wasn't stolen, nothing was apparently stolen from him. There were no witnesses. It probably happened very fast, a single bullet. The crime could have been related to the ongoing protests in Jakarta, the people in the streets rebelling against the corrupt regime. But then again, it could have been a random act. No one could say definitively. No one had been apprehended. All of this happened so far away. Read the crime the way you want to read it—either way, Will was gone.

I know I could imagine the scene more completely, the way Will died, and try to make sense—I don't want to, I doubt I ever will. Instead when I need to think about Will in the end, I picture him waking up in the country house after Jorie and Nico and I were gone:

He rolled onto his back and wondered how he could have slept so long. His eyes adjusted to the light. He knew that he was alone. He got up and looked out the window and saw only one car out front—yes, he was alone. He did not understand. Truly, he didn't get it, not yet—why had we left him? Would we— would I return? He went downstairs without putting on clothes. In the kitchen, he could smell the food that had been cooked but didn't find any dirty or drying dishes. He gazed out at the field, the dried-out rye, the desiccated meadow, blond in the morning heat. He could walk out into the tall grass. The wind would make him arid. He would blend in. He would fade, vanish. Leave no trace.

I suppose that every man we make a hero inevitably returns to the station from which he rose; that is a lesson we never learn, and now we inhabit an age of accelerated disillusionment. Or perhaps our heroes don't really change at all, and it is we who change in relation to them, in how we regard them, in the codes we apply—a man like Will Law can only carry us a certain distance before we overtake him—and some might call this pattern tragic, but I am willing to admit that quite possibly it also allows for progress. That said, my days were still gray and I yearned to find meaning in some legacy Will left behind.

All of us know someone whose absence defines us, who gives form to our longing. But that absence more often than not exists as an abstraction: If we carry on a conversation with our lost love, if we compose a letter to him, we do believe that the conversation could take place, the letter could be sent. And what happens, then, when even the most remote possibility for any letter-reading, for any conversation, no longer exists? What do you do when this absence that has shaped you for the better part of your life is made real?

I don't know yet. Time has passed, and I don't know.

Jorie woke me late in the afternoon.

"Nico and I are going for a walk," she said. "There's a cliff not too far from here where you can watch the sun set over the Mediterranean."

"Wait," I said. "I'll join you."

We headed out through the olive grove and into a forest of ancient height. All the conifers lined up in clean rows, and for a while, we followed a beaten path. Then Jorie led us across less trammeled ground, the carpet of needles unparted. We walked up a hill. Jorie held Nico's hand. The forest was dark, one tree shadow falling on another tree shadow, but before long, I could see the sun. The trees thinned out. We reached a bluff. Jorie pulled Nico to her side. The land collapsed away from us, and as promised, I could see the coast in the distance, the great sea.

The sun reddened as it dropped toward the water. We waited.

"I'm glad you were there that morning," I said. "If you weren't, I don't know if I would have left him."

"I didn't see that I had a choice," Jorie said. "I had to go back to Paris."

"You had a choice," I said. "So did I."

"But you're still not sure you made the right one," she said.

"No," I said. "I did what I had to do."

I followed the sun in its descent, but then in a blink, it was entirely gone. The sky matched the sea, they were the same blue, and the air and the water were separated by only a brilliant white line—the radiant curve of the earth illuminated for a moment before there was no horizon in sight at all, nothing but a blur in the distance, evening now, to which we surrendered ourselves with practiced yet uneasy trust.

We headed down the slope away from the bluff. Jorie let go of Nico's hand and he bounded ahead of us. He appeared to be in a good mood. There was still light in the sky, but not for long. We walked quickly. It was getting cold.

Before we hit flat ground again, Jorie must have realized that Nico had slipped away from her, out of sight.

"Nico," she said.

I couldn't see the boy.

"Nico," she called.

I couldn't find him.

"Pedro, do you see him?"

I looked around in every direction. We were deep in the woods, and all I could make out were the darkening trees. I began to worry.

"Nico," we both called out. "Nicolas."

Then I heard a snap of twigs and the swift gallop of a small animal behind us. Birds flapped from the higher branches. I looked back up the hill and saw the boy flashing through the dim colonnade of trees, appearing and disappearing, his arms rising at his sides, his body falling forward without faltering, his short legs fleet and lighter with each step.

He shouted, "Look, look, I'm flying."

Nico spoke.

He said, "Mom, look."

And he ran down through the forest, his feet a hard beat on the ground, past us and beyond. Chased, fugitive, free.